DARKNESS AT PEMBERLEY

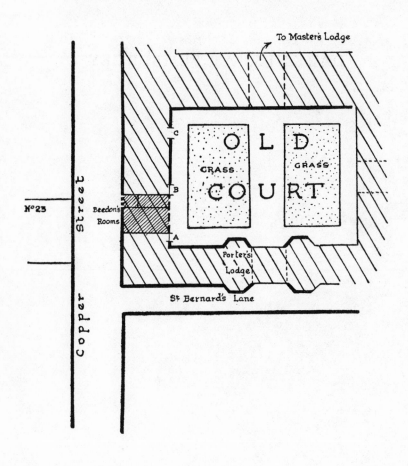

DARKNESS AT PEMBERLEY

by

T. H. WHITE

DOVER PUBLICATIONS, INC.
NEW YORK

NOTE

When this book was in page proofs it was suggested to me that the rather obvious local identification with a real college was unfortunate, not so much on account of possible libel against particular members of the college (for no real person in the college could possibly be identified with anybody in this book) as because it might tend to give a curious idea of the college in general, to those who were not acquainted with it. It therefore seems best, although it scarcely seems necessary, to state explicitly that the only connection which the college in this book has with reality is the local one. No person in the real college would be in the least likely to write incriminating letters, or to take drugs, or to commit blackmail or murder. These are the figments of the detective story convention. Imaginary characters and events were grafted upon a real place because it seemed amusing to plan a fiction within the local limits of a fact.

This Dover edition, first published in 1978, is an unabridged and unaltered republication of the work first published by Victor Gollancz Ltd., London, in 1932.

International Standard Book Number: 0-486-23613-7
Library of Congress Catalog Card Number: 77-20549

Manufactured in the United States of America
Dover Publications, Inc.
180 Varick Street
New York, N.Y. 10014

PART I

CHAPTER I

MR. MAULEVERER stood in the middle of the Old Court and shouted upwards to the occupier of C4. The latter poked his head out of the window and answered: "Coming!" Then the head disappeared; the light swallowed itself with a leap; footsteps echoed on the wooden stairs. Mr. Mauleverer was taking the occupier, an undergraduate named Weans, to the Festival Theatre. He was also taking Mr. Beedon, the history don whose rooms were on A staircase.

As they moved up the court Mr. Mauleverer said: " There's a light in Beedon's room. Just run up and see if he's ready." Weans ran up the stairs and turned to the right at the first landing. Mr. Beedon's rooms were on the first floor, with windows looking over the court on one side and across Copper Street on the other. The landing opposite Mr. Beedon's door was very narrow and unlighted. Weans could scarcely make out the white letters MR. BEEDON above the door. The door was sported, and he knocked. There was no answer. Weans conscientiously said the Lord's Prayer and knocked again. After a minute he clattered down the stairs to Mr. Mauleverer and

said : " Mr. Beedon's door is sported. I can't
make him hear."

The two stood on the cobbled pathway opposite the lighted window and shouted " Beedon ! "
in unison. Still no reply.

" How very remiss of him," said Mr. Mauleverer. " I do think he might have remembered an
invitation to the theatre. I expect he's in his
study : the one with the window on the other
side."

Weans asked helpfully : " Shall I go round to
Copper Street and shout from there ? "

" No, no ! We'll go up and see if we can't make
him hear through the door."

Two pairs of footsteps clumped up the stairs
again and halted in the darkness of the tiny
landing. Mr. Mauleverer called " Beedon !
Beedon ! " and thumped the door with his umbrella. He stooped down and tried to pull the
door open—there was no handle—by inserting
the tips of his fingers into the T-shaped keyhole.
But it was locked.

" What a nuisance ! " exclaimed Mr. Mauleverer. " How very boring ! One more shout
together " :

" Beedon ! Bee-don ! "

In the silence which followed, a gramophone
began to play inside the room.

" Really ! " said Mr. Mauleverer, " if we can

hear his gramophone he can hear us. How stupid! I suppose he's forgotten all about the theatre and thinks this is a rag or something." Then, raising his voice and giving another bang with his umbrella : " Beedon ! What about the theatre ? "

The gramophone went on playing without interruption. Muttering something about rudeness, Mr. Mauleverer led his companion down the stairs again : started for the Festival Theatre in an irritable frame of mind.

The serious undergraduate in the rooms above Mr. Beedon's shut his book with a sigh, switched off his light and came lumbering down the stairs. He had worked nine hours and felt that a walk to Grantchester before eleven would do him good. He knew that he must be careful not to overdo it. There was a car in Copper Street, and a small crowd of people. He passed by on the other side, since he disliked accidents, and tramped the boring road to Grantchester, thinking about Byron's "Don Juan" and its Relation to Restoration Comedy.

The Master of the college pottered into the Old Court five minutes later and made for Beedon's rooms. He stood on the dark landing for some time, wheezing a little, and slipped something into Beedon's letter box. There was silence inside the room, except for a thin scraping or

swashing noise, like somebody mowing rhyth-
mically with a scythe, only fast and quietly. The
Master tiptoed down the stairs, looked out under
the archway, and, seeing nobody about, walked
quickly to the centre of the Court. There he
resumed his shuffle and disappeared in time
towards his own Lodge.

At about half past ten the Chaplain, biting his
fingers nervously, made his way up the stairs and
stood opposite Mr. Beedon's door. He did not
knock. As he waited, the telephone bell rang
inside. There was no answer. The Chaplain looked
over his shoulder and, taking his sport key out of
his pocket, fitted it into Mr. Beedon's lock. It
fitted. The Chaplain opened the door half an
inch, so that a beam of light struck across the
landing. Apparently intimidated by this, he stood
hesitating for a moment. Then, closing the door
again with infinite precaution, he also tiptoed
down the stairs.

Finally, at midnight, the porter Rudd went
round to turn off the lights on the staircases. He
did not content himself with turning off the light
at the bottom of A staircase, but went up to the
landing and stood for a few moments opposite
Mr. Beedon's door, in silent reflection.

.   .   .   .

Some four hours earlier the telephone had rung in the local police station. The Inspector took off the receiver, and answered briefly. After the thin voice had trickled and clattered for a minute he said : "What address?" His pencil moved over a pad which he had drawn towards him. The tinny voice stopped, and the Inspector repeated : "23 Copper Street. Right. I'll be over." He replaced the receiver and reached for his hat. Considering that he had just been told of the discovery of a murdered man, the Inspector's phlegm was admirable. His seamed muscular face betrayed no excitement ; the jaw set with no more than its usual taciturnity. Inspector Buller moved through his duties as a policeman without faith in his fellow men, and with some doubts of the world in general. He had seen so many witnesses shaken that he believed the testimony of his own senses only with difficulty. He had been told there was a murder. Very well. There might be, and there might not. He would be sure of it when he had seen the murderer hang. Meanwhile he reached for his hat, tersely summoned a sergeant and two constables, and drove to Copper Street.

The constable in charge saluted respectfully, and the Inspector gravely returned the salute. "Well," he said, "what happened?"

The constable opened his note book and began : "When passing over Copper Street bridge on my beat at 8.3 p.m. this evening I was accosted by a woman who gave her name as Mrs. Button, lodginghouse-keeper of 23 Copper Street, who stated that there was a dead body in her house. I immediately accompanied witness to the above address and found the deceased as stated. I proceeded to lock the door of the room in which the body lay and telephoned the police station from the provision merchant's at Number 24 Copper Street. Whilst awaiting the Inspector I stationed myself outside the door of the deceased's room, having cautioned Mrs. Button not to leave the house."

"A very good report," said the Inspector. "Did you 'phone for a doctor?"

"No, sir. I deemed from the condition of the deceased that it would be unnecessary."

"Very good. Go and 'phone for the police surgeon now. Where is Mrs. Button?"

"Mrs. Button is weeping in the dining-room, sir."

"Well, we'll give her time. Where is the body?"

The constable opened the door behind him. The group of men, who had been standing on the first floor landing, filed in carefully. The body was lying on the floor, huddled and suddenly collapsed. On its face was an expression of surprise and fear, accentuated by the blue hole of a bullet directly between the eyes. The back of the head lay neatly upon what remained of its brains, barely staining the carpet. Nothing in the room seemed to be disordered. There was no weapon. Buller locked the door with the key which the constable had left, and went downstairs to the dining-room.

Mrs. Button was a small straggling woman, much more like a bedder than a proprietress in a prosperous thoroughfare like Copper Street. She had dried her tears by the time the Inspector came down and, though still slightly hysterical, was agog with curiosity. However, she made an effort to remain distressed.

" I'm sorry, Mrs. Button," said the Inspector, " to have to trouble you with questions after a shock like this, but we must get to the bottom of it. Can you give me a little information ? "

" I'm sure I'll answer anything as I can, sir, for the poor young gentleman's sake. He was a real nice spoken young man, and never gave no trouble for a moment. Whoever can have had an interest in doing away with him is more than I can say ! "

" Ah, no motive," Buller replied tactfully. He pretended to make a note of it. " Now I gather from his things that he was an undergraduate from St. Barnabas. What was his name ? "

" He was a Mr. Frazer. These was his first lodgings."

" A freshman called Frazer from St. Barnabas. Now would you tell me how you found him ? "

" Oh, Inspector ! " exclaimed Mrs. Button tearfully. " It do seem like a judgment, for I was out at the Crown Arms just round the corner for a drop of brown ale ! Mr. Frazer, he would have been to first Hall, and I'd heard him come back quite usual, something after half past seven it must have been, and go up to his room ! " Mrs. Button dissolved into tears again. After a patient pause the Inspector prompted her.

" Well, what happened ? You went round to the Crown Arms."

" I can't have been there more than twenty minutes, for I had it on me mind that Mr. Frazer's fire needed seeing to, and he wasn't one that remembered to put the coal on himself. So I only had a glass of brown ale, for I remember Mr. Rudd remarking on it, and came right back at once to take up the scuttle. I had it on me mind to go back again afterwards, if need be. And then, when I took it up, there was no answer to the door, and I found the poor fellow lying there horrible. Did he kill himself, Inspector ? "

" That's what I want you to tell me, Mrs. Button. Had he any reason for doing so ? "

" Not the least in the world, he hadn't," said Mrs. Button. " He was that cheerful always, and that respectable ! Why, I'd as likely kill myself ! "

" Had he a revolver, or anything of that sort, do you know ? "

" That he hadn't. I know, for I did all his drawers for him."

" He hadn't anything of a queer shape, had he ? Anything like a flat sort of revolver with a contrivance on the end of it ? "

" He hadn't an automatic with a silencer, if that's what you mean," replied Mrs. Button, with the dignity of a confirmed cinema goer.

" Oh," said the Inspector. " What sort of friends had he ? "

" Just the usual sort. Only two or three. He was a freshman."

" Nothing strange about him, or them ? "

" Nothing at all."

Nor did the Inspector gain any further information from Mrs. Button.

.   .   .   .   .   .

Inspector Buller was ushered into the senior tutor's room at St. Barnabas. When he had told the senior tutor the news, and given him time to recover his balance, he asked for information.

" Did you ever meet the boy's parents ? " he asked.

Mr. Witherspoon, the tutor, had resumed his air of a hostile solicitor. " No," he said, " I never met them. I corresponded with them. Colonel

Frazer was in the Indian Army. I believe they were both quite ordinary people."

" No chance of a vendetta, or a diamond stolen from the idol's eye, or anything of that sort ? "

" Not in the least, I should think. They live at Croydon. Frazer was reading Agriculture."

" Well, it seems a most extraordinary crime, Mr. Witherspoon. There is no weapon, and the police surgeon says he can't have shot himself from the nature of the wound. He seems to have been a perfectly normal young chap, and nobody can give me any motive for a murder. Have you any theory or suggestion which would help us along ? "

" I was not trained as a detective, Mr. Buller."

CHAPTER II

Mrs. Grigg, the senior bedder of A staircase, allowed herself the prerogative of arriving
nearer seven than six o'clock. The college gates
opened at six, when the bedders were supposed to arrive, but Mrs. Grigg had been a
servant of the college so long that she was allowed
a little latitude. Thus it fell to the lot of Miss
Edgeworth, Mrs. Grigg's help, to perform the
preliminary ministrations alone. Her routine was
to begin with the fireplaces, starting at the bottom
of the staircase. She reached Mr. Beedon's room
at twenty past six, put down her brushes, and
fumbled with the key. At twenty-one minutes past
six a horrible scream swept through the sleeping
court, followed by a clattering of feet and the
debouch of Miss Edgeworth on the cobbles, in
hysterics.

Mr. Beedon was sitting in his favourite chair,
stone cold, with a bullet through his head.

.   .   .   .   .   .

Inspector Buller, whose night had been a sleep-
less one, stood in the room on A staircase and
listened to his sergeant. The latter was a slow
speaker, like the Inspector, but a more ardent

theorist. He was younger, and open to conviction.

The sergeant said : " But doesn't this clear it all up ? The surgeon says it was probably the same weapon."

" Suppose you tell me what happened," said the Inspector.

" Well, sir, I wouldn't rush to any conclusions, but I see it this way. The wounds were inflicted with the same weapon : the automatic with silencer on the table there, which was found in this man Beedon's hand. Both men died at about the same time, as near as the surgeon can make out. Beedon's wound seems to have been self inflicted ; it was fired from close up, and from his right side, with the muzzle against the temple. The boy Frazer was shot from a distance of some feet, so he couldn't have been the one who shot himself, quite apart from the fact that a dead man couldn't have brought the automatic back to Beedon's room and put it in his hand. There are no fingerprints on the stock except Beedon's. If the shots were fired from the same weapon then Beedon must have fired them. He shot Frazer and then himself.

" We don't know," the Inspector pointed out, " that the shots were fired from the same weapon. We shall have to have a microscopic report on the bullets."

" Mark my word, sir, it'll turn out as I say."

" It may do," said the Inspector. " You never know. Why should he have done it ? "

" We don't know the motive yet. It'll crop up. You get some queer fish in these universities."

" Well," said the Inspector, " you may be right. I suppose I shall have to see the Master."

The Master was in his study at the Lodge. He rose courteously from his writing-table as the Inspector entered. In appearance everything that a Master should be, patriarchal and benevolent, he constantly gave the impression that he had just laid aside a treatise on the Hebrew gospels. He shook hands with his well-known hospitality and feebly motioned the Inspector to a chair.

" Well, Mr. Inspector," he said, " this is a terrible shock to all of us. I hope you will be able to throw some light upon it."

" I'm sure it s a dreadful thing to happen in a college," replied the Inspector sympathetically. " I was hoping you might help us clear it up."

" Everything in my power to tell you, Inspector, I shall hasten to say. I only hope it will throw no discredit upon poor Beedon. He was such a nice fellow, though a little reserved from the other members of the college."

" You don't know of any oddity which he may have had, anything which might have proved a motive for killing himself ? "

" No," replied the Master with the slightest

perceptible hesitation. " No. He seemed to live in a very respectable way."

" There is some sort of theory that he may have killed this undergraduate from St. Barnabas, and then shot himself. Would you agree with that ? "

" I should think it unlikely," said the Master honestly. " Mr. Beedon used to go up to London every Friday. I believe he was not—ah—unsusceptible to the charms of the other sex."

" There might be any number of motives. You don't know whether he was acquainted with this undergraduate ? "

" As far as I can say, he was not. I have looked it up, and find that Mr. Beedon had no pupils from St. Barnabas. He was not a man who met many undergraduates except with regard to their studies."

" This makes it much more difficult. You don't know whether he knew the boy's parents ? "

" He may have done. I am not in the habit of concerning myself with the private affairs of the Fellows of my college. But he did not know them to my knowledge, so far as that goes."

" Well, we shall have to follow the usual routine and interview anybody who may have called on Mr. Beedon last night. Thank you very much, sir, for your assistance."

The Master detained him as he rose to go. " I called on Mr. Beedon myself," he said, " at about eight o'clock. I meant to give him some papers, but the door was sported, so I posted them in the letter-box. I expect you'll find the envelope there."

" Did you hear anything, or notice whether the lights were on ? "

" The lights were on. Yes, I certainly noticed them."

" You heard nobody talking ? It must have been somewhere round eight o'clock that Mr. Beedon died."

" I heard nothing," said the Master, " except —there was a sort of swishing noise, I fancy. It may have come from somewhere else. I may have been mistaken."

" What sort of swishing noise ? " asked the Inspector. " Could you be more definite. Was it a noise like heavy breathing."

" Oh no, a much more mechanical noise."

" Like a carpet sweeper ? "

" No," said the Master. " It was soft and regular, and there were no bumps. Swish, swish, swish ! "

The Inspector cast his mental eye round the room as he remembered it. " Was it a gramophone running down ? " he enquired.

" Yes ! " exclaimed the Master. " That was

what it was. The needle on a gramophone disc after it had finished the music ! "

" Somebody must have been alive within five or six minutes of that anyway. Could you give me the exact time ? "

The Master said : " It must have been about eight o'clock—within a quarter of an hour either way."

" What time did you dine ? "

" I dined in the Lodge on Tuesday. I was feeling rather tired. Dinner would be at half past seven."

" It wasn't late, by any chance ? "

" No, Anson gives me my meals very punctually. I don't take much at night."

" How long does it take you to dine ? "

" Not more than forty minutes. I had some soup, then fish, chicken and then custard. I was alone. My wife was in London for a meeting of the Child Welfare."

" Very well, say you finished dinner at ten past eight. What did you do then ? "

" I went into the study for a cigar. When I was lighting it I remembered Beedon's papers, so I took them over."

" Immediately after dinner ? "

" Not quite immediately. I opened a new box of cigars. I don't move very quickly nowadays, Inspector."

" Say you left the Lodge at a quarter past eight, then ? "

" Yes, that would be about the time. I daresay it was twenty minutes past before I got to Mr. Beedon's rooms. I walk rather slowly."

" So somebody was alive inside as late as fourteen minutes past eight, or thereabouts. Thank you very much, sir. That will help us a great deal."

" I wonder," said the Master as Inspector Buller was going out, " if you would let me have the papers back which are in Mr. Beedon's letter-box : as soon as you've finished with them, of course."

The Inspector came back into the room. He said : " By all means, sir, only we shall have to look at them first as a formality : that is, if you don't object. Nothing private, I hope ? "

" Not at all, Inspector ; look at them as much as you like. Simply papers relating to a pupil of Mr. Beedon's."

The Inspector hesitated. " Would you take offence, Master, if I asked your permission to look at your glasses ? "

The Master gave him a startled look and took them off. " A regular Sherlock Holmes ! " he remarked pleasantly, handing them across. The Inspector turned them over absently and passed them back, looking the Master in the eyes.

" Thank you very much," he said. Then he wished the Master good morning and walked out into the wintry sunshine.

Back in A4, he addressed the sergeant : " We shall have to see everybody who came up this staircase last night. The Master had some evidence which bears out your theory to this extent, that somebody—presumably Beedon, but it might be his murderer—was alive in this room when we were looking at the dead body over the way. Will you give me that envelope in the letter-box ? "

The sergeant fetched it and watched it carefully opened. Inside was a blank sheet of paper.

" This is from the Master," the Inspector said. " He told me that it contained papers relating to a pupil of Beedon's."

" I suppose the old geezer slipped the wrong sheet in by mistake."

" Very likely. Will you go to the Lodge now, give him my compliments, and tell him what we've found. Ask if we could see the actual papers."

The sergeant came back with three or four printed forms, a syllabus of a revised Tripos examination torn from the pages of the University Register.

" Well," said the Inspector. " These might

apply to a pupil of his, I suppose. But I see Mr. Beedon took in the Register himself, and who would put a single sheet of paper into an envelope, in mistake for three or four ? "

" You might," replied the sergeant. " If you were unconscious enough to make a mistake at all, you might just as well make a big one. These old gents all get rather loopy."

" Yes, I daresay they do," answered the Inspector wistfully, looking at his blunt nails, " what with knowing such a lot. But would they write their names in invisible ink before they enclosed the paper by mistake ? "

The sergeant looked suspiciously at the piece of paper which was held out to him. There, in the middle, was a ghostly signature, faint and blue.

" This is the cheap sort of ink which they sell to amuse children in toy shops like Hamley's. You just warm it by the fire. I suppose dons are rather children. They never stop being at school all their lives. First Nanny to protect them in the nursery, then the governess and the head master and finally the Vice-Chancellor. A guinea-pig, now, is independent of its parents after three days."

" Are you getting at anything," asked the sergeant resentfully, " or is this just uplift ? "

" I don't know. You never can tell. Children

have games and are sometimes naughty. Now would you say this was one of the Master's games, which we've come across by mistake, or would you say he was being naughty ? "

" After all, the old man may be senile or something. He may have a passion for playing with invisible ink. It might be a joke. It might still be a mistake. Perhaps he wrote his name on it and forgot, and then put it in by mistake as we said. If you asked him, he would probably explain it quite easily."

" So I won't ask him, sergeant," said the Inspector, with a smile, whose point the sergeant missed. " We'll have to steal a clean sheet of paper from the Lodge when it comes to giving this back. Have the photographers finished ? "

" Yes."

" Just have them microphotograph the catch and tone-arm of the gramophone. I suppose they've done the door ? Send the search-party's tabulation to my room. I'll be there directly. Oh, and ask the surgeon whether anything else besides narcotics would contract the pupil of the eye ? "

At the Porter's Lodge, Buller borrowed a pen and paper. He asked the porter to display his notice on the screens. It read :

" Will any person who attempted to visit Mr. Beedon on Tuesday night after seven o'clock be so kind as to offer his evidence at the police station? The matter is urgent."

Then he went to the nearest call office, and 'phoned the Chief Constable with the request that the matter should be turned over to Scotland Yard.

CHAPTER III

A WELL-TAILORED young man in a green hat
came down from London, driving an 8-litre
Bentley. He was very polite to the Inspector, and
agreed absent-mindedly with everything he said.
The Inspector laid before him lists of everything
found in either of the two rooms, a résumé of the
evidence up to date, and the surgeon's report.
The young man decided to supplement the latter
by calling in Sir Loftus Boneface. He also interviewed Mr. Mauleverer and the undergraduate
Weans, who came forward in response to the
Inspector's notice. Next day he drove away again,
having instructed the Inspector to ask for a verdict of murder and suicide against Mr. Beedon.
He apologised for not being able to stay for the
inquest, which was fixed for two days later, but
promised that Sir Loftus would come down again
to give evidence—which would ensure everything
going off satisfactorily.

Mr. Beedon, according to his reconstruction,
had shot Frazer for reasons unknown (and, considering the strength of the other evidence, unnecessary) at five to eight. He had then returned
to his rooms, played a record on the gramophone
whilst Mauleverer was shouting at him through

the door, and shot himself at about 8.15. The conclusive evidence in favour of this theory was provided by Sir Loftus, who proved that the bullets were fired from the same weapon, which was found in Mr. Beedon's hand bearing no fingerprints but those of Mr. Beedon. It was decided that the Master's invisible signature was a mare's nest, or at least a matter unconnected with the crime under consideration. Sir Loftus pointed out to the Inspector that evidence must be discriminated. A lot of evidence, he explained, would always crop up without relevance, and it was the mark of the great detective to be able to separate the germane from what was not. Among matters set aside by Sir Loftus as irrelevant were : The Master's signature, the photographs of the catch and tone-arm of the gramophone, a set of unidentified fingerprints on the door, and a tiny piece of typewriting-paper ash still clinging to a piece of coal in the dead fire. The Inspector saw Sir Loftus off by the mid-day train, after thanking him very much indeed for his assistance.

Then he went back to his room in the police station, where he was coldly received by the sergeant, and sent for the police surgeon.

The two men were old friends.

" Well," said Dr. Wilder, " I suppose his highness has cleared everything up ? "

" Sir Loftus is very quick on the uptake," said the Inspector defensively.

Dr. Wilder smiled affectionately and offered a cigar, which Buller refused.

After a pause, " Did you agree unconditionally with Sir Loftus's post-mortem ? " asked the Inspector.

" I think so."

The Inspector pushed the photograph of the tone-arm across. " Why," he asked, " did Beedon put on that gramophone without leaving any fingerprints on the catch or arm ? "

" There must be some sort of mark."

" The arm has been carefully wiped, finishing with a single sweep which leaves an unbroken grain along its whole length. A cloth has been pulled down it from top to bottom to finish off. Underneath, this grain is disturbed by a very slight smudge. The catch has been wiped in the same way, and is also marked underneath (and on the two narrow sides) but this time by a distinct line. This line is about an eighth of an inch thick. The catch was released by means of a piece of string. How the arm was lowered I don't know."

" Very well."

" Why," pursued the Inspector, " did the Master, who is a drug addict, post a letter to Beedon containing a blank sheet of paper with his signature in invisible ink ? "

" Actually," said the surgeon, " I knew the old man took cocaine. But how did you ? "

" His eyes struck me as curious, so I got him to take his spectacles off and had a good look at him. The pupils were contracted to pinpoints."

" People who take drugs are sometimes very cunning," put in the doctor reflectively.

" I know."

" Did he do it ? " asked the surgeon humbly.

" How am I to know ? How am I to know anything ? That isn't half the evidence."

" Well, go on."

" Who went to the door after Mauleverer, and probably opened it with a key ? And why hasn't he come forward ? "

" Did somebody ? "

" The three latest sets of fingerprints are Weans's with Mauleverer's over them, and then an unknown man's on top of Mauleverer's."

" Anything else ? "

" Ten or twelve million things, I suppose, but Sir Loftus tells me you have to discriminate. So, cutting all of them out, there's one more thing which may be on my mind. Who has been busy spring cleaning in A4 ? Because whoever it is has a queer method of doing things. The keys of the typewriter in the study looking over Copper Street are all printed with Beedon's fingers. But

the little wheel thing which you turn to make the
roller revolve has been wiped like the gramophone. All waste papers, notes and so on have
been torn once across and dropped in the waste-
paper basket—just the day's correspondence, you
know. And yet one piece of typewriting-paper has
been burnt in the fire and carefully powdered.
Lastly the automatic. It is as clean as the tone-
arm except for a smudge on the barrel and *one*
clearly defined set of fingerprints as transferred
by the hand in which we found it. The smudge
on the barrel really resolves itself into a second
wiping which does not quite correspond with the
grain of the first one. But the extraordinary thing
is the single sharp definition of Beedon's grip. If
you had carried an automatic across the street,
shot somebody, put it down to play the gramophone, picked it up and shot yourself, would you
have left only one set of prints ? "

"He may have wiped it for some reason or
another between playing the gramophone and
shooting himself."

"Quite likely. I think if I were going to shoot
myself I should nurse the gun, and wipe it, and
think it over. But even then, when I picked it up
for the last time, I should change its position in
my hand—to get a grip of it, you know, and that
sort of thing. This stock has only been gripped
once, and in one position."

" Well," said the surgeon, " now tell me who shot them both ? "

" You be damned," replied the Inspector crossly. He went out of the room.

. . . . . .

But that afternoon he was still talking to the doctor. There was something excited now, straining under the reserve of his tired face, and something which made him look younger and enthusiastic. He was almost garrulous, and talked on to his friend without paying him much attention. Nor was he attending principally to what he was saying. His attention hurried on in advance of his words, like somebody hastening through a big untidy warehouse matching coloured cloths just beyond the lantern's circle of radiance lighting those who followed him.

" Why ! Why ! Why ! " he exclaimed. " Why did Beedon play the gramophone when Mauleverer was outside the door ? If he didn't want to go to the theatre, and wanted Mauleverer to go away, why should he advertise his presence by putting on a record ? "

He did not wait for an answer. " Why," he continued, " did Mauleverer take the trouble to go up those stairs with an unbiased witness ? "

The doctor felt it was his duty to break in. " Mauleverer went up to see why Beedon wasn't

Cp

ready for the theatre. He went with Weans because they were on their way to the theatre together. That's natural, isn't it ? "

" Quite natural. It gives Mauleverer an absolute alibi, for the gramophone proves that somebody was alive inside the room when Mauleverer was outside it, bound for the theatre. By the way, Mauleverer admits that he was with Beedon at about seven o'clock, so he would have been the last person to see him alive if it wasn't for this gramophone—that's supposing that the man who played it was Beedon's murderer. Mauleverer gets out on the ground floor either way—on Boneface's explanation. Either Beedon was alive and playing the gramophone when Mauleverer started for the theatre between 8.10 and 8.15—in which case he can't have killed him—or else there was somebody else in the room, who had come there since Mauleverer left. The gramophone proves either that Beedon killed himself, or that somebody else did who was in the room while Mauleverer was on his way to the theatre."

The Inspector puffed fiercely at his pipe until it sparked. " Why do people start gramophones with string ? " he asked. " String," he answered himself after a pause, " is the basis of mechanics. Pulleys, ropes, chains, cranes. String is also used for fastening and for operating from a distance. We pull a string to discharge a cannon or to work

marionettes. In this connection string is a link
between the operator and the thing operated. A
link may exist in order to join or to separate. If
to join, then the string was used because the
operator could not make contact with the thing
operated by other means, i.e. he could not reach
it. This is the principle embodied by people who
shoot themselves with rifles and have to reach the
trigger by means of string. On the other hand, if
the link was used as a separator rather than as
a joiner, then the person who started the gramophone didn't want to touch the catch. He wanted
to leave no fingerprints. But it would have been
easier to push the catch sideways with a pencil
or something of that sort ? "

The Inspector wrote on his pad :

(*a*). Inspect the room for traces of mechanism,
i.e. screws in wall, etc., over which string might
be passed to form some sort of rigging, e.g. the
sort of rigging that some people put up in their
bedrooms so that they can switch off the electric
light by the door without getting out of bed.

(*b*). Inspect the whole gramophone very carefully, not only for traces of apparatus. How did
the tone-arm come down after the catch had
been pulled with string ? (If it was.)

The Inspector read this through distastefully

and then said : " I don't believe the gramophone had anything to do with it."

" What about the third visitor ? " asked the doctor.

" Yes. What about him ? Why hasn't he come forward ? Three possible reasons. One, he hasn't seen the notice. This would mean that he wasn't a member of the college. A member of Christchurch, for instance, might very well have visited Beedon and equally well might not have seen the notice on the screens at St. Bernard's thereafter. Two, his visit to Beedon—though not necessarily connected with the murder—was one which he would rather not have talked about. Three, he was the murderer. Beedon need not have been killed before Mauleverer left, or even before the Master's visit at 8.20. What a pity the Master left no super-imposed finger-prints when he posted that letter ! We could have timed the visits then. As it is, we don't know whether the unknown came before or after 8.20. We only know he came after Weans and Mauleverer."

The Inspector made another note :

(c). Enquire at Porter's Lodge, for information about people seen in Old Court between eight o'clock and midnight. N.B. Autopsy shews that Beedon could not have died later than nine o'clock.

"I suppose undergraduates can do murders just as much as anybody else," ventured the doctor. "The boy below Beedon's room was out dining in Mary's, and didn't come back till midnight. His alibi's sound and natural. But this fellow above says that he went for a walk to Grantchester, starting at a quarter past eight. We have no check on him."

"It comes to this," said the Inspector, "you can suspect anybody once you entertain suspicion. It's an extraordinary thing how remote human beings are from one another. We go here and there like cats, meeting, fraternising, diverging. Sometimes we have alibis and sometimes not. But always, inside, everybody is incalculable and secret, always locked up and impenetrably alone. The heart is deceitful above all things, and desperately wicked."

"You ought to have been a poet," said the doctor.

"Not nowadays," replied the Inspector, and shook his head.

The telephone thrilled startlingly at his elbow and he took off the receiver. He listened, replied "Speaking," and listened again. Then he said "Right" and hung up the receiver. "Well," he said, "that's that. The Master of St. Bernard's went up to London to-day and I had him shadowed. We lost him absolutely."

" Do you mean that he's got out of the country ? "

" No. I should think it very unlikely. He'll be back to-night or to-morrow morning. I shall have to go and see him." The Inspector looked round the room and added : " Meanwhile I think I'll go and see that porter." At the door he turned round and smiled pathetically.

" I wish you'd think over that post-mortem again, doctor," he said. " Any little thing, you know. I don't understand this case at all, not at all, and anything may mean anything. I'm dead sure Boneface is wrong." He came back and sat on the table by his friend's chair. " Listen," he said. " I'm not keeping anything back—that sort of thing's all bosh. I haven't any theories, and I'm lost. But those men were murdered, both of them, and I don't stand for cold murder like that. I don't want to catch the man for the sake of my reputation. I want to catch him because he's all wrong. I don't care whether he ought to be punished or pitied, and I don't know whether murderers ought to be hanged. But I want to catch him because I've a feeling for England, and that's an odd thing to say. This case is all ends up, and anything may be significant or nothing, So I should just like to be sure of that autopsy, like everything else. There may be something we ought to have noticed and haven't. Perhaps one

or other of them was poisoned and shot afterwards. I take it that Sir Loftus confined himself
to the local wounds. Perhaps one or other or both
or neither was dead before he was shot. In fact,
perhaps anything. So I'd like you to be very careful, would you? If you could, I should like you
to look into it again. Don't take offence at me.
The man who did these murders was a scientist."
He stopped abruptly and got off the table.

"Mauleverer," he said, "is a lecturer in
chemistry."

CHAPTER IV

Rudd, the porter who had been on duty on Tuesday, was off duty when the Inspector called at the Porter's Lodge. He ran him to earth in the under-porter's cottage on the other side of the river.

The two men sat solemnly in the parlour, shaded with aspidistras, bowered with lace. Between them was a red serge table-cloth.

The Inspector said : " I've called because I want you to give me some information. Were you on duty between seven and midnight on Tuesday ? "

Rudd was a stout surly man with an expression not altogether pleasant. His eyes were close together and evasive. He was above the common height. When the Inspector asked him this question he replied with another : " Who said I wasn't ? "

" Nobody did," replied Buller patiently. " I was asking you a question."

" Well, I was," said the porter. " It's my duty."

" You were in the Porter's Lodge all the time ? "

" See here, mister, what are you getting at ? Are you accusing me of the murder or asking for information ? I don't know as you've any right to pry into my private affairs without a caution, nor I don't know what reason you could have for wanting to. If you think it's me I can tell you you're wasting your time."

" I don't think it was you, Mr. Rudd. I asked because I want information about the people who passed through the Old Court between seven and midnight, and naturally I wondered whether you were there all the time first."

" Well, I was," said Mr. Rudd defiantly. " But if you want to know who went through the Old Court you can get a college list. Why, both Halls would pass through between them times."

" What time are your Halls ? "

" Six-thirty and seven-thirty."

" Well now, between seven-thirty and eight you can help me ; for the second Hall would be in just then and few people about. Can you remember anybody in the courts between those times ? "

" Nobody went through the Old Court at all."

" Not a soul ? "

" Not a soul ! I was there, wasn't I ? "

" You couldn't by any chance have missed anybody ? "

" I tells you I was standing in the gateway all the time ! "

" What happened after eight ? "

" The second Hall came out, that was all "

" You didn't notice any dons ? "

" The Fellows of the college was having their coffee in the Combination Room till half past eight. That is, all except the Master. Come to think of it, I seen him come into the Old Court about twenty past, but I never seen what he did there for I had to go for something in the Lodge.

" You didn't see any of the other fellows ? Mr. Meacock ? Mr. Bell ? Mr. Mauleverer ? "

" I tells you the Fellows was in the Combination Room ! And Mr. Mauleverer wasn't in college anyway."

" How do you know ? " The question came out like a palm slapped upon the table. Rudd paused, and amended weakly :

" He didn't come out of the Combination Room with the others in any case."

The Inspector suddenly got up and said pleasantly : " Well, thank you very much. That will help me a lot, I think."

The porter seemed no longer at ease. " I could tell you some more," he said, " about Mr. Beedon. He had a quarrel with the Chaplain on Tuesday morning, according to the Chaplain's bedder. And I saw the Chaplain go to Mr. Beedon's room at about half past ten. I noted the time, for I put a telephone call through to Mr. Beedon just then. He didn't answer it. The Chaplain was there five minutes."

"What was this quarrel about?" asked the Inspector.

"Mrs. Duckworth only heard the end of it. She heard Mr. Beedon say, as he came out of the Chaplain's room: 'And don't you try to threaten me, because I should have no more qualms in squashing a creature like you than in squashing a white slug!' That was the very words."

"I suppose I shall have to see Mrs. Duckworth. Was there anything else?"

"Nothing else about the Chaplain," said Rudd, as if he were sorry to admit it.

"Anything else you can remember before midnight?"

Mr. Rudd paused. "I went up to Mr. Beedon's landing myself," he said, "when I was doing the staircase lights. His lights was on."

"What made you go up?"

"I don't know," said Rudd slowly. "I hadn't seen him about, and I wondered why his light was still on."

The Inspector said "Ah!" a little encouragingly.

Rudd made up his mind and assumed a virtuous air. "There was something up between the Master and Mr. Beedon," he explained with rather nauseating candour. "I happened to come across——"

"I know all about that," said the Inspector

unexpectedly. " So when you saw the Master in the Old Court you guessed he was bound for Mr. Beedon's room with the usual letter. I expect you hid and spied on him, and you thought you might be able to make a little out of it ? A little blackmail, perhaps ? "

" I never thought of such a thing, Inspector, and you've no right to say it ! If there's a law in this land——"

" O.K.," Buller put in. " The point is, did you or didn't you make up your mind to do anything ? I needn't ask. You were thinking of trying to work it out of the letter-box, but the light being on put you off ? So you just stood there and then went away. Thank you. I'd like to see you again later, if I may. Try to cast your mind back to eight o'clock."

" I tell you I was in the gateway ! " shouted the porter, but shouted in vain, for the Inspector was making his way sedately back to college.

.   .   .   .   .   .

Before calling on the Chaplain, Buller waited to collect himself. He stopped on St. Bernard's bridge and, taking out his little note book, began to write, resting it on the wooden edge.

He wrote :

Frazer, undergraduate, St. Barnabas : dead : not known to be acquainted with anybody in this college.

Beedon, Fellow of St. Bernard's : dead.

Master of St. Bernard's : drug addict : ordered drugs through Beedon (?)

Mauleverer, Fellow of St. Bernard's : alibi rather pat : No motive yet.

Chaplain of St. Bernard's : quarrelled with Beedon. Why not come forward ?

Rudd, porter : blackmailer : but why lie about people in Old Court ?

Weans : party to Mauleverer's alibi.

Undergraduate in A5 : why should he ?

Undergraduate in A2 : alibi.

Then he wrote down in block capitals : " FEAR, ENVY, GAIN," scratched everything out, rolled the page into a ball, and tossed it impatiently into the river. The sluggish flow carried it slowly away.

.   .   .   .   .   .

The Chaplain received Buller with the laboured surprise of one who had been expecting him. He was a sallow man in the early forties, whose brown eyes hesitated before Buller's and fled away. He asked the Inspector to sit down, in a voice calculated to be hearty, but miserably without success. Then he walked nervously round the room, cleared his voice to speak, and broke down entirely. He looked at Buller, pleading mutely for mercy, for a lead in conversation.

Buller said sharply : " If you tell me every-thing at once, it'll do you good and help me. The inquest is on the day after to-morrow, unless I have to put it off, and the verdict won't be murder and suicide against Mr. Beedon. I take it you're sensible enough to prefer some other kind of charge to a charge of murder."

The tonic acted effectively. " There is no possible charge against me. What I have to say might damage my reputation or tend to lose me my position, but no legal evidence exists which could put me on a criminal footing. You will have the goodness to bully somebody else."

" That's better," said the Inspector. " That makes it much easier for both of us. If there had been any crime of fact, outside the sphere of the present case, I should have been forced to follow it up. But if as you say it's an extra-legal matter of reputation, there can be no harm in making a clean breast. It goes no further."

The Chaplain looked at him calmly. This aspect of the situation had made him brave again.

" I don't require a confidant."

" Very well. And I don't require confidences Will you explain why you have not come forward in response to my notice on the screens ? "

" My visit to Mr. Beedon was in no way con-nected with his death, and I have no evidence which bears upon it."

" You must kindly convince me of that, sir."

The Chaplain was in difficulties again.

" I called on Mr. Beedon over a private matter . . . "

The Inspector stood up and shook his head. " I'm sorry," he said, " but you must be a little more explicit. I must warn you that I know something about your experiences on Tuesday, and I don't propose to tell you what. If you are going to fabricate a story, fabricate it so that it bears a close relation to the facts. Then I may not know anything to contradict it."

The Chaplain swallowed.

" You must swear not to say anything about what I am going to tell you to anybody."

" I won't swear anything of the sort," replied the Inspector. " But if you are criminally in a safe position it makes me unable to say anything. There is a law of libel, you know."

" Well, I shall have to begin at the beginning. I suppose I've no choice."

" No," said Buller. " You haven't. I don't believe you had anything to do with the murder or I should have to warn you. But I do believe you can clear one or two things up. Now go ahead."

" Beedon was a very difficult man to get on with, for clergymen especially. He had no principles and his own kind of vice. He always made his ideas very painfully clear. Although he was not a religious man himself he believed that clergymen ought to be. He felt contempt for us if we were—er—religious, and greater contempt if we were not." The Chaplain paused and added : " This is very painful to me. Can't you accept my assurance that I know nothing about it ? "

" Just give me the outlines of the story."

The creature plucked up courage : " Briefly," he said, " a letter written by me came into Beedon's possession by a stupid accident. On Tuesday morning he brought it to my room and behaved very ratingly. Er—he was very cutting and contemptuous. He was an Irishman and we had never got on with each other. I believe he was delighted to have the opportunity." The Chaplain stopped speaking. The scene was repeating itself behind his eyes. " I hated him," he added, and his white hands clutched and un-clutched themselves on his lap. " He was an intransigent man, and thought he was God Almighty. He came with the definite intention of taunting and humiliating me, and he tortured me past bearing. Besides, I was frightened because I didn't know what he would do with the letter. I became hysterical, I think, and threatened his life. After all, one isn't a worm."

The Chaplain's eyes followed the course of

events again in silence. " In the evening," he resumed, " I went to Beedon's rooms to end the suspense. I still didn't know what he meant to do with the letter. I meant to ask him, or to apologise, or to do anything that might suggest itself rather than remain in uncertainty any longer. I didn't notice from the Court whether his light was on or off. When I got to his landing the door was sported. You may or may not know that the sport keys sometimes fit different locks. I tried my own and it opened his door. I found that the electric light was on. I had only opened the door a fraction and the light daunted me. I swear that I closed the door and went away again without doing anything. I swear that, Inspector, by Jesus Christ our Lord."

Buller felt disgusted. " There's no need," he said. " There's no need. It's a plausible story already."

The two men faced each other in silence.

Buller said : " There was no such letter among his effects."

" When I got back I noticed the white of an envelope in my letter box. It was a letter from Beedon enclosing my own letter. He must have delivered it himself after tea, when I was out."

" So everything fits in beautifully," said the Inspector.

Dp

" Oh God ! " exclaimed the Chaplain. " You don't believe me ! But I swear it's true."

" I suppose you burnt the letter ? "

" I did ! Oh, you won't believe me, but I did ! It was natural, wasn't it ? I didn't keep the covering letter either. Why should I ? It was beastly."

The Chaplain suddenly became calm and urgent. " Listen," he said, " what I've told you is true. If you don't believe it you must face other facts. I didn't visit Beedon till half past ten. Whoever told you that they saw me must have told you that. I read detective stories. Surely your autopsy proved that Beedon died before or after that hour ? The coincidence would be too cruel otherwise. And then, am I the sort of person that would go about committing murders ? Does it strike you that I have the nerve ? "

The Inspector said : " Everybody says that. But it isn't a question of nerve, it's a question of nerves. However, I believe you. If it hadn't been for the autopsy I wouldn't."

He stood up abruptly, and took his hat off the table. " You said that Beedon had his private vice. Will you tell me what it was ? "

The Chaplain stared in the fire. " No," he said. " I don't believe it had anything to do with it and I refuse to get people into trouble."

" Thank you," said the Inspector. " I believe your story. Anyway I shall see the Master as soon

as he comes back." His stern face suddenly melted
a little. " Good night," he said. " I'm glad you
got the letter."

When he had gone the Chaplain walked slowly
into his bedroom and knelt on a rather ornamental prie-dieu.

.   .   .   .   .   .

After this interview the Inspector realised that
it was time for dinner and that he had had nothing
to eat all day. Without calling at the police station,
he went back to his rooms.

Buller was in many ways a strange man. He
was a man without education in the university
sense, and yet he was tactful and perceiving. Most
curious of all, although he was an ordinary
policeman and the son of a pork-butcher (perhaps because ?) he had a private income and knew
how to spend it. He loved his work and did it for
that reason only—a boast open to few. He was
what is so very misguidedly called a self-educated
man, and yet he was neither bumptious nor in-
sincere. He played the flute with sentiment and
execution, because he enjoyed it. His flat, looking
over Parker's Piece, was furnished for comfort
and for beauty. Very few people had ever been
inside this flat, not because Buller was falsely
diffident or secretive, but because he preferred
solitude like an animal.

He did not write poems or literary biographies or abstruse books on matters of vertu, nor was he addicted to solving his cunning problems in a flowered dressing gown with the aid of narcotics and a violin. Actually he seldom had the opportunity to solve a problem. The criminal scope in Cambridge has not, until recent years, been wide. Buller was that almost unique phenomenon : a man of sincerity and restraint who enjoyed being alive, was too sensible to worry about being dead, and who was not defeated by his own company.

He let himself into his flat, glanced at the dinner-wagon which his charwoman had left ready for his meal, and wandered into the sitting-room. There he looked at the clock and put a record on the gramophone. It was Myra Hess, playing " Jesu, Joy of Man's Desiring." In the middle of this he went out to the kitchen and poured two fingers of whiskey into a tumbler of milk. After drinking this he turned the record over and listened to the Gigue. His hands curved in front of him, wrists upwards, over imaginary reins. When the record had curveted in half a dozen paces from a trot to a stand he switched it off and stood still, looking about the room. He picked up his flute and began to play without intention. What he played was " John Peel." Then he put down the flute, dragged the dinner-wagon into the dining-room, and began to eat ravenously.

His meal took him ten minutes, after which, without conceding a moment for digestion, he rang up the Porter's Lodge at St. Bernard's. He asked whether the Master was back, and was told that he was. He gave a message asking that the Master should see him in a quarter of an hour. He lit a cigar, which he cut with a penknife produced rather unexpectedly from a pocket at the back of his coat, and started for the college.

The Master received him in the long gallery, apologising for being late. He had only just finished his dinner.

The Inspector said : " I hope you had a good day in London, Master."

" It was a beautiful day. Quite warm for the time of year, and I really believe the plane-trees were budding. But I expect you haven't come to discuss the weather."

The Inspector sighed. He was faced by an antagonist whose powers were not inferior, like the Chaplain's. He decided not to beat about the bush.

" In a case like this, Master," he said, " a lot of cross-currents crop up which have no bearing upon the matter in hand. I daresay it must be so everywhere. If we suddenly burst into any room where there was a gathering of people we should find troubles and secrets abounding, all irrelevant to the mere fact of our entrance. A murder makes an entrance, and we spend our time clearing away the cross-purposes which don't apply to it. Now, I will be perfectly frank with you, because it would be useless to be anything else. Why did you sign your name in invisible ink on the sheet of paper which you delivered at Mr. Beedon's door ? "

" Since you've already tried to track my movements in London, Mr. Inspector, I suspect that you are rather interested in this question ? "

" Yes."

" But you must concede that my private behaviour belongs to myself, and that it might be against my wishes to explain a course of action to you which I have already attempted to hide ? "

" You leave me in a difficult position, Master. Either you must choose to explain your actions in private—but without the assurance that it won't be made public—or you must be content to make your explanation before the Coroner. If your actions have been illegal and I can prove it, then I shan't hesitate to prosecute them, whether you tell me about them or not. If on the other hand, I can't prove it, then it might be to your advantage to explain your methods of getting cocaine, to me instead of to the Coroner."

" I'm an old man, Inspector," said the Master,

" but I must assure you that I've seldom met a person with more perception than yourself. You put the matter precisely, and yet broad-mindedly."

" Not at all," replied the Inspector.

" And since you've had me followed once without catching me out, I daresay you might do so again."

" If I might return a compliment, your evasion was positive disproof of your claims to age."

The conversation began to bore the Master. " Very well," he said, " we'll stop all this talking. You want to know why Beedon shot himself, and I'm afraid I can't tell you."

(" I don't believe he did," the Inspector put in parenthetically.)

" Whether he did or not, I know nothing about it. Now I am sorry to put you under an obligation, for I can perceive that you are a man who appreciates them. I don't give you an explanation of my conduct because I fear to give it to the Coroner. Between you and me, Inspector, I could invent satisfactory explanations for any Coroner between now and the day after to-morrow. I give it you simply because I should like to help you with your case."

" If you will excuse my interrupting," said the Inspector, " how would you explain your signature to the Coroner ? "

" I have a daughter," answered the Master cheerfully, " who teaches in a Sunday-school. The little boys there are very fond of invisible ink. It's a sort of craze just now. She bought some as a present for one of her pupils and I had the curiosity to experiment with it. I must have written on more sheets than I noticed. In any case, the blank sheet of paper which I inadvertently enclosed to Beedon must have been overlooked when I warmed the others to bring out the signature. This is perfectly untrue, but it is what I should tell the Coroner. The point of it is that I have got a daughter who does teach in a Sunday-school where invisible ink is a craze. You see, I started the craze." The Master smiled at Buller without rancour.

" Go on," said the Inspector.

" Having established that point I'll proceed to lay you under my obligation. Actually, there's no earthly reason why I should trouble to explain at all. And if I do explain, I expect you not to pester my future activities as a result of the information which I shall myself give you as vaguely as possible. It is true that I am addicted to opiates, and for that I don't answer to anybody but my Maker. Beedon was, too. Since I'm no longer so active as I used to be, it seemed convenient that Beedon should order my stores for me. The ordering, you see, entailed going up to

London and making a rather circuitous journey in which I was fortunate enough this morning to evade your spy. But you will have heard that persons addicted to my habit are inclined to be unscrupulous in obtaining stores for themselves. There was nothing to prevent Beedon, for instance, giving my name in order to get a double ration. Cocaine is difficult to import, you know, and has to be rationed carefully among old customers. So the retailer used to prefer that Beedon should bring with him some token from myself, and then the stuff would be sent to me direct. It made for honesty on all sides. Hence my signature. I used invisible ink as a sort of reserve against mischances such as the present. Also it ensured the authenticity of the token, for anybody could cut my signature in ordinary ink out of a letter. My enclosure to Beedon was in the nature of a sign that I was running out of stores; and I did run out of them. Beedon having failed, poor fellow, I had to go up to London myself to-day." The Master stretched his legs luxuriously, in token of an errand well performed. He waited for Buller to go away. The Inspector, however, had other questions to ask.

" Your story confirms my own theory, Master. It was kind of you to explain everything so clearly. Now may I ask you a few questions? " The Master nodded.

" Do you think that Beedon's death could have had any connection with the drug-traffic ? "

" No. He was always able to keep himself in stores, and would have had no reason for killing himself through scarcity."

" Suppose he didn't kill himself. Can you tell me frankly whether there is anybody else who was equally addicted, and who might have plotted to kill Beedon over some imbroglio connected with the drug ? "

" Actually, Inspector, I should have doubts about betraying my peers to you if there were any. But there were not. As you know, cocaine is scarce and illegal. We hardly have the opportunity to form coteries of devotees. Mr. Beedon and I were the only people I know of in this University who dealt with my particular retailer."

" Very well, Master. I can't see daylight at all. Mr. Beedon was murdered, I'm sure of it. Have you any theory whatever which would account for the motive ? "

The Master put his finger-tips together and stared thoughtfully into the fire.

" Beedon," he said, " was a quarrelsome man. He made enemies easily, because he seemed unable to say anything but what he thought. So there is the possibility of murder in hot blood, carefully re-staged afterwards. Unfortunately there is nobody in this college whose blood would be hot enough to commit a murder of that sort. Then there's the drug theory, but we've ruled that out. Except for these two I can think of no motives peculiar to Beedon's case."

" You mean that the motive will have to be one of those common to the human race ? "

" Exactly. And what are they ? "

" What would you say they were ? " countered the Inspector.

" Hatred," replied the Master, counting on his fingers, " due to sexual causes : money matters or thwarted ambition. Greed, due to sexual causes, money matters or general ambition. Fear, due to sexual imprudence, financial imprudence or imprudence about the reputation. Madness. One could go on splitting one's subdivisions for hours. It boils down to love, finance and reputation. That is, if we exclude madness. You haven't felt, by any chance, that Beedon may have been killed by a maniac ? "

" No," Buller answered. " This is the murder of the century, so far as premeditation is concerned."

" I know nothing about Beedon's sexual affairs," said the Master. " His finance and prospects of reputation were rather interwoven. Beedon was a very rich man, so far as dons go, and though he was not what you might call a popular man his monetary position made it

likely that he would—er—step into my shoes.
So he may have been murdered for his money.
(I suppose you will look into his will.) Or he may
have been murdered by my friend Mr. Mauleverer, who was the second favourite for the
Mastership until Beedon's death. And now,
Inspector, I really must ask you to let me go to
bed : or the Mastership will be vacant before I
intend it to be."

The old man shook hands and bowed him out
of the Long Gallery.

. . . . . .

Buller did not go home. He walked slowly
across the Old Court to A4, and let himself in.
The constable on duty threw away his cigarette,
stood up and saluted.

The Inspector said " Carry on, constable, I
just want to take a look at this gramophone."

The gramophone was a cabinet model, standing open just inside and on the right of the door.
To the right of the gramophone again was a sort
of oak dresser ornamented with glass, china and
two calceolarias in pots. Beyond the dresser was
the door of a cupboard. This door reached the
end of the right hand wall as you went in. The
next wall in rotation had two stone windows
opening on to the Old Court, with a high book-
case between them. Under each window was a

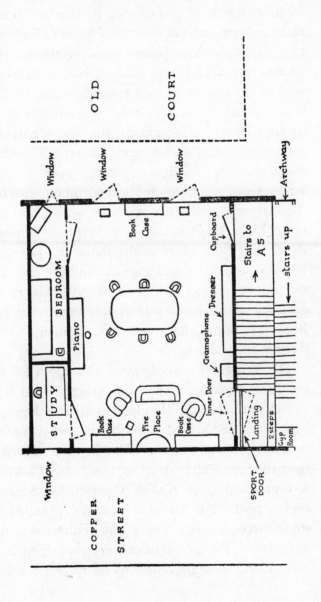

table with a bowl of bulbs on it. Beedon seemed
to have been fond of flowers. The next wall had
two doors, with a piano between them : that
nearest the Old Court leading into a bedroom
with a tin tub in it, and the other one leading
into a small study. The latter was entirely taken
up by a large desk and chair, the former carrying
a typewriter and various card indexes. This little
room had a window opening over Copper
Street. Coming out of the study again one reached
the last wall of the sitting room, which had two
more high bookcases and a fireplace between
them. The floor space of the room was taken up
by two easy chairs and a sofa round the fire, and
by a large table further back with six chairs
grouped about it. It was at this table that Mr.
Beedon's pupils had been accustomed to sit
during supervisions.

The Inspector looked round this room for the
twentieth time in silence before he moved over
to the gramophone. He glanced first at the chair
in which Beedon had been found—the armchair
nearest the study door. Then his eye travelled
over the four walls : there were only two pictures,
a reproduction of Blake's Canterbury Pilgrims
and a portrait of three buxom dairy maids by
some Swedish artist. There was neither hook nor
nail visible, for the pictures were supported by a
rail. That, thought Buller as he turned towards

the gramophone, rules out the idea of a string and pulley system.

The gramophone stood as it had first been discovered. The tone-arm was across the face, with the needle resting on the trackway into which it would naturally run at the end of the record. On the left hand side, by the speed indicator, was a small pool of water which corresponded to a couple of pools under the calceolarias on the adjacent dresser. Whoever had done the watering must have done it promiscuously.

The Inspector tried the handle and found that the engine was run down. Whoever put on the record had not taken it off. This confirmed the Master's story. The record had been set going by means of a piece of string (though it was difficult to say how the tone-arm was lowered—for both Mauleverer and Weans had been emphatic that the record started abruptly, not with the slow groan which would have resulted if the catch had been released whilst the needle rested on the disc) and had gone on running until the engine was exhausted. The tone-arm was the crux of the situation. The catch shewed the marks of the string and was therefore accounted for. But how could the tone-arm have been lowered without being touched ? The evidence of Mauleverer and Weans shewed that it must have been lowered.

And yet it was clean from beginning to end, carefully wiped. It would not be possible to wipe it effectively after it had been lowered to play the record. The only time at which it could reasonably have been wiped was after the record had been played. In which case, if there was somebody waiting to wipe it, why did he wait till the engine had run down ?

The Inspector peered at the thing again. The grain of the wiping was unmarked, top and bottom, except for a single blur underneath, where a small drop of water splashed from the calceolarias still hung. That seemed to mean that the calceolarias had been watered after the tone-arm had been wiped : not that it led one very far.

Buller sat down in the dead man's chair and stared at the gramophone with baffled curiosity. Then he dragged himself to his feet and went into the study, from whence he stared through the window at No. 23. Mrs. Button had pulled down all the blinds.

The Inspector was so pre-occupied that he left Beedon's rooms without acknowledging the constable's parting salute, an omission of which he had never been guilty before. The night air failed to clear his head. He ploughed his way back to the police station through a miasma of conflicting evidence.

In his own office he found a mass of papers
waiting on the table. His sergeant had employed
the day nobly. There was a copy of Beedon's will,
leaving everything to his sister without preamble
or admonition, and a dossier of the sister as far
as her local police could provide it. She lived in
Devonshire and grew roses. There was a note
from the sergeant saying that she had arrived
that afternoon by the 4.15 train and might be
interviewed at the University Arms. Pinned to
this note was a brief history of Mr. Beedon as she
had detailed it to the sergeant. Beedon, it seemed,
had never done anything extraordinary. He had
gone straight from the University to the War, in
which he had acquitted himself with ability as an
intelligence officer on the staff, and straight from
the War back to the University. His financial
affairs were sound and enviable. He was in the
habit of passing his vacations with his sister. She
could throw no light upon the tragedy.

A pile of papers next door to this dealt with the
undergraduate Frazer. His father and mother had
come up in the morning. Frazer, so far as their
knowledge extended, had never met Mr. Beedon.
He was a normal and healthy boy, whose letters
had so far dealt only with the prospects of his
College fifteen and with a few clumsy opinions of
his tutor and the University in general. There
was something pathetic about the brevity of this

dossier, its childish particulars of school achievements, even in comparison with the not very wide
experiences of Mr. Beedon. Buller read everything
through carefully and replaced the files. Then he
switched off the light and made for his flat. In
the middle of Parker's Piece the chimes of the
University assailed him from all sides, counting
the hour of twelve.

CHAPTER V

The Inspector was early up the next morning and found the surgeon at the police station, waiting in his room.

The Inspector said : " I'm sorry I worried you about all that, doctor, there's nothing in it. I was a fool to think I knew more than Boneface and the big bugs from London. Beedon shot the boy and then himself. There's no evidence for any other conclusion, and very little reason why there should be. Beedon must have wiped the automatic just before he shot himself, and for some reason he didn't alter his grip. As for the gramophone, there must be faulty evidence somewhere. It *must* have been started with the needle resting on the record, and I suppose Beedon used a piece of string to start it, so that he could have music to die to, whilst he was sitting in his chair." After a pause he added : " Though God knows what he did with the string ! I suppose he swallowed it." He glanced at the surgeon with a look of ironic misery and shrugged his shoulders. " I shall just have to learn to discriminate."

The police surgeon patted him on the arm. " You're very selfish about this," he said. " You haven't asked what I was doing all yesterday."

Buller's eyes leapt to his companion's face.

" I even had to buy and brutally slaughter a live pig," continued the surgeon, " though his epidermis was not characteristically human."

The Inspector said : " Well ? "

" You'd better come to my rooms and I'll show you. I'll explain on the way."

" First of all," pursued the surgeon as he walked along Scroope Terrace, " I've got rather a piece of news for you. Beedon was shot before Frazer. I can corroborate that statement from the microscopic examination of the bullets alone. There is a faint mark on the Frazer bullet which does not correspond to any on Beedon's. The firing of the bullet which killed Beedon made a fresh mark on the bore of the automatic which has transferred itself to the bullet which killed Frazer. But the marking is infinitely small and too dubious to impress a jury. Luckily there's another point which bears it out. I've re-dissected both wounds and found twice the percentage of oil and cordite in Frazer's that there is in Beedon's. This means that the barrel was already fouled when Frazer was shot. It's a complicated question, for the bullets were fired from different distances. The bullet which shot Frazer was discharged from a distance of several feet and had already outstripped its gasses. Beedon was shot with the muzzle against his temple, so, since the gasses were still in front of the bullet we should naturally expect more of the waste products inside the wound. And they are present in great quantity. But the fact that the barrel was stopped up, as it were, by Beedon's head evidently tended to foul it more than usual and when the second bullet was fired, although the distance prevented it from carrying its gasses with it into the wound, Frazer got the benefit of this extra fouling. If Frazer had been shot first, and from a greater distance, we should expect his wound to be much less fouled than Beedon's. Whereas the actual fact is that, although Beedon was shot absolutely point blank, Frazer's is the dirtier wound. This left no doubt in my mind that Beedon was shot first. However, I thought it best to make a practical demonstration and you must come and see my dead pig."

The Inspector allowed himself to be led into the house and stared uncomprehendingly at the animal's corpse.

" I shot it dead first of all at a distance of four feet. Immediately afterwards I shot it point blank without cleaning the automatic—(by the way, I used one borrowed from the armoury). These wounds I call in order A and B. Then I cleaned the weapon and shot it first of all point-blank and again, without cleaning, at four feet. These wounds I call in order C and D. D was more fouled than C, B more fouled than A. That is to

say, in each case the second wound was fouler
than the first no matter what the distance of the
discharge. They vary comparatively, but that is
not important. The point is that the fouler wound
is the second, and that Frazer's was the fouler.
Beedon was shot first."

The Inspector came out of his trance and
thumped the doctor on the back. However, he
was still not completely jubilant.

" Can you convince Sir Loftus when he comes
down to-morrow ? "

" I shouldn't try to for a moment," replied the
surgeon. " I shall show him my experiments as
if I didn't quite understand where they led and
ask for his opinion. Then I hope he'll explain it
all very carefully, compliment me on my able
work and tell the Coroner all about it. You don't
understand how to manage these things."

" Well," said the Inspector. " That settles that.
Now we'll sit down and talk it out. Let X be the
murderer. . . ."

.   .   .   .

Mr. Mauleverer lectured from ten till eleven ;
then he walked back across the Courts to his own
rooms, his gown flowing out imposingly behind,
and deposited his paraphernalia in the study. His
rooms were less luxurious than Mr. Beedon's. Instead of the old glass, china and statuettes which

ornamented the dead man's dresser (with the calceolarias) Mr. Mauleverer had a medium priced tea service and a tobacco jar with his college arms on it. The college had been George Augustus Hall.

Mauleverer went to a cupboard in the sitting-room and fetched out a bottle of sherry with some biscuits.

He turned round as Inspector Buller knocked on the door.

" Come in ! "

Buller said : " I have a grave matter to discuss with you, Mr. Mauleverer. May I see you for some time in private at once ? "

" Certainly. Come in and have some sherry."

" Thank you, I'll do without a drink."

" As you like," said Mr. Mauleverer. " I hope you won't mind if I drink myself. I've just been lecturing, and it makes one thirsty."

He proceeded to pour himself a liberal glass, looking at Buller over the top of it with an inscrutable expression. Buller fidgeted with his hat uneasily. After a pause he said awkwardly : " I scarcely know how to begin. All this is very irregular. I ought not to have come to you."

" Well," said Mr. Mauleverer pleasantly, " now you've come I hope we'll have a pleasant chat."

" I believe," said the Inspector, enunciating his

words with difficulty, " that you are the murderer of Mr. Beedon."

" My dear Inspector ! What an idea ! What an unwarrantable remark ! I hope you don't go about saying this sort of thing to everybody ? "

" I'm sorry. I shouldn't have come." Buller rose to his feet. " I thought you might have taken it differently. I'll go away at once."

" Well, I'm relieved at least that you haven't brought a constable—even if it is irregular. And oughtn't you to have warned me ? "

Buller was quite red with mortification. " I'm sorry, sir," he said (but stiffly). " I had no right to speak with you. I apologise for my remark. If you wish to, you can report me to my superiors."

" Now don't go off like that. I don't take any offence, but I insist on an explanation. You can't go about accusing people of murder without telling them why. Are you free for an hour ? We might take a little walk towards Grantchester while you explain yourself. I haven't any pupils till twelve o'clock."

" Why," said Buller, " I have nothing which will come to any good by explanation. I've made a great mistake in coming."

" Nevertheless," replied Mr. Mauleverer, " you won't retrieve it by going. You must explain yourself, you know, in common decency."

" I have no common decency, not in my profession. I'm afraid I shall have to leave it as it is."

Mauleverer said persuasively : " Come along, just a short walk. If you expected to get something out of me in conversation when you first came, why shouldn't you expect to get it still ? " He walked to the door and looked out, as if he expected someone to be outside. But the landing was empty. " Come, take your hat," he said. " I have something to tell you after all."

In Copper Street Mr. Mauleverer said to the Inspector, without change of tone : " I'm sorry to have had to drag you out. Walls have ears, you know (have you seen the ear in the dungeons at Hastings Castle ?), and we scientific criminals get to be a little pernickety. This constant attention to minutiæ has the effect of making one over-careful. I'm sure it's a fault, really. Eventually one will get to the point of not seeing the wood for the trees. What a lot of proverbs ! "

Buller was at a loss for reply, but Mauleverer ran on. " Even now," he said, " I'm suspicious of a trap. Could you have a microphone in your button hole, for instance, with all the Roberts at Scotland Yard listening to my little confidences ? I hardly think so, and, besides, conversation heard over the wireless hasn't yet been admitted as evidence in a court of law. One would be sure to get it suppressed."

Buller was still silent.

" You'll admit, however," Mauleverer went on, " that I had to get you out of doors before we could really talk. After all, you might have had a constable listening on the landing. I could hardly, in those circumstances, have agreed with your accusation enthusiastically."

Buller said : " You were unwise to drink that sherry."

" Not at all," replied the don. " My loquacity is due to other reasons than a mere glass of sherry. I have been ready to talk to you since last night, and I've nothing to hide. Perhaps the *gaiety* of my *tone* may be attributed in part to the intoxicant (though of course it's mainly nervous reaction) but you may be sure I'm not putting myself in any difficulties."

" I understand," said Buller halting. " Now I'm going home."

" Don't be a fool." Mr. Mauleverer laid his hand on the Inspector's arm. " You cannot allow a personal and illiberal dislike to tear you away just when you might be able to pump me advantageously. I gather from your behaviour that you haven't the evidence to convict, since you haven't even warned me. Your call was just an effort to startle an advantage. Well, go on with it. After all, there may be something to be gained, if only in studying my mentality as revealed by conversation."

Buller made no reply.

" Besides," added the other, " I enjoy pulling your leg."

" I don't enjoy," replied Buller evenly, " having it pulled. Good-bye."

" What a waste of time ! Now that you've dragged me out on this pointless walk I insist on talking to you. I shall tell you exactly how everything was done. I suppose you've established the priority of wound by the autopsy ? "

Buller grunted non-committally.

" You'd never have thought of looking into that so closely if it hadn't been for an accident." Mr. Mauleverer sighed with what seemed an almost genuine regret. " It was that wretched tone-arm and catch," he added and began to justify himself with vehemence.

" I wanted to kill Beedon because I believed the Master was getting shaky. Beedon would have got the Mastership if he'd survived the Master. Now I shall get it. I'm poor, you know—by damned fortune. That's your motive. I wanted to make it a suicide. Beedon had a faintly shady past, and suicide would have gone down all right. I went over to Holland and got an unregistered Belgian

automatic. (You know they have a type manufactured with a silencer.) It might just as well have
belonged to Beedon as to me. Then, about a fortnight ago, I called on Beedon in the evening and
got talking about typewriters. He let me try his.
I wrote on a slip of his own paper : " I am sick
of it. Good-bye," and slipped it in my pocket.
He didn't notice. He was in the other room,
making coffee. I had asked to try the typewriter
just when the milk began to boil."

" Then I made my plan about the gramophone.
I proposed to prop the tone-arm up on a thin
tripod made of ice—standing on the record, so
that it would be knocked over when the record
started. Then, if the engine was fully wound up,
one only needed to release the catch for the needle
to fall on a record which was already revolving
fairly fast. It is the initial drag which slows records
up when released with the needle lowered. I was
to release the catch by means of a loop of string
through the T keyhole of the sport door. (When
released you merely let go of one end of the
string and pull the whole length out. Then you
burn the string.) Your companion has heard
a record being played inside the room, with you
outside it, and he can swear you were with him
all the rest of the evening. Ergo, somebody was
alive inside the room when you were at the Festival Theatre, and there's a bullet-proof alibi

which isn't likely to be required in any case. For you shot Beedon with the automatic pressed to his temple, you have left no finger marks on the weapon except Beedon's, and the slip of paper is in the typewriter.

The gramophone would have borne a very close inspection, for I proposed to touch no part of it except with a pencil or the string itself (which would only mark the under surface of the catch, and you'd have had no reason to be suspicious enough to look there). And—this is the important point—I proposed to leave Beedon's own finger marks on both catch and arm. I did not propose to give them that suspicious wiping, as I was later compelled to do. The thin ice-bridge on which the arm rested was made by myself in the University laboratories so that it would melt in twenty minutes. Beedon's room had a fire in it. To account for the water on the gramophone which the melted ice would leave I put the calceolarias on the dresser by its side and watered them clumsily. I used the same water for both bridge and watering, so you won't prove anything by analysis.

" And that was the whole of my operation orders at zero-hour. But the best-laid schemes, etc. I went into Beedon's room and shot him according to plan. He was more surprised and vexed than anything else, and couldn't believe his senses—

whilst he had them. Then I turned at once to the arrangement of the gramophone. Perhaps rather morbidly I had myself given Beedon the record which I proposed to play for his funeral march. But my main reason in giving it him—a couple of days before—was to encourage him to play the gramophone and make nice fresh fingerprints. The record itself didn't matter in my calculations for I proposed to wipe it before putting it on with a silk handkerchief. You see one often wipes gramophone records.

" Well, I went to the gramophone to put the record on and so forth. I found it was on already. This made me look at the tone-arm through my magnifying glass—I was doing the thing scientifically, you must admit—and I was horrified to find my own fingerprints. That wretch Beedon actually had not touched the machine since I gave him the record, and played it to him myself, two days before. I recognised my own fingerprints because I have studied them. Many people can tell you what colour their own eyes are, but few are familiar with their fingers. I think this is an omission. Anyway I was confronted with Beedon dead and my own prints irreparably on the instrument. It would have been impossible to carry him across and make prints then and there, for what with the blood and other matters liable to microscopic examination I'd have messed up the

verisimilitude too much. So I just had to wipe
the arm and catch altogether. I still don't think
you'd have noticed it but for the other mis-
carriage of plan. Both miscarriages, I claim, were
unforeseeable.

" Having wound up the handle—allowing it to
turn in my palm so as to blur beyond recognition
even such imperfect prints as one gets from the
main body of the hand—and set up the tone-arm
on its ice rest, I went to the little study which
faces Copper Street in order to put the typewritten
sentence into the machine. I had picked up the
automatic as I went, and carried it in my hand,
putting it down by the typewriter. The paper was
already in place and I had wiped the wheel which
turns the roller—of course I had been forced to
get his ' confession ' typed some days before, so
that Beedon should have used the machine *after*
me and thus left his own prints on the keys—
when I picked up the automatic and glanced out
across Copper Street. That unfortunate undergraduate was standing at the window of his rooms,
on a level with myself, staring at me open
mouthed.

" I went straight out—I had to chance it—
walked into Number 23, climbed the stairs, and
found his room. He was waiting for me with an
expression of horror and expectation. I shot him
dead.

" I went back to Beedon's rooms—there was nobody to be seen in the Porter's Lodge on either trip—and took the slip out of the typewriter again. I put it in the fire. Then I took a last look round, wiped the automatic, and put it in Beedon's hand, holding it by the barrel with a silk handkerchief as I did so. Afterwards I gave the barrel a second wipe to make sure. I went to the door and fixed my piece of string round the catch so that both ends just came through the keyhole. Then I sported the door and went to find Weans.

" When we were outside Beedon's door together I pulled the loop under the pretence of trying to open the door. The catch was released with the engine at high pressure ; the record revolving overset the ice prop and dropped the needle on the disc, which started playing with the slightest perceptible groan. I noticed it, but Weans didn't. He wasn't on the look-out for it. It is dark on that landing and neither my actions nor the string were visible."

Mr. Mauleverer paused abruptly and looked at the Inspector. " That's all," he added.

Buller said, rather cheerfully : " Well, if you've finished I'll be going." He turned round eagerly and began to walk towards the college. Mauleverer called him back.

" You should have seen that porter before," he remarked.

Buller looked at him with horror.

" He saw me coming out of Number 23. I saw him too, though for some reason I thought he hadn't noticed me. He was coming out of the Crown Arms, where he ought not to have been. You see, he was on duty at the time. I expect you interviewed him and found him reticent on the subject of his whereabouts at eight o'clock. He didn't mention that he'd seen me for two reasons. First, because it implied that he must have left the Lodge when on duty—he did so because everybody was in Hall—and second because he had not actually connected me with the crimes : his mind was full of the Master's imbroglio with Beedon, and with the Chaplain's quarrel. He was a stupid man. In any case he thought best not to mention it : I may say fortunately, for his would have been the one tangible piece of evidence you could have offered against me at a trial. Without his evidence, even on the full reconstruction which I've offered you, you will realise that of course no jury will convict. Now the evidence is negative only."

" Now ? " enquired the Inspector, with his first trace of emotion. He looked as if he could strike Mauleverer to the ground.

" Yes," replied Mauleverer, " now. But don't let me keep you from going to see him."

" What have you done to him ? " Buller said, rather than asked, in a voice of cold passion.

" Tut, tut ! Run along and see."

Buller turned on his heel and made off towards the college. Mauleverer's voice called after him triumphantly.

" Don't hurry," it cried. " Don't hurry ! "

CHAPTER VI

Buller turned in at the back gate of St. Bernard's, a wrought iron contrivance which led into the part of the college on the Grantchester side of the river. Here was the Fellows' Garden, with some decaying lecture rooms and the cottages which lodged the senior college servants. The Inspector made for Rudd's cottage.

At the door he found a constable. Inside, talking to Mrs. Rudd, among the aspidistras and bowers of lace, were the police surgeon and the sergeant. Mrs. Rudd was in tears.

The surgeon took Buller by the arm and led him into the passage. " I came along," he said, " in the hope of seeing you. Did you get the sergeant's note ? "

" No," said Buller. " I've been walking to Grantchester with Mauleverer. What's the matter ? "

" Rudd hasn't been in all night. His wife didn't let me know before because apparently he's done the same thing once or twice already. She seems to think he has a girl in Swavesey. But this morning one of the gardeners found a lot of blood on some clothes which he leaves in the gardening shed on

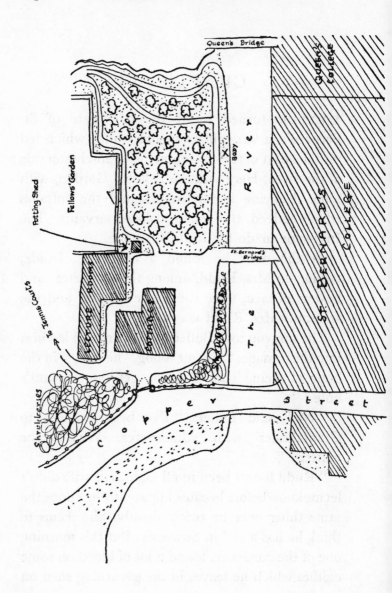

GROUNDS OF ST BERNARD'S

Queen's Bridge

QUEEN'S COLLEGE

The River

X Body

St. Bernard's Bridge

ST. BERNARD'S COLLEGE

Fellows' Garden

Potting Shed

To Tennis Courts

Lecture Rooms

Porters' Lodge

Shrubberies

Copper Street

the Backs, and she got frightened. She sent for us just after you left."

The Inspector called the sergeant out of the room.

"Talk to Mrs. Rudd quietly," he said, "and find out everything you can about her husband. Try particularly to get her talking about the Beedon murder. I want to know if Rudd happened to mention to her that he saw Mauleverer coming out of Number 23 at about eight o'clock. I'm going to see this gardener." He tapped his teeth for a moment and then turned to the surgeon. "And I wonder if you," he added, "would 'phone up for reserves from the station? Tell them to bring something to drag the river with."

．　．　．　．　．　．

When the surgeon got back from the telephone he found the Inspector standing half way down the path which bordered the Backs. St. Bernard's bridge was a hundred yards to their right, and Queen's bridge about the same distance on the other side. In front of them, across the river, rose the crumbling red brick of the Master's Lodge, and behind them dripped the early spring foliage of a dense grove of trees traditionally planted by Duns Scotus. Since the schoolman's initial effort very little care had been lavished on this part of the grounds, so that the two men seemed to be standing between barbarity and civilisation. The bowers and weedy thickets behind them crept untidily towards the University with something of a tropic surge. The trees hid, somewhere in their bosky heart, the brick wall of the Fellows' Garden (mainly vegetable) and, with their Copper Street wing, the outbuildings of the college. These included the lecture rooms, bicycle stores, porters' cottages, and two or three seedy tennis courts. It was a desolate spot, seldom frequented except in summer.

Buller was standing on the river bank, looking down at his feet.

" Look at this," he said, when the surgeon came up. " I suppose it's blood ? "

There was a wide and murky stain, rusting the blades of grass, which spread down the bank to the stone parapet of the river and trickled down to the water in cracking rivulets. The surgeon bent down and investigated with his finger. He plucked a blade of grass and tasted it. It was blood.

" Don't move about," said Buller. " There are plenty of footprints and so on. It was a damp night." He seemed inert and uninterested.

The surgeon asked helpfully : " Shall I 'phone for Chambers to make a plaster cast ? "

" Yes, and send the sergeant to keep people off.

I want to see that gardener's shed as soon as I can get away. You'll find me there."

The gardener's shed stood beside the cottages, at the edge of the stretch of gravelled drive where the Fellows left their cars. The place was at the very fringe of Scotus's plantation, just outside the walls of the Fellows' Garden. The surgeon, after he had completed his errand, found Buller talking to the under-gardener. On the potting table lay a coat, an apron and a pair of heavy boots : all bloodstained. Buller was looking at them without interest, whilst the gardener told his story. The latter was a black-haired Welshman with the expression of a baboon.

" Indeed, sir, yes," he was saying, " a change of vestment I keep throughout the winter months. The clay in these parts is very clinging, look you, and I am a poor man sir, look you, indeed, so that I must needs cover my outward parts with a beggar's raiment, yes, and preserve my decent apparel against the Sunday, look you, yes, indeed ! "

" You left your working clothes hanging up here last night," said the Inspector, " and found them in their present state this morning ? "

" Morning or no morning," said the gardener, " look you——"

" Is that so or not ? "

" As I was saying——"

"Well, I'm afraid you'll have to leave them for the police."

"I am a poor man, sir, in an alien country——"

"However poor you are," answered Buller grimly, "you'll have to wear your decent apparel on weekdays as well, till after the inquest. Or else get some beggar's raiment off the next scarecrow you see. I'm sorry, but there it is."

Buller folded up the exhibits and walked out of the shed. In the drive he bundled them into the police car and sat down wearily on the step. The surgeon sat down beside him and lit a pipe. He waited for his friend to break the silence.

"Well," said the Inspector at last, "now we're up against it. We shall have to look into everything, of course, according to routine. But if I know Mauleverer there won't be anything to find."

The surgeon made a noise to indicate his sympathy and attention.

"I went for a walk with Mauleverer," said Buller, "and he confessed to both murders. He detailed the whole proceedings to me in full. There isn't a scrap of evidence which would carry weight against him in court—not a scrap of positive evidence at all, and even the negative evidence is equally applicable to the undergraduate Weans or even to the Chaplain and the

Master. There was only one loose end which he'd left over, and that was this porter Rudd. Rudd was coming out of the Crown Arms, where he'd been paying an illicit visit, as Mauleverer came out of Number 23. They saw each other. I guessed something of the sort, and I intended to get a signed statement from Rudd this morning. Now Mauleverer has tidied up."

" Perhaps you will be able to get Mauleverer over this second affair ? "

" Too neat. The inhuman swine ! Three poor blighters turning into worms, without guilt or preparation." The Inspector stared moodily at the ground.

" How did he do this last one ? "

"They'll find Rudd's body in the river, there, I suppose. We can't be sure till we've seen it. But it's fairly clear. Some time after dark last night he must have let himself out with his Fellow's key and hidden himself in the plantation. Then, in the darkness, he changed his clothes for those left by the under-gardener. I expect he wore nothing else but the coat, apron and boots. He wouldn't have wanted to risk even the smallest splash on his own things. I can imagine him there, like an animal in the shade of night, half naked, waiting. . . . Rudd was on duty in the college. When he came out, over the bridge, Mauleverer whistled to him. I don't know about the whistle, but he induced him away from the drive on to the path by the river. Rudd was a little on the shady side himself. Perhaps he thought it was his book-maker or his fence or an accomplice or a victim in blackmail. (They don't like to meet their vampires very publicly.) We shall never know. Anyway, he got him to the path and slit his throat like a butcher—coolly, like a snake with a fascinated rabbit. Poor devil ! This last one has upset me more than the others. I should have stopped it if I'd been sharp. Imagine that gross wicked man quivering before Mauleverer in the damp darkness. Mauleverer slit his windpipe at the same time, so he didn't make a human sound. Then he rolled him into the river, warm and dead, and probably chucked the knife in after him. It will have been a Woolworth production, bought for sixpence along with the thirty thousand facsimiles which must have been purchased in this country last year. Quite untraceable, and carefully wiped.

After that Mauleverer will have gone back to the potting shed and changed into his own clothes."

" But surely," the surgeon said, " we must be able to find *some* circumstantial evidence ? "

" I fail to see how. The plaster cast now being made will show Rudd's footmarks and those made by the gardener's boots. The knife won't help us. Nobody saw or heard the thing done."

" Even if Mauleverer wore the gardener's boots from the shed to the path, he must have worn his own boots to and from the shed. That's something, isn't it ? "

" Unfortunately not. The shed stands here at the edge of the drive, which is gravel and won't hold footprints. Nor will the bridge. Mauleverer reached the shed without leaving a trace, and from the shed to the bank he left only those of the gardener."

" At least he can't have an alibi ! "

" Unfortunately you can't hang people for that. Mauleverer will say that he spent the evening reading quietly in his rooms. He won't need an alibi, for there's nothing to connect the business with him."

As Buller stopped speaking there was a hail from the river. The two men got up and walked towards the scene of the murder. Over the path and grass where the bloodstains had been found lay a white coat of plaster of Paris. Next to this was the wet bundle which remained of Rudd. His head was nearly severed from the body, and rolled to one side over a bloodless wound, with bloodless lips coloured by the river. The sergeant held an object in his hand, which he offered to the Inspector. It was a cheap razor, marked from Woolworth's.

" Here's the weapon," he said. " Rudd never told his wife anything about Mauleverer. Shall I arrest that gardener ? "

Fortunately the gardener had an alibi.

PART II

PART II

CHAPTER VII

A FORTNIGHT later Inspector Buller was making a comfortable dinner on a westbound train. The spring was drawing on, and the panorama of sunset over the English fields soothed and elated him. He was free.

The telegram which lay in his pocket had surprised the post office officials. It read simply : " Can you fight next week end zero Saturday noon Darcy," and was addressed from Pemberley in Derbyshire.

Two years before, Inspector Buller had been taking a holiday near Derby. He was driving his car at the lowest possible speed along a rutty deserted lane at the back of Pemberley, when, with a rather loud explosion, something blew up under his off fore tyre. At the same time a voice spoke from the other side of the old brick wall which bounded the lane.

" Kingdom," it said, " look over the wall and see if you've killed anybody."

A stately head, ornamented with white walrus moustaches (uncommon in a butler), dawned solemnly over the brickwork, surmounted by a bowler hat. The whole creation slowly became a deep scarlet and disappeared. There was a whispered colloquy, and a new head popped up. This one was fair haired and fine drawn, the head of a man in the early thirties.

" I beg your pardon ? " it said.

" I didn't speak," said the Inspector in an amused voice.

" Then why don't you go away ? "

" Well," said the Inspector, " one of my front tyres has just blown up, and my spare wheel is punctured."

" What a relief ! " exclaimed the fair haired man. " I thought Kingdom had shot you with a 5.9."

" Probably he has. I don't see why the tyre should blow up otherwise. It was a perfectly good tyre. In fact it was brand new. It was my spare wheel half an hour ago, until I had a puncture and changed wheels."

The blue eyes considered the Inspector solemnly, and then suggested, " If you would care to come in and have a drink I could send somebody round to see to it."

Buller accepted the suggestion with alacrity. He was of an enquiring turn of mind, and wondered who could be firing 5.9's in a private park during the piping times of peace. His host explained that one of the gates was a little further down, and began to walk on the inside of the wall whilst Buller trudged along the road. The

Inspector heard him address a parting remark to the butler.

"Kingdom," he said, "go and fetch Smith from the garage. You might have killed that gentleman. In future I shall discharge your pieces for you myself. And don't go prying at my positions whilst I'm away. Remember you're on your honour, Kingdom."

And Kingdom replied: "Very well, Sir Charles. Shall I fall out the Welch Fusiliers or leave them out till after tea?"

Whilst they were walking up the drive Sir Charles Darcy made his explanation.

.   .   .   .

Sitting in the restaurant car and watching the careful allowance of gin slopping in his glass, Inspector Buller thought about Sir Charles. He had pieced out the story from Elizabeth Darcy—the Christian name had been in the family since the famous Elizabeth in 1813—and it was an odd one. The present baronet had been married in 1918 to a beautiful and charming wife. With the War ended, almost as soon as he had found himself pitchforked into it, and with the broad acres of Pemberley in which to beguile his wife, Sir Charles had had cause to suppose himself a fortunate man. He was gifted and irresponsible, and consciously happy. The wildness of the years

immediately following upon the Armistice delighted him. The newly married couple stayed little
at Pemberley, which was dull even in peace time,
but amused themselves perseveringly in the lights
of the metropolis. They hoped that they were
completely immoral.

One night Charles was rather drunk in a night
club. His wife was sober. One of their acquaintance, a fat man who was said to be something in
the City, came over to their table and talked to
Charles in whispers. He knew that Charles was a
sport, he said, and he had a job of work for anybody who had the guts to do it. It was dangerous,
he said, and just the sort of thing for anybody
who was out for a bit of fun. He and some friends
of his, to put it shortly, had smuggled a small
cargo of liquor from Holland. It was now lying
at Tilbury, waiting to be taken away. They
wanted a really fast car, in case of trouble with
the police, to run it up to town. Was Charles
game to call for it in his Benz ? Of course it was
quite illegal, but everybody was doing that sort of
thing nowadays.

Charles and his wife were delighted to under-
take the adventure. After all, there was nothing
nasty about liquor : it wasn't one of the things
which were " not done."

The fat man explained to Charles that he and
his friends were afraid the police were more or

less " on to " their own car. They believed, indeed, that the police would be on the look out for the cargo in any car travelling the necessary route that evening. It was vitally necessary that the stuff should be fetched at once, before the police traced it to where it lay. Charles would have to keep his wits about him on the return journey, and go by a route which the fat man explained to him. The fat man himself would be unable to come, as he had to make things ready at this end. He gave the directions for locating the cases at Tilbury, and a sort of countersign for the man who would be waiting to deliver them there.

Charles's wife insisted on coming too, and drove the car down herself, as he might have driven rather erratically. On the return journey, when he was more sober, Charles took the wheel. He was volleying along at sixty miles an hour when he came round a slight curve at Purfleet and found a police car drawn across the road. Four policemen with lanterns were waving him to stop. It had been raining. Charles had a confused idea of the interior of his own car, of the road and policemen swirling to the left and then to the right, of the dark police car rushing at him broadside on.

When he woke up he was in a hospital ward with a policeman sitting beside him. Lady Darcy had been killed outright, and the cases in the wrecked car contained many thousand pounds' worth of cocaine. Nothing was ever seen again of the fat man, and nobody believed that he existed. Charles went to prison for two years.

When he was released, he came to live at Pemberley with his sister Elizabeth. It was not a very pleasant life, for the usual country pleasures were impossible. The county no longer consented to attend his shooting parties, and it was impossible to hunt. The unpleasantness of his first day made that abundantly clear.

He laid out a stiff point-to-point course in his own grounds, and rode round and round this for hours, trying at first to break his neck. But he broke the neck of his favourite grey mare instead, and gave up his crazy riding out of shame. He still went round the jumps every morning ; but now he was riding, instead of charging his fences.

As time went by, the curious neighbours heard that he was getting decidedly crochety. He amused himself by launching a miniature fleet, electrically controlled, on Pemberley Lake. With these he fought noisy engagements, which were heard for quite a distance round, until they were all too battered for action. Then he turned himself to warfare on land and elaborated a game which had some of the interest of chess. He used the most realistic lead soldiers imported from France, and miniature artillery specially manufactured for him by Bassett-Lowke. These pieces fired real shell, made of china, and had a very natural effect.

The battle ground was divided by a high canvas sheet into two halves, and on either side of this sheet the combatants—Charles and Elizabeth, or the butler—entrenched their armies for two days prior to the battle. At zero hour the canvas was removed, and, after tossing for the initiative, the battle began. The rules became increasingly elaborate.

The contending armies moved in turn, each turn being reckoned at twenty-five points. These points were controlled by a table of movements. Thus for the loss of one point one cavalryman could advance ten yards, or one infantryman could advance three yards. The discharge of a howitzer cost five points. The white army might select to expend its turn by discharging five shells from the howitzers, and the black army might reply with a ten yards charge by twenty-five dragoons or a five yard charge by fifty. Or either side might split up its points ; firing one shell, advancing five cavalrymen ten yards, and fifteen infantrymen three yards. The adjustments became more and more delicately balanced, and the rules of capture more and more specialised.

The impetus of the attacking force was allowed for in a charge. Moves could be commuted and saved up for a mass attack. Tanks, machine guns, mines, flammenwerfers and even poison gas were introduced. Elizabeth and the butler found that protection was necessary. The combatants operated thereafter from behind triplex screens.

It was to one of these actions, as Charles explained while they were walking up the drive, that the Inspector owed his introduction to Pemberley. It was not entirely to these actions that he owed his continued reception there. Sir Charles had taken a quiet fancy to him, it is true, and enjoyed a change of society. They were soon fighting battles with concord and interest ; but the Inspector would not have gone back to Pemberley solely on that account. He went back because he had instantly fallen in love with Elizabeth Darcy.

He knew that a match between a police inspector and the hostess of Pemberley would be an impossible one, but he managed, as most lovers will, to justify himself in seeing her at any rate. She must be lonely, he argued, seeing nobody in that vast mansion : and she seemed to enjoy talking to him. It was his plain duty to cheer her up ; not expecting anything, of course—in fact carefully retreating from the intimacy which he longed for. Inspector Buller conscientiously saw her not more than fifteen or twenty days in a year ; and thought about her on all the other days from the safe distance of work in Cambridge.

Elizabeth was worth thinking about. She was tall, with mouse-coloured hair. Her lips were Louis Philippe, and she was lovely—a natural champion of the divided skirt. How she could put up with the lonely splendours of Pemberley was more than Buller could understand. At first-nights, driving fast cars with a white cigarette between those formal roses, at house parties and grouse moors, hunting in Leicestershire, bored at Cowes, or chattering in the Royal Enclosure at Ascot, she would have been indistinguishable. And she might have stayed in all these situations. Her brother's disgrace need not after all have affected her. Yet she had followed him to exile. She was a natural creature, and she loved him. She also loved Inspector Buller, and had done, from his second clumsy visit ; but he was not the man to suspect that startling coincidence.

. . . . . .

The Inspector reached Pemberley at ten o'clock, and was bundled off to bed almost at once in preparation for the morrow's action. All the next day was spent in fortification and planning of trenches. Nobody mentioned his affairs until the table had been cleared after dinner.

Then Charles looked guiltily at Elizabeth, cleared his throat and began.

" Liz was reading in the papers," he said, " about this case of yours in Cambridge. I hope there's no truth in this talk about your resignation ? "

" Miss Darcy is right. I resigned before I came away."

" But why ? " exclaimed Elizabeth impatiently. " It isn't your fault if you can't catch the murderer. Besides, you can't be expected to find out who did it straight away ! "

" The trouble is, Miss Darcy," replied Buller, with the old fashioned respect which drove her nearly to desperation, " that I have found out who the murderer is, and I can't prove it."

" But why resign ? They can't have kicked you out for that, can they ? "

" No, I've not exactly been kicked out. They weren't best pleased with me, for I've saddled them with an Unsolved Murder Mystery when the affair might have passed off quietly. They don't want any more unsolved murders at present. But I could very well have stayed if I'd wanted to."

" Why," asked Charles, " did you resign then ? "

" General disgust."

" What at ? "

" At my profession. I'm afraid I've been a fool,

It's a good profession and it probably does quite as well as it possibly could. In fact it's a magnificent profession, and I have been a fool. What really drove me to it was disgust with myself."

"You must tell us about it," said Elizabeth.

"I suppose I resigned because I might have saved this last victim, the porter, if I'd acted promptly. At the time I thought I was resigning from general despair, because we couldn't bring it home to the murderer. But that would just have been pique, and I hope it wasn't the reason."

"Do you mean to say," asked Charles, "that you know who the murderer is?"

"Yes."

"And he got away?"

"No, he's there in Cambridge. We can't prove anything against him."

"Do tell us about him!"

"Well," said Buller, "I'm not a policeman any more, and I can trust you. You're my friends and won't repeat it, I know. Why shouldn't I? The three men were killed by a Fellow of St. Bernard's, a man called Mauleverer. He says he did it (only to me, mind you; he'd deny it to anybody else or in a court of law: but he admitted it to me privately, to gratify his vanity) in order to get the Mastership of his college when it falls vacant. The don whom he killed stood in his way, and the other two got tangled up and had to be finished off. But that's all my eye and Betty Martin really. He did it because he's a born murderer : just for its own sake. He's as clever as hell, and self centred. Beedon did stand in his way and the idea must have occurred to him that he could get rid of him by murder. It's a curious thing, and we generally refuse to admit it, but most of us have had thoughts like that. Only we dismiss the thoughts, through idleness and timidity and, I suppose, through inherent decency—whatever that may be. Mauleverer thought this out, and decided that there was no such thing as any problematical decency about it. He decided that we don't commit murders, because we're afraid to. He wondered if he had the brains to match himself against the Yard. Also, it struck him that there might be a great deal of myth about the fear of consequences which deters most of us. He figured it out that the murderers who don't get found out don't get heard about. Perhaps half the people who get doctors' certificates of death from natural causes have really been murdered. Quite a neat little percentage of the population may be murderers, and nothing known about it, while the small number of persons hanged imposes on us the belief that murder is too dangerous a pastime. Having got this far, and being naturally vain and cruel, he was too proud not to murder Beedon. If he had refused to chance it, it would have looked like squeamishness or timidity. Besides, he had a tremendous belief in his own cleverness. He set to work to plan it out with the crazy enthusiasm of a maniacal chess-player."

Buller considered a moment and then added : " Well, I'm afraid he's pulled it off. We can't bring it home to him."

" But what a wicked state of affairs ! " exclaimed Elizabeth. " Do you mean to say that in this country, in this century, a man can be known to be a murderer and not be punished ? "

" I'm afraid so."

" Then I think you were perfectly right to resign. If that's all the law and the police can do, then I'm glad you're not a policeman ! "

" I think you're wrong about that, Miss Darcy. Things must be proved to the hilt before we can hang a man. Otherwise think of all the poor wretches who might be hanged innocent. It's better that a hundred such as Mauleverer should get away than one man should suffer without deserving it. No, my only excuse for resigning is that I might have saved that porter."

Charles interrupted. " Tell me," he said, " some more about this blighter Mauleverer."

" Well, what would you like to know ? "

" More about him, himself."

" Oh, I don't know. He's a small man, rather petty and neat, with a sharp face. I daresay he feels inferior about his personal appearance and that contributed to his motives—to re-assert himself physically, you know. It's partly on account of his unappetising physique that he's so vain about his mental powers. Rather a common little man. I should think he bullies his pupils. I'm not good at describing people."

" He doesn't sound very much fun," said Elizabeth.

" No. Not very nice."

Buller added : " Do you know I really hate him—quite personally. I've never noticed it with anybody before. Perhaps it's because he's scored off me. I don't think so, though. He reminds me of a snake or a vicious boar, both malevolent and obstinate. What I'm afraid of is that he'll do it again. He's the sort of creature who'd get a craving for the excitement and the mental stimulus. And he'll feel much safer too."

There was a lull in the talk, till Buller took it up again anxiously.

" You mustn't think I'm so bitter about it for personal reasons. After all I don't think I do really hate him as a man. I ought to be sorry for him. I don't hate him. I'm afraid of him, because he isn't human. You see, if he does do it again he'll keep on with it : he'll be a maniac. That's where I'm afraid of him : it's the tiny light of insanity, of incomprehensible chaos behind his eyes, that frightens me into primitive loathing. He's so much cleverer than I am. Oh, I can't explain it, but he's *wicked*."

" Some men are wicked," said Charles quietly, and suggested a game of billiards.

CHAPTER VIII

Next morning Buller was awakened by Kingdom in person. After Charles's disgrace the footmen had given notice—they were a post-war generation in any case—and there was no valet. Nobody had troubled to engage new ones, since Kingdom, who had been a groom when Charles's father was a boy, preferred to gather the duties on himself. Next to Elizabeth he had been his master's greatest stay.

"Miss Elizabeth's compliments, sir," said Kingdom, putting her back into the nursery pinafore by vocal powers alone, " and if you would care to ride before breakfast the horses will be ready in half an hour. Miss Elizabeth wanted to speak to you particular about Sir Charles."

Elizabeth was beautiful, in a blue jersey and red lips. Buller never ceased to be delighted that she did not ride astride. She was mounted on a horse called Vitty Kerumby—a name deviously derived from Webster's White Devil—a huge white mare with a bold eye who leapt her fences like a battleship, and had been round Olympia with half a fault. Buller's mount was a kindly hunter, who had never refused anything, but was gone a little in the wind.

As they rode through the park, Buller waited for Elizabeth to speak about her brother. But she seemed inclined to let the matter wait. Buller would never have understood that she wanted to enjoy her ride with him, without perplexing discussions. So they rode down to the big field in an awkward silence, and there forgot about Charles entirely, for an hour of delight.

While the horses walked home side by side, Buller asked : " What is this about your brother ? "

Elizabeth said : " Oh, it's nothing. I don't know. Let's wait till after breakfast."

Charles was not at breakfast, and the two, after a hearty meal, stood side by side on the thick carpet in front of the fire—glutted with kidneys and coffee, arrogant with early rising and exercise.

Elizabeth said : " This about Charles. My dear, I believe he's gone to murder that don of yours."

" Why do you think that, Miss Darcy ? "

" Well, after you went to bed last night he came to talk to me in my room. He always does when he's worried. He sat on the bed and talked round and round the subject, edging up to it from every side and refusing at the last moment. Now, this morning, Kingdom tells me he's gone off. It's the first time he's been outside the grounds for eight years."

" Do you mean that he told you he was going to kill Mauleverer ? "

" Oh no. He didn't say anything about it. He said that he was bored with life : that he had nothing to live for, no friends. That there were too many crooks going scot free nowadays."

" But surely he isn't mad enough to take the law into his own hands ? He wouldn't be such a prig as to elect himself the instrument of justice. He's never struck me as a person who would be smug enough to do that."

" Well," said Elizabeth, " this Four-Just-Men business is pretty conceited, I admit. But then Charles's motives aren't puritanical. If I'm right, he hasn't gone off because he believes in justice, though he may think he has. You mustn't forget that he adored and still thinks about his wife. She was murdered, to all intents and purposes, by that swine who wanted the drugs smuggled. Charles personally hates all crooks. It's quite painful sometimes to see him read the newspapers. And then he's sick of life here. He wants something to *do*. . . ."

" Even then, I can't see him turning to murder as a pastime."

" No. I hope not. I don't think he could murder anybody. But still, I'm frightened. He hasn't been away for eight years."

Buller puffed his pipe in silence.

.   .   .   .   .   .

Charles came back in the evening and Buller caught him in his dressing-room before dinner.

" Well," he said, " did you tell him you were going to kill him ? "

" Yes," said Charles.

" Would you mind," Buller asked, " telling me all about it ? "

Charles looked guilty, obstinate and embarrassed.

" I suppose I've been a fool," he said. " It seemed possible last night. Now I don't know."

" What happened ? "

" I went straight to St. Bernard's and asked to see him. He'd only just finished breakfast."

" Well ? "

" Well, I just told him what you'd told me and one or two of the things I thought about him. He was surprised at first. Then he began to get angry. I can be rude at times, and that warmed me up. He was sarcastic and I was more so. We had quite a tiff."

" What did you tell him ? "

Charles suddenly looked cast down.

" I told him that I should kill him at the end of a week."

" What did he say to that ? "

" He went absolutely mad."

" And then ? "

" Then I went away."

HP

" And now you're not so pleased with your-self? "

" I had a lot of time to think it over in the train."

" And now what are you going to do ? "

" I don't know," said Charles, " it wouldn't be impossible in a fair fight. He's an utter little cad. But I can't just hide behind a bush and pot him sitting. And if I don't do it secretly I shall get caught and hanged at once. I don't know how to manage it."

" He plotted to murder people without a fair fight. Wouldn't it be fair to do the same by him ? "

" It would be fair enough. But I can't do it."

" So now you're stuck ? "

" Yes. You seem to like rubbing it in."

" Oh, I'm delighted of course. The best fun will be explaining to my late colleagues how you came to be murdered."

" What do you mean ? "

" If you want a fair fight, my dear man, you're going to get it. Only it won't be fair. Great heavens, man, do you think you can go and talk that sort of stuff to a homicidal maniac and get away with it ? There won't be any trouble about potting him sitting, if that's any consolation. You say he went absolutely mad. What exactly did he say ? "

" Oh, some balderdash or other. He was actually frothing at the mouth : little bubbles at the corners, which slurred his utterance—the first time I've ever seen it, except in a man who was slightly drunk. He called me a bumptious little puppet and told me to make my will. He was rather fine about it, in a way. He certainly believes in himself."

" And has it occurred to you that he may have meant it ? "

" I don't think so. He was angry."

" Listen," said Buller. " Mauleverer is a killer. He has committed a triple murder with complete success, and has no reason to believe that he will be caught if he commits another. He enjoys his success. He would be delighted to increase it. He is a man of tremendous vanity. A young man whose intelligence—I hope you won't mind my saying so—cannot have impressed him, arrives out of the blue and announces that he proposes to execute him in a week. He is also very rude. Don't you realise that, even apart from his pride, Mauleverer is actually looking about him for somebody to kill ? He's tasted blood."

" If you think that the fellow will try to kill me, I'm very glad to hear it. It will make it much easier. But I don't believe it. Full term ends tomorrow, and he'll sneak off to hide himself somewhere on the Continent."

" May you long continue to think so. I must send a telegram."

Buller stumped out of the dressing-room in a very bad temper.

.   .   .   .   .   .

Next day it poured with rain. Elizabeth was jumpy at luncheon and Buller taciturn. Charles had been out to the stud farm—he still bred his own horses though he never ran them in any race —and was in a good humour. He was sipping a glass of light madeira when he remarked to Buller, à propos of nothing :

" By the way, your friend Mauleverer nearly got his chances spoilt for him this morning. A tile came off the stable roof just as I was passing. It missed me by inches and broke in eight pieces at my feet. They're heavy things. It must have been coming at a tremendous bat."

Buller walked straight out into the rain without a coat on. He came back in ten minutes.

" I must ask you," he said, " now that you've got yourself into this position, to listen to me sensibly. This is for Miss Darcy's sake as well as your own. I got a ladder and looked at that roof. The tiles are as sound as they were when they were first put on, and the single tile which came down hadn't the least excuse for doing so. Are you going to insist that the thing happened by accident, and be dead to-morrow morning, or will you face the position as if there were something going on ? "

" Really," said Charles, " on the strength of one tile——"

" Now be sensible, Chiz," Elizabeth interrupted. " Let's hear what he has to say."

" I've got nothing to say except what I told you last night, and what I told you after dinner, Miss Darcy. Charles has raised a hornet's nest and I don't know what we can do about it. All we can do at the moment is to guard him as if he were the Bank of England."

Charles said : " I absolutely refuse to be coddled on the off chance that a miserable maniac may be after me. And I don't believe it."

" Very well, then," replied Buller, " I shall leave by the next train."

All three were conscious that he did not mean it.

" What have we got to fear ? " Elizabeth asked.

" My friend Mauleverer told Charles to make his will. He is now busy, somewhere, arranging to make it necessary. How he will do it, now that the tile effect didn't come off, God only knows. We know that he's somewhere in the neighbourhood at least."

" What are we to do ? "

" Well," said Buller, " I'm afraid it's a question

of psychology. We've got nothing to go on except our very hazy idea of what's inside Mauleverer's mind. As soon as I heard Charles's story last night I sent Mauleverer a telegram apologising for the threat and saying that I had notified the police. The apology won't do anything, of course, but the second half of the message was its *raison d'être*. If Mauleverer thinks that the police know of the feud between him and Charles then he will have to be extra careful that Charles dies without any possibility of implicating himself. The mere fact that Charles does die may be suspicious. So Mauleverer will have to kill Charles in some way which leaves himself beyond suspicion. This narrows his field. Charles will have to be killed—— I hope, by the way, that you don't find this a depressing topic, Charles ? "

" Not at all. I get quite a kick out of it."

" Charles will have to be killed, as I was saying, either so that he seems to have died a natural death, or by an accident which might happen to anybody (such as tiles), or by murder at a time when Mauleverer possesses an alibi. Now Mauleverer has already worked the alibi racket, and he probably won't be interested in it. He's proved his ability as an alibi-framer with Beedon's gramophone, and he'll be out for fresh fields to conquer. So I should plump for the natural death or the act of God. Do you agree with me so far ? "

" My dear," replied Elizabeth, " I suppose it will be all right when one gets accustomed to it."

" Either these things happen or they don't, Miss Darcy. It's a mad world when they do, but we've got to live in it. Remember nobody will ever understand people like Mauleverer. You can't argue normally, or there wouldn't be any murders at all. But there are murders. We shall just have to pretend we're in a detective story."

" Granting that the situation is as you say," Charles interrupted, " what are you going to make me do about it ? "

Buller replied with another question.

" Are you going to do it ? "

" Please do, Chiz," said Elizabeth.

" Let's hear it first."

" No. Listen, Charles. I've been a detective for a long time and I've had the pleasure of frank conversation with Mauleverer. I swear I'm not vapouring. Either you must believe me and consent to act under orders, or you must go your own way."

" Very well. I utterly disbelieve you. I hope you won't force me into mutiny."

" Not if you want to go on living. You're going to do as you're told ? "

" Go on, for heaven's sake, and don't bully."

" Right," said Buller. " The first thing we're going to do is to search the house and grounds.

The second thing is that you're going to be locked up in your bedroom till further orders, with a guard inside and outside it."

" Splendid. I hope I shall be allowed out occasionally : every third Armistice Day, or something of that sort."

" Seriously," said Elizabeth. " We can hardly keep the poor thing locked up for ever."

" I know," said Buller. " He deserves to be, but we can't. And the trouble is that we ought to. Mauleverer may kill him to-morrow, or this time next week, or in ten years' time."

" So what is the solution ? "

" Well, to begin with, Mauleverer would probably prefer to kill you within the week at the end of which you said you were going to kill him. That would strike him as a neat joke. We shall have to be doubly careful for the next six days. And after that, if you're still alive, we shan't be any nearer the solution. He has the patience to wait for years."

" So you do propose to keep me locked up for the rest of my natural life ? "

" No. After this week we shall have to do what you said."

" And what was that ? "

" Kill Mauleverer."

Elizabeth said urgently : " Mr. Buller, I can't let you be mixed up in this."

Charles said : " Fancy a suggestion like that coming from an ex-minion of the law ! "

Buller exploded. " Damn it, Charles ! Do you think I want to kill the man ? Do you think I want a skeleton like that in my cupboard ? Do you think I haven't seen enough of the seamy side to hate being mixed up in it myself ? You poke your stupid head into a hullabaloo like this and then refuse to believe in it, or make ridiculous jokes. What else can we do but kill him, God damn it all ? "

" There doesn't seem to be much else, granted that the tile didn't fall off by itself," said Charles reflectively.

" No, there isn't. You go about the country lightheartedly telling murderers that you're going to kill them, and then you damn well have to if you want to go on living yourself. Don't you see you've let yourself in for it properly ? If you don't kill him now, he'll kill you."

" But you can't kill people," exclaimed Elizabeth. " You can't be a common murderer."

" Apart from the fact that it isn't done," said Buller coldly, " it's a hundred to one we shan't pull it off, and it's in self-defence when you come to consider it."

" You can't do it ! "

" Remember he's murdered these people in cold blood."

" That doesn't make it right for you to do it."

" Remember that if we don't do it he may murder your own brother, Miss Darcy, any day for the rest of his life."

" Even then, it's nothing to do with you. Chiz must do it himself. It's his funeral, not yours."

" A precious lot of good that is to anybody ! So long as I'm privy to it I might as well be in at the death."

" That's a lie. You needn't be privy to it. You could always swear that you thought Chiz was joking."

" If Charles tries to do it alone there'll be another lot of death duties on Pemberley. He isn't safe with a pop-gun."

" Thank you," said Charles. " I'm going to find Mauleverer now, alone, to kill him with my bare hands."

He got up.

" Don't be a fool," said Buller. " This isn't a theatre. All this argument about who's going to kill him can wait. The first thing is to prevent him killing you. Let's search the house."

Charles consented out of politeness to his guest.

CHAPTER IX

THE staff at Pemberley had diminished almost yearly since Charles's imprisonment, and nobody had troubled to engage new servants. All that could be assembled in the hall, including Charles, Elizabeth and Buller, was a party of sixteen. The gamekeeper, the cook, the boot-boy, and Smith the chauffeur, stood marshalled with the gardeners, grooms and maids under the dignified patronage of Kingdom's white moustache. Buller took command of the whole party.

The house was dealt with first. Each one of the innumerable rooms in its Georgian façade was entered in turn. The cupboards and hiding-places searched. Then the windows were fastened and the door shut and locked. Every room was thus secured, except the few bedrooms actually in use, three living-rooms, and the servants' quarters. Throughout the search Kingdom stood on guard in the big hall ; the gamekeeper waited on the principal landing upstairs ; and a maid stood on each of the two main staircases. Nothing was found, nothing stirred.

When the house had been combed thoroughly Kingdom was left to guard it and the party beat the grounds, posting sentries at favourable view-points in case the quarry should break back. Again nothing.

Buller had been walking with Elizabeth.

" All this searching," she asked, " does it mean that you think Mauleverer is in the house ? "

" No. I don't think anything. All I know is that Mauleverer was on the stable roof this morning, or I'm a Dutchman. It's best to make sure he isn't in the castle before we pull up the drawbridge, so to speak."

Meanwhile darkness had fallen. Kingdom had stood alone in the gathering dusk of the old house whilst the great hall sank about him impercep-tibly through waves and waves of gloom. The invisibility welled up from the distant corners and sank downwards from the domed ceiling, gradu-ally stealing its last glints from the chandelier. At last only the silent ghost of a white moustache hung suspended in the night.

Kingdom had made a mistake in not turning on the lights. The old man had lived at Pemberley all his life, and knew the house like his life itself. He was part of it, soaked in its feelings and not at enmity with its ghosts. He enjoyed its quiet dusk. All this locking of doors and the supposed danger of his master was at variance with the feeling of the house. He did not believe in it. There was no occasion for alarm, no need to live by electric light and peer in corners. Such things could not happen at Pemberley.

Upstairs the gloom was equally peaceful. Down the long corridors of the closed façade there was perfect silence and a faint smell of pot-pourri. In the oldest part of the house, at the back, where Charles's bedroom was, the darkness was deeper. Here the walls were panelled and the ceilings low, giving little purchase to the dying twilight. The locked doors were mute sentinels of darkness. Only in Charles's dressing-room there was a faint click, the rattle of a toothbrush against a glass. Then, to eyes accustomed to the darkness, a deeper darkness seemed to move across the room.

Kingdom was never able to give, to the end of his life, any account of the attack upon him—or no coherent account. He said that he had been standing silently in the middle of the hall, thinking about nothing, when a pair of white hands appeared before his face. There was a soft but unpleasant chuckle of laughter, and something cold was thrust between his fingers. He ran at once for the switch of the electric light and wheeled round as he snapped it on. There was nothing in the room. Only, on the floor where he had instinctively dropped it, was a white toothbrush.

Kingdom opened the front door and shouted to

the search party, which, on its way back, was already half way up the drive.

Buller arrived at the double and asked what was up. When Kingdom had told him he swore softly and turned round to the others.

" We shall have to search the house again," he said. Then, turning back to Kingdom : " Was the front door open when you came to call us ? "

" No, sir, it was locked on the inside."

" Go round to all the other doors on the ground floor and see if any of them are open, or could be opened from the outside without a key. And you, Smith, go round the outside of the house with a torch and see if any of the windows are open."

The search of the house was begun again. The villagers of Pemberley who could get a glimpse between the trees saw the whole house starting into light. Every window blazed uncurtained, from floor to roof, and the green lawns were rayed outwards with yellow beams. Inside the house, doors banged, keys turned in the locks and footsteps plodded along the passages. As each corridor was cleared the searchers called out to Buller on the main staircase. Kingdom came back from his inspection of the downstairs doors, and reported that they had all been locked and bolted. Shortly afterwards Smith came from his outside tour.

" All the downstairs windows were shut," he

said. " But Sir Charles's window, and yours, sir, and Miss Elizabeth's, were open at the top."

Nobody was found in the house, and the doors were locked again as before. Charles took the keys.

Buller drew Charles and Elizabeth into the morning-room.

" Do you think Kingdom is prone to hallucinations," he asked Charles, " or are you going to believe me now ? "

" It looks as if you were right," said Charles, " but why the toothbrush ? "

" Why, indeed ! Have a look at it."

Elizabeth exclaimed : " Why, that belongs to Chiz ! Doesn't it, Chiz ? "

" Yes," said her brother. " When we were looking through the rooms I found mine had gone. Why on earth ? "

Buller said : " I'll send this to a friend of mine if you don't mind. The sooner we can get it done the better. I wonder if Smith could take it over to Cambridge in the car and be back before breakfast to-morrow ? "

" Certainly, if it's important. Smith won't mind. He's a good fellow."

Smith was sent for, and set off without delay.

" Now," said Buller, " we've started in earnest. I'm going to sleep in your room, Charles, and we'll take it in turns, four hours at a stretch. You, Miss Darcy, must go and live in the village."

" I certainly shall not."

Buller became quite agitated.

" Now don't be heroic," he begged. " There's nothing to stay here for. It'll only make it worse for everybody——"

Elizabeth was quite final. " Of course I shan't go. I should be terrified in the village."

Buller was at a loss for reply.

" If I leave the house," she added reasonably, " I shan't know what's happening and I shall be scared into fits. I'm not in the least nervous whilst I'm here," she tried to say " with you " but it turned out as—" with everybody."

Buller said, " Well, you must lock your door and keep the window shut. This fellow's a cat burglar or a ghost. Either he got in by a second floor window to get the toothbrush, or he filtered through the wall. By the way, are there any secret passages or such like ? "

" Not that I know of," said Charles. " I should think it was very unlikely. There's the priest's hole, of course, but you've seen that. It's now the little cupboard off the library."

" Have you any literature about the house ? "

" There's a bit in Blundell's *Relicks* and one or two county histories. It's not the sort of house that would have secret passages. All this part is very old, of course, much older than the front, which was done up in about 1750. But there aren't any legends to speak of, and it never was a priory. No secret entrances to the nuns' quarters half a mile away, or anything of that sort."

" Any ghosts ? "

" I don't think so. It's a singularly peaceful house. We don't feel our ancestors at all, although some of them were a queer lot. They've died in all manner of ways here, but we never feel conscious of them."

" I don't see," said Elizabeth, " how Mauleverer could know about any secret passages if we don't know about them ourselves."

" Well, it's very unlikely I admit. But then you may not have studied the history of the house, and he may have done. He might have spent yesterday afternoon at the British Museum and turned something up which the family itself has quite forgotten. Still, it's unlikely. It's only in story-books that houses have secret passages."

Charles asked : " How on earth did the blighter get in an out again so quick, if he had to climb out of the bedroom windows ? Shouldn't we have noticed him as we came up the drive ? And Smith was sent round outside at once. How did he get away ? "

" Don't ask me. It was *possible* to get in and out of those windows, I suppose. But he must be a very slick mover."

" The interesting part," said Elizabeth, " is the

white hands. Why didn't Kingdom see a white face as well ? "

．　．　．　．　．　．

Before dinner Buller made a last attempt to persuade Elizabeth.

" Miss Darcy," he said, " won't you go away just for a week in case anything nasty crops up ? I don't want to be unkind, but you can't possibly be useful, and wouldn't it be much better if you weren't here ? I don't mean in case anything happens to Charles—if it happens, it doesn't matter where you are—but in case we get a chance of potting Mauleverer ? I don't want you mixed up in a murder."

" No, I'm sorry : I absolutely couldn't go. I should be perfectly wretched. And besides, you know you can't try to kill Mauleverer even if you do catch him."

Buller said gruffly : " Well, if you can't go you must stay." In his heart he was delighted.

．　．　．　．　．　．

They sat down to dinner amicably and were just dipping their spoons in the soup when Buller made an exclamation.

" No," he said. " Don't touch it. What a fool I am ! "

The candlelight shone on two spoons half way to two open mouths, and four startled eyes looking at him over the rims.

" I'm sorry," he added. " It might be poisoned, you know."

The spoons descended slowly to the plates.

Charles suddenly exclaimed : " Damnation take it ! This is the twentieth century. I'm to be locked up in my bedroom in my own house because a tile falls off the roof, and then I'm not allowed to have my dinner because my butler says he's been given a toothbrush ! The soup can't be poisoned."

He seized his spoon, splashed his shirt-front and swallowed a vigorous mouthful.

" Well, we shall see now in any case," Buller said pacifically, and watched his host. Elizabeth tried to take some too, but he held her wrist firmly against the plate.

Charles began to splutter into his napkin and turned round furiously on the butler.

" Kingdom ! What the devil is in this soup ? "

" I couldn't say, I'm sure, sir. Cook made it as usual, I believe."

" What does it taste of ? " enquired Buller. " If it's strychnine you'll have an agonising pain in about five minutes, and if it's a large dose of cyanide, your head will begin to curl over backwards till it touches your heels."

" Blast you ! It's soap."

Charles began spitting in his napkin and frothing between oaths. Then he drank successive glasses of brandy, gin, lemonade, and anything else that appeared to have a taste. He sat down furiously and said :

"Well, what do we do now ? "

"We might go on with dinner," said Buller. "Unless you want some more soup."

"I'm not going to have *any* more dinner. Ask cook to come up."

Mrs. Bossom arrived in a state of agitated indignation.

"I didn't put no soap in your soup, Master Charles," she said. "I've been in service in this house since ever you was born, and I never done such a thing ! "

"Of course you didn't, cook," said Elizabeth. "Nobody thought so for a moment. But do you know who can have done it ? "

"I made that soup," said Mrs. Bossom, "from the very best stock, such as I'm always using. There's nothing in that soup but what was in my kitchen all day, under my very nose ; except when we was trapesing about a-looking for the burglar."

"I wonder if we could see the stock ? " Buller asked.

When it was brought he tasted it, and asked the cook to do the same.

"Well, upon my word ! " she exclaimed. "If some ruffian hasn't been putting soap in it ! "

She dredged about in the bowl with a spoon and brought up the remains of a cake of that commodity.

" Good," said Buller, " now we might as well go on with dinner ? "

" But is it safe ? "

" I should think so, perfectly. Unless there's cascara in the petits poussins. This is in the nature of a joke and a warning. If Mauleverer meant to poison us he wouldn't have given us the hint. I should think the rest of the meal would be perfectly harmless."

When Mrs. Bossom had retired grumbling to her den, Buller went on :

" This incident is rather a relief in one way. It may mean that Mauleverer doesn't wish to kill Charles by hole-and-corner methods. He's just saying : Look how easy it would have been to poison you, but I'm not going to do that, I'm going to get you properly, on the wing."

" I suppose he got into the kitchen whilst we were stumbling round the grounds. That's three places he visited : the kitchen, my bedroom and the Hall."

" Chiz," said Elizabeth, " this is awful. It didn't seem real before this. What a horrid joke ! Why, it means we aren't safe anywhere, at any moment. If we sit down we may be sitting on a poisoned pin."

" Exactly," said Buller. " Now you begin to understand why I want you locked in your bedroom. No more meals downstairs, Charles, and, just as a precaution, we'll feed you on tinned foods from now on."

CHAPTER X

IMMEDIATELY after dinner Charles, who was now ready to submit to Buller meekly, commandeered a parcel from the Times Book Club and announced that he was ready to be incarcerated. Buller had a word with Elizabeth before they went up.

" When you go to bed—and I wish you'd go now," he said, " lock your door and sleep with the window latched. It'll only be for a week. Don't open the door unless you're sure who is outside. Promise me to do this. There isn't any danger, but I like to know that everybody is acting according to schedule. Good night, Miss Darcy."

When she was gone he added to Charles : " I wonder if you realise that this scrape of yours may embroil your sister as well ? It isn't only you that can drink soapy soup or sit on poisoned pins. And if I know Mauleverer, it's fifty-fifty whether he doesn't decide to get at you through her. He's the sort of man who might murder your whole household, one by one, saving you till the last."

" I'm sorry, Buller," said Charles stiffly, " that I've muddled you up in this annoyance. But after all you needn't stay."

Buller laughed. " I apologise," he said. " Don't get grumpy. I might be in love."

.　　.　　.　　.　　.　　.

Four hours later, just before two o'clock in the morning, Buller was sitting in Charles's dressing-room with the door into the bedroom standing open. He was reading *Mr. Sponge's Sporting Tour*.

There is an odd stillness and definition about the hours before sunrise, when the body is at its ebb. The electric light seemed to acquire a personality of its own, something aching and attentive ; motionless, but imperceptibly stealthy and indued with sound and movement. The floor boards creaked under its watchful footfall. Charles's breathing from the next room sounded strange and irregular : the movement of a being removed from human thought by sleep.

The night life of things surrounded Buller in widening circles, focused upon his light. He was in the middle of the room, under the down beam of the lamp shade. Immediately about him was the green silence of the carpet, tired and ashy from his cigarettes. A wider circle of consciousness brought him to the inhuman patience of the clock, on his right, and to the weird breathing from the other room : equally inhuman.

Then, outside, was the silence and tangible

darkness of the passage, leading, further off, to the hall's absorbing void, and to all the great and little deserted clocks of the household, ticking in separate persistence : unwatched, tenacious, uninforming. All the wainscots of all the rooms concerted about him in their stealthy rustle. The heart beat slower and slower. At tedious and regular intervals the brown hand moved mechanically up the right hand page and turned it over : the blue eyes flashed up, skirted the room, dwelt on the doorway and the clock : then they dropped to the left hand page and recommenced their timeless to-fro sidling.

A chapter ended like a cycle of ages, and the clock's hands stood at five past two. Buller shut the book with a startling noise, and stood up, breaking the charm. He went into the bedroom and shook Charles by the shoulder.

In Elizabeth's room the windows and doors were secured according to order. The curtains were drawn, so that the room was as dark as pitch. There was a faint smell of scent, the suggestion of feminine proximity. Otherwise nothing, except the softest regular breathing, and a gentle scraping from the dressing-table. The mirror creaked, ever so little, and a greasy surface squeaked against the glass.

In the absolute blackness an acute and trembling ear might have imagined that it detected a second ghostly breathing, a footstep upon wool.

. . . . . .

Buller rang for Kingdom to relieve him in Charles's room, and went downstairs to breakfast. The short but heavy sleep of the night had put him back into the mood of old campaigns, and, after a cold bath, he felt elastic and looked rosy.

Elizabeth was waiting for him.

" Come to see my room, would you ? " she said. " I've got something to show you."

" What is it ? "

" Come and look at it. I locked my door and bolted my window last night, as you told me to. Also, on my own account, I looked in the cupboards, under the bed and up the chimney. I was absolutely terrified, but I did. That was the only kick I got out of it until this morning. Then I got this one."

She opened the door into her room.

On the cheval glass of her mirror was a rough sketch drawn in lipstick :

Buller walked over and examined it dispassionately.

" Were your door and window still fastened when you woke up this morning ? " he asked.

" No. The door was open, but the key was still under my pillow."

Buller stood biting his thumbnail.

" It isn't very nice for you," he said.

" No. It made me feel horrid when I first found it. That man walking about in my room and drawing pictures in Louis Philippe ! It's the other things he might have done—perhaps did do. . . . But any way we're still alive. How on earth did he get in ? "

" I don't know. Locked doors can always be unlocked, you know. He may have a master key, or be clever with his fingers. He may have hidden himself in the rhododendrons when we searched the house for the second time last night, and let himself in again later on. We shall have to have bolts put on all the doors to-day, and from to-night onwards we'll set guards in the passages and in the hall. Will the servants stand for it ? "

" Yes. All that remain now are devoted to Charles, and wouldn't leave him for anything. We've gradually let the staff whittle itself down to the ones who would still be here after an earthquake. Does this little picture mean anything in particular ? "

"No," said Buller. "Let's get down to breakfast. Perhaps we'd better rub it out first, for the sake of the servants—though I suppose your maid has seen it already?"

"Yes. We didn't say anything, though. She may have thought I did it myself."

Buller took his clean handkerchief from his breast pocket and wiped the glass. This red stuff, he reflected, is Liz's lipstick : I shall be able to kiss my handkerchief because it shares the same colour with those lips. Out loud he said : " The picture is simply an attempt to make our flesh creep. We mustn't let it. I don't think it applies to you at all. The man simply wanted to rub it in that he could get into anybody's room with impunity. Now for some breakfast."

They were just finishing their coffee when a knock was sounded on the door and Smith came in with the police surgeon from Cambridge.

"Hullo, Lucifer," said the latter. " I thought I'd come and see how you were doing since you fell from heaven."

Buller said : " Miss Darcy, this is Dr. Wilder, a very old friend of mine. He's the fellow I sent the toothbrush to."

"How d'you do ? " said the surgeon. " As a delicate hint I thought it in rather bad taste."

"Won't you sit down and have some breakfast ? " Elizabeth asked. " You must be absolutely exhausted. And you, Smith, you'd better go and have something to eat too, and a rest, you've been splendidly quick."

Smith shuffled off looking proud of himself, and the surgeon proceeded to fill his mouth with bacon.

"There's nothing like driving through the dawn, and that sort of thing," he said, "for giving one an appetite for bacon. Now what about the toothbrush ? "

"What about it ? " asked Buller.

The surgeon drank a large cup of coffee.

"You can't have expert opinion," he said, "without fee. Your chauffeur told me something about the excitements going on here whilst we were on the way. If I tell you about the tooth-brush I insist upon being let in on the ground floor."

Buller said : "I'm afraid the excitement isn't public property."

"If you're going in for bootlegging or murder, you can confide in Uncle. I'm on holiday."

"It isn't my secret," said Buller.

"Well, the toothbrush is mine and unless there's a fair exchange it's likely to remain so. Forgive my abruptness, Miss Darcy, but Buller's so punctilious that he has to be stampeded into everything."

Buller said slowly : "Actually we're terribly

short-handed if it's going to be a question of guards in the passages. I think you'd better come and see Charles." He drew Elizabeth aside. " Wilder's a good man," he said. " He might be useful if you don't object. Do you think you could put him up ? "

" Why, certainly, if he'd like to stay. But this isn't exactly a house-party."

" If it was," said Buller, " he wouldn't stay."

" Now that you've arranged it," remarked the surgeon cheerfully from the sideboard, " let's hear about the toothbrush. Is Miss Darcy the murderess or are you ? "

There was such a twinkle in his eye that Elizabeth couldn't resist him for long. " My dear," she said, " the whole house is a shambles."

" Splendid ! Naturally I shall give everybody a certificate of death from natural causes."

" Don't talk so much," said Buller, " and finish your breakfast. I want to take you upstairs to see Charles."

" Whilst I'm eating, you might give me an out-line of the position. You forget that I don't even know whom you are proposing to murder."

Buller looked at Elizabeth and, receiving her nod, proceeded to explain.

When he had finished, the surgeon drummed on the table, with a grave face. " We'd better go and talk to Sir Charles," he said.

Charles was standing in the dressing-room, staring moodily out of the window. He was delighted that Wilder should join the garrison.

" Stay and talk to me," he said. " You can't imagine what hell it is being locked up in this piffling little room."

" Actually," said Wilder, " there are several things to talk about. First of all that toothbrush was simply crawling with diphtheria. Now why was it given to the butler ? "

" It was given," said Buller, " as a hint. It was Charles's own toothbrush taken from this room. Mauleverer meant us to realise that he might much more easily have simply left it here for Charles to use and possibly die of."

" It's extraordinary," said Elizabeth, " how Mr. Buller mentioned the death-from-natural-causes kind of attack when we were talking it over yesterday, before the search."

" You don't think," said Wilder slowly, " that this man may have heard you talking it over ? He seems to be pretty well at home in this house...."

The house seemed to stand still and catch its breath about them.

" If he had overheard," Wilder went on in a lower voice, " the procedure might have been a little different. I'm inclined to think that he had already treated the toothbrush and left it for use.

Then he heard Buller vapouring about his probable methods and very naturally changed his mind. He was too proud to give Buller the chance of saying : I told you so. So he went back and took the toothbrush away again and gave it to the butler to show what he could have done."

" But it's preposterous," said Charles. " How can we have been overheard ? "

" How can the man get into any room he likes, with all the doors locked ? You haven't been told about Miss Darcy's looking-glass."

They told him.

Charles said : " Liz, you've got to go away at once."

Elizabeth said : " If you turn me out I shall walk about the grounds in my nightgown, and if you turn me out of the grounds I shall sleep in the road outside the gates. Wouldn't it be safer to stay ? "

Her tone of voice made further argument useless.

" What I can't understand in you, Buller," said the surgeon, " is why you don't plump for police protection."

" Simply because we can't. I'd give my soul to be able to, but the circumstances are peculiar. You know what police protection is, and, even if we could get it on our flimsy story, it would only work for a few days. The nation can't afford to support a posse of constables simply to protect Charles. They would have to let up sooner or later and then the man would step in and finish it off. Mauleverer has the patience to wait for any length of time, and the ingenuity to kill Charles safely in the end even if the police knew that he was trying to kill him. I sent a telegram to Mauleverer saying that we had informed the police—though we hadn't—so as to make him be careful at any rate. We've got the moral protection of the police, in so far as he won't dare simply to shoot Charles from a distance, unless he's worked up an alibi, but that's all we can afford to get."

" Actually," put in the surgeon, " I doubt if he would want to shoot Sir Charles from a distance. From what you've told me of him, I should think he would be very keen on letting Sir Charles know that he was in his power before he died."

" Quite so. But to get back to this police protection business. We should have a couple of country Roberts sitting about the place, and we should have the moral support of Mauleverer's knowing that he would be suspected if Charles died. That's all we should have. The Roberts would have to go and Mauleverer would work out an assassination which couldn't possibly be connected with himself, even on presumptive evidence. Then the real snag crops up. If we ask for police protection and *Mauleverer* disappears, Charles will be suspect. Protection makes it impossible for us to protect ourselves by the only hopeful method—that of polishing off Mauleverer before he finishes Charles. You see, we're up against a man who has the tenacity of a viper and is more or less above the police. We get a regular mediæval feud forced upon us by the special circumstances of our adversary."

" So our late detective is going to countenance an attempt to murder a Fellow of St. Bernard's? "

" Yes. It comes down to that. About murdering Mauleverer I haven't the least compunction. It's a case of self-preservation, not a social case at all."

" And how do you propose to get him ? "

" That's absolutely beyond the horizon so far. The bait is here in Charles, and if we can make it a trap we must do. We can only sit over the bait and hope that Mauleverer will betray himself."

" I don't object to being a bait," said Charles, " not in the least. But I do find it boring being shut up in this cursed room, away from all the fun. Also it's bad for the nerves, you know."

" Nerves ! " exclaimed Buller. " In a couple of days nobody will be able to hear a door slammed without screaming."

As if to confirm his statement a door slammed in the hall and they all jumped.

" Couldn't I get out a bit ? " pleaded Charles. " I should be just as good a bait in a motor-car every afternoon, or taking a short walk round the grounds."

" Too good a bait, I'm afraid. We should find the cheese gone and the trap empty. Seriously, Charles, you won't see what you're up against. You are thinking about murders with knives and pistols and that sort of straightforward stuff. You forget that you've got a madman against you who is also a recognised intelligence at one of the leading Universities. As Wilder says, Mauleverer will probably prefer to get you in some way which will leave you time to understand perfectly that you've been beaten and by whom. And I should think, myself, that he will probably try to get you in some bloodthirsty way. You see, he was blooded over this unfortunate porter. But, if he can't get you like that, he has the whole of modern science to play with. He can induce blood poisoning in several ways. The whole world is a potential arsenal of things that might puncture or poison you : of tetanus, and meningitis and chronic diseases. He may gas you, or electrocute you or even blow you up like Darnley. I'm trying to put the wind up you because it'll do you good. You're too lazy about it. I wish you'd realise that when you light a cigarette, or cross your knees, or turn over in bed, you may be touching off the spring. The only safe position for you is lying flat on your back and motionless. And then you'd be in grave danger. Yet you talk about strolling round the grounds."

" You don't make great efforts to improve my morale."

" No, and I won't till you realise that you're not safe in this room even. It isn't pleasant to have to say these things in front of Miss Darcy, but you make me."

" Why don't we go away ? " asked Elizabeth. " Surely Chiz might be safer travelling about, instead of sitting still where the man can lay his traps just where he's sure to catch him."

" I've thought of that. But it isn't so really. Charles would be on the move, certainly, and it wouldn't be so easy in one way to locate him for the *coup de grâce*——"

" You don't, if I may say so," put in the surgeon, " stint yourself of expressions likely to encourage the invalid."

" —I'm sorry. There it is. We must face it. But as I was saying, it might be better to keep Charles moving except that he has to move in a large space. The bigger the crowd which Charles shoulders through, the easier Mauleverer can hide in it—with a little pin. If we took Charles to London, for instance, imagine the increased chances of ambush ! No, he's safest in the smallest room,

CHAPTER XI

" It's only some soot from the chimney," said Buller guiltily. " You'll have to have your chimneys swept, Miss Darcy, if we're going to keep sane." The tense atmosphere gave place to one of slight hysteria.

" My dear ! " said Elizabeth. " Actually they've just been swept. I did my spring cleaning early when I heard you were coming to stay." She giggled weakly. Wilder began to whistle the Spring Song and they all laughed—nobody knew why.

. . . . . .

The mellow old brickwork and peaceful scenery of Pemberley seemed to take on an air of menace and exhaustion under these new conditions. The three men became secretly tiresome to one another. Charles began to find the continued presence of one or another of them a *memento mori.* Elizabeth could have screamed when, for the hundredth time, she came upon the white moustache of Kingdom discreetly hovering just outside her range of occupation. It was not that there was any antipathy between the members of the beleaguered garrison, but that each reminded the other, simply by his presence, of an unpleasant doubt. The silence was sinister with possibilities.

Buller, when it was the surgeon's turn for duty upstairs, could bear it no longer. He went in search of Elizabeth.

" Here," he said, " I can't stand this. Let's go for a drive or something. I don't think anything can happen during the day in any case. We're not really needed here, and we owe our nerves a rest."

" Where shall we go ? "

" Anywhere, so it be out of this whispering."

. . . . . .

Elizabeth had insisted that Buller should drive, though it was her car ; and he did drive : at a pace which was hardly in keeping with his usual solemnity. The beautiful engine huskily purred beneath his foot. The roads were shining with rain, the sun was out, and the drenched buds unclasped themselves in green and bursting ecstasy.

" This is better than stuffing at home, isn't it ? " asked Buller. He thus temperately expressed the sensation of driving a powerful coupé through the spring sunlight, with his heart's sun and moon sitting alone beside him.

" Yes, isn't it ? " replied Elizabeth, in the attempt to phrase adequately the melting of her limbs.

Beyond these declarations the rest of the drive was uneventful.

.   .   .   .   .   .

The day dragged itself out in futile discussion. They dined together in Charles's room, and there made their last dispositions. It was arranged that the sleeping quarters of all four of them should be confined to a single passage, into which, though it was in the old wing and by no means straight, all the doors opened fairly conveniently. In this passage Buller and Kingdom were to remain by four-hour spells. Wilder was to sleep that night with Charles. He would change places with Buller every other night. Smith, the chauffeur, was instructed to sleep in the passage outside the maid-servants' rooms in the other wing. The gardeners and gamekeeper had to look after themselves in their own cottages, though one or another of them was to be about the grounds all night.

" Wouldn't it be a good idea," asked Elizabeth, " if we got some of the dogs inside the house ? "

This was done.

Meanwhile the early spring twilight had come down in rain again, bringing the battlements of neutral clouds to brood over Pemberley. The darkness which had never weighed upon the house before, in four hundred years of English weather, gathered above the eaves and crept up the great staircase. The clocks began to steady themselves for their lonely concerts of the night, and the less durable human creatures took themselves with a final clatter to their beds or vigils. The house congealed again into silence and the life of things.

Charles, who was taking the first watch this time, sat in the dressing-room where Buller had sat the night before. He also was reading a book, but with different mannerisms. His progress through it was less absorbed, the movement of his hands and his attention to the duties of his guard less measured and automatic. His eyes would stray from the page before he was ready to turn over. He played with a paper-knife. The electric light poured down, not upon an absorbed or taciturn and efficient watchman, but upon a restive manhood : upon a yellow head which moved perpetually like a bird's, and a frame which rose and walked to the windows each time that the silence seemed to gain an ascendancy. There was nothing to be seen outside the windows, for it was as dark as pitch. Charles would stare gloomily at his own reflection, stamp about the room for a moment and drop back into his chair with a disgruntled sigh. He would open his book, shift in his seat, read a few sentences, and shift again. Round this restlessness the same room that had surrounded Buller's absorption pursued its identical interests. The clocks counted as usual, and Wilder's unconscious breathing sounded from beyond the human mind.

At two o'clock the guards changed over. Charles heard Kingdom whispering to Buller in the passage outside, and woke Wilder. In five minutes the house was still again.

The passage was L-shaped, leading at one end to a staircase, at the other to the upstairs morning-room which had another staircase beyond it. Down one side of the longer arm were four bed-rooms. On the other side a series of large windows looked across a leaded roof to the sundial of the formal garden, and, beyond the garden, to the windows of the opposite wing. The back of Pemberley was shaped like an irregular U with a very long base.

Buller walked up and down this passage quietly. He was a man who gained in dignity by being alone. In the unwinking glare of the electric bulb and the stillness of the house, he seemed at home, and satisfied with his own devices. He walked along the passage steadily, halting opposite the pictures for a lengthy and attentive examination. He stopped opposite a lacquered cabinet, and, after a minute, put out his hand to stroke the surface. One could almost see him thinking. He read the titles of the prints, in French and English, and to whom they were dedicated. Opposite each of the family pictures, especially the women, he stood for a long time. Elizabeth's distinctive feature was her profile, and all of these were full face. He turned away from the last of them with the ghost of an untheatrical sigh. The Georgian grandfather downstairs boomed out the quarter and left an accentuated silence. Buller sat down in a brocaded chair and tapped his upper row of teeth with a fingernail.

Except for the tiny movement of his finger he was absolutely motionless, his eyes fixed in front of him on a pot of flowers. The clicking of the fingernail stopped, and he was listening. He stood up as the scream split the silence.

He was across the passage in two strides as a window in the opposite wing was thrown up.

The screams came in an unfaltering succession, like gasps for breath, but fierce and piercing.

Buller could see the bright square of the window opposite, framing the cook in a flannel nightgown, clutching the window ledge and panting between yells.

He threw open the door of Kingdom's room— the old man was already struggling with a dressing gown—and said quietly : " Stay here. Tell Dr. Wilder to stay with Sir Charles." Then he took to his heels. The lights sprang into being as he raced through the rooms. The cook's door was still locked when he reached it, with Smith outside holding a poker. He tapped, and said in a normal voice : " Open the door, Mrs. Bossom. It's all right." There was no reply.

He put his shoulder to the door and, taking the handle, drew back to the stretch of his arm. He grunted as he rammed it. The door shook. He drew back, and, with the heavy heel of his boot, kicked downwards and forwards at the lock. It was a beautiful kick and the door shuddered open, with bolt and lock wrenched away.

Mrs. Bossom was lying at the foot of the window in a tousled heap. He turned her over, felt her pulse, splashed cold water on her face. Mrs. Bossom began to mutter.

Buller stood up and looked at Smith. " Only a faint," he said. " Now why——"

Smith pointed at the end of the bed. An ancient and peaceful-looking skull was perched on one of the uprights.

Mrs. Bossom came to at that moment. Her first thoughts were of decorum. " What's this ? " she said, and, struggling to her feet, invested herself in a quilted dressing gown. Buller had slipped the skull under the bedclothes.

" Why, Mrs. Bossom," he said cheerfully. " You screamed so, we thought you were being murdered. What was all the fuss about ? "

Recollection came back to Mrs. Bossom.

" He's gone ! " she said. " His teeth was gleaming from the grave ! "

Buller said to Smith over his shoulder : " Get Mrs. Bossom a glass of brandy ; and just slip over to the other wing and tell the others it's all right." Then he turned back to the cook.

" Now come, Mrs. Bossom," he said. " Somebody's been playing a joke on you. What happened ? "

Mrs. Bossom said : " Oh, my poor heart ! He was a dreadful one, I can tell you ! I woke up in the dark of night feeling the cold of death upon me, and there he stood in all his cerements, a-gnashing of his teeth and glittering with his eyes."

Buller shook her by the shoulder.

" Wake up, cook," he said. " Don't tell me these fairy stories. You woke up and saw a skull. Here it is. Just an ordinary skull from the museum, with a printed ticket pasted on the top. Now tell me what you can remember ? "

Mrs. Bossom eyed the exhibit with aversion, but seemed heartened. When Smith came with the brandy she was coherent and even vivacious.

" It was a little noise that woke me, I think," she said. " I took it for the clicking of his teeth, but it might have been that he was knocked against the bedrail. I'm a light sleeper. Then I sat up in bed and switched on the electric torch as Laura gave me for Christmas. The very first thing I caught in the beam was *him*,"—she nodded to the skull—" a-staring at me face to face, so to speak. So I turn on the lights, and he is still there. Then I run to the window and shout blue murder.''

" Your door was locked and bolted when we came to it.''

" I bolted it myself, sir, before I went to bed—and the window too, for I had to undo it with that thing a-grinning at me from behind. I thought he'd leap upon my back.''

" You didn't see or hear anybody in the room when you switched on the torch ? ''

Mrs. Bossom was doubtful.

" Nothing that you could speak to. But I could take my Bible oath somebody'd been here. The darkness was a-moving.''

Buller said : " Well, it's all over now. You'd better go and sleep with Laura. And, Smith, light fires in all these rooms, will you ? Now, Mrs. Bossom, I must get back to see Miss Elizabeth. There's nothing more to be frightened about to-night.''

Mrs. Bossom was declaring that she'd never sleep another wink when he departed.

.   .   .   .   .   .

Buller found everybody awake when he got back. Kingdom was in the passage. Elizabeth was sitting with Wilder and Charles in the latter's room. She was in green pyjamas and a man's thick blue dressing gown.

Buller said heartily : " Well, how are the refugees ? "

" Perishing and terrified," said Elizabeth. " What was it all about ? "

" More fun and games. Our friend has just entered Mrs. Bossom's room with the door and window bolted and deposited one of the skulls from the museum (also locked and bolted, for I did it myself yesterday) on the bedrail. Mrs. Bossom is of a nervous temperament."

Charles had lost all his restless incredulity.

" I don't believe in ghosts," he said. " But you seem to have been right about this creature. How did he get in if everything was bolted ? "

" In the same way," said Buller cheerfully, " as he got into Elizabeth's room last night. Now will you two keep in this room to-night, and get Kingdom to light a fire ? I want to have a long talk with Wilder, and I don't know when I'll be back."

He took Wilder by the arm and led him into the passage. Then, instead of halting in the morning-room, he took him straight through and down into the hall.

" Get a coat," he said, " we're going for a walk."

They crossed the drive and made their way across the tennis courts to a green garden seat. The sky was a little lighter with the approach of dawn.

Buller said : " You were right about being over-heard. Of course one can't be sure of saying a word in that house with secrecy. So I thought we'd better come outside. He can't get within range of this seat at any rate, without being seen."

" I gather that you suspect the chimneys ? "

" Yes. Look at them."

Against the ever so faintly paler sky the four towers of brickwork were visible.

" It stands to reason. Up till now there's al-ways been a door unlocked or a window open : always the chance that he may have got in by legitimate methods. But that cook's room was hermetically sealed, and yet he got into it. He must have got in by the only other entry, and that's the fireplace."

" I admit they're large," said Wilder.

" Large ! Why the whole house was designed so that you could roast an ox in your bedroom. Even the tops haven't got pots on them. This is the only house I've ever believed in Father Christmas in."

" We ought to be able to catch him on the hop somehow, if we know where he is."

" That's just the trouble. You see we can't muster more than twenty beaters and there must be at least three times that number of fireplaces— not all of them negotiable, I admit. The fact is that the place is too much of a warren, even apart from the chimneys, for us to comb through properly. We should want three people to go up each of the four chimney stacks (to explore the side entries properly) besides a person in each room to see that he didn't bolt, and a complete ring round the house outside to pot him if he made for the roof. It's impossible without a regiment."

" Well, what's the object of this conference ? "

" I was wondering if you could suggest anything. You see, now that he's located—unless we've guessed wrong—we have the chance of taking the initiative. This is the moment when we change defence into attack, if only we can think how."

" I have a friend near Manchester," said the surgeon slowly, " who is an experimental chemist working for the government. He's a good fellow and would trust me."

The two men drew at their pipes in silence.

" We can't use a real poison gas," said Buller eventually, " for we don't know where it will go to after it's been through the house. We don't want to wipe out the whole of Derby owing to a change of wind."

" No. We should have to use laughing gas, or tear gas, or something of that sort. Preferably something lighter than air. That would go up the chimneys well, and dissipate itself without spreading destruction or annoyance in the neighbourhood."

" Well," said Buller, " if you could go and see this fellow to-morrow ? "

" I'm sure he'd give it me. We were in the same regiment."

" In the meantime it's vitally important that Mauleverer shouldn't smell a rat. We won't mention chimneys indoors, and we must be careful not to lower our voices if we want to say anything important. We just mustn't say it. Mauleverer must go on thinking he has us puzzled, and the more he eavesdrops the better, for we can fill him up with misleading information if the occasion arises. So can I leave it to you to tell Elizabeth "
—the name slipped—" before you go to-morrow, and *out* of doors, what tack we're on ? Give her the same instructions, and tell her not to act as if there was any suspicion of the chimneys. We'll discontinue this business of keeping fires going tomorrow morning. You can leave Charles to me. I shan't be able to whisper to him, for if Mauleverer overhears a whisper he may guess that we have reasons for whispering. I'll write my message to Charles and give it him with a finger on the lip. After all, even if chimneys are good places for acoustics you can't see from them."

As they rose to go indoors a figure detached itself from the bushes on their right.

"Whilst you gentlemen was talking," said the gamekeeper with a kindly smile, "I thought I'd keep an eye around in case of eavesdroppers."

CHAPTER XII

NEXT day Buller conveyed the news to Charles as he had said he would. Then, after luncheon, leaving Kingdom to keep his master company, he took Elizabeth into the garden.

As they walked towards the lake, the wildfowl left the lawn and took to the water, paddling distrustfully away towards the overhanging vegetation of the further shore.

" Wilder gave you my message before he went, didn't he ? " he asked.

" Yes."

" There's one thing we can thank our stars about, and that's Mauleverer's vanity. He's set himself to break Charles's nerve before he finishes him off, and all this child's play with skulls and pictures on your looking-glass is calculated to do it. Fortunately he's given us time to locate him—for I'm sure I can't be wrong—before he's done any real harm. What I mean is that if he'd chosen to polish Charles off without a preliminary fanfare we wouldn't have stood a dog's chance. Now, as it stands, Wilder ought to be back before dinner with enough poison gas of one sort or another to clean the place up by to-morrow afternoon."

" Couldn't we use it to-night, as soon as he comes back ? "

" I'm afraid it will be too dark. You see, we must do it by daylight so that if he bolts we can pot him."

" You aren't really going to kill him ? "

" Yes. We are. Honestly, Miss Darcy, neither you nor your brother really believe in this man. You think to yourselves that a skull drawn in lipstick on a mirror and a practical joke played against your worthy cook are not sufficient reasons for panic. But I've seen three dead bodies behind him, and he's told me about them. He's having a preliminary flutter just now : a little harmless enjoyment before he comes to the big spectacle. And I honestly assure you that if we don't knock him off first your brother is as good as dead. Will you believe me ? "

The urgency of Buller's pleading had brought them to a more intimate pitch than he could ever have reached on his own account.

Elizabeth said doubtfully : " Well, if you say so . . ."

" But I do," said Buller. " It's our only hope."

" I wouldn't believe anybody else."

The suddenness, and, as far as he could expect, patent hypocrisy of this statement threw Buller into confusion.

" Er—yes," he said. " Yes—quite." And then

with a hurried change of topic : " The problem is how much the servants will stand for, and how much they can keep their mouths shut. When we do use this gas, whatever kind it may be, and supposing that Mauleverer does bolt—as I suppose he must—we shall have to have a cordon right round the house. Charles, Wilder, Smith, Kingdom, the gamekeeper, the gardeners and myself : we shall all have to be armed, and we shall have to shoot on sight. Will your people do that, and will they keep their mouths shut about it afterwards ? "

" They'll do it, even if it's rank piracy. You see we have a very close feeling with what remains of the staff. They've all stayed with Charles, through his imprisonment and everything, and they all love him as a sort of martyr. When he came out of prison he got them all together, told them the story of the fat man in the night club, and offered them three months' wages if they wanted to leave. Those that will ever leave us left then. They'd do anything he asked them. As to their keeping their mouths shut afterwards, I don't know."

Buller said grimly : " The best reason for keeping one's mouth shut is self-interest. Once they'd helped in the hunt they'd have that, for they'd be accessories to the fact."

" I think it's very unfair on them," said Elizabeth.

" Not only is it unfair on them, but it's an act
of banditry which may get me personally hanged.
We've got to chance that."

Elizabeth said inadequately : " It's very sweet of
you to stay and help. I'd much rather you didn't."

This also, together with the remark about not
believing anybody else, Buller stored away in his
bosom, to be puzzled over in the hours of night.

" The question of firearms is rather difficult,"
he said. " Wilder and I have got our revolvers, and
I understand that Charles's father used to shoot
big game. Smith could have one of the rifles and
the gamekeeper—he'll be the marksman of the
party—ought to have the other. Do you know, by
any chance, whether Charles has a revolver for
himself ? "

" He has his army revolver somewhere."

" That's good. That means five of us will have
something pretty lethal. The gardeners will have
to carry the shotguns in case of accidents. Even
then it's a difficult house to surround with such a
small party. However, anything that gives Mauleverer a sporting chance is welcome in one way.
My God, I do hope he'll put up a fight."

Elizabeth turned on him suddenly.

" Look here," she said. " If the gas does bolt
him you've got to catch him alive. You can't kill
him. I'd rather he killed Charles."

" But, Liz——" Her eyelids flickered. " But,

Miss Darcy—— It would be suicide. What could we do with him if we did catch him? I assure you he wouldn't repent and promise to live happily ever afterwards. He'd be much more furious than ever. He'd never sleep again until he'd wiped off the defeat."

" I don't care," said Elizabeth, her chin sticking out defiantly. " I'd rather have Charles murdered, and I'm sure he would too, than have the master of Pemberley taking to cowardly murder himself. If it's in self-defence that only makes it worse."

This side of the question struck Buller for the first time.

" Well——" he said.

Elizabeth went on excitedly.

" I'd rather," she said, " that you were murdering him for revenge or hatred, or just for fun, than that you should be compelled to kill him at a distance out of fear that he will kill you."

．　．　．　．　．　．

When Wilder got back from Manchester in the evening he found Buller waiting for him in the Hall. They walked out into the twilight.

" He'll give it, all right," said the surgeon, " but he has to make it. He hasn't got any on hand. We shan't be able to use it before to-morrow afternoon. He's bringing it down himself by the first possible train."

Buller asked : " Is it a poison or an irritant ? "

" It's an irritant of his own invention. In fact he invented it for us on the spot, this morning, when I outlined our requirements. By the way, I thought it only fair to tell him what it would be used for—I knew I could trust him—and he's completely callous. In fact, I think he's delighted to have a chance of human experiment. He says he's making some stuff which will go upwards, instead of rolling along the ground, and which won't go up too quick. Then there won't be any fear of damage in the neighbourhood."

" You're sure it won't do Mauleverer any permanent harm ? "

" No," said the surgeon, looking a little surprised, " the fellow said that if Mauleverer stayed in it he'd choke, and finally be rendered insensible. But he said it wasn't a lethal gas at all."

" Why I ask," said Buller, " is because we've now decided that Mauleverer must be taken alive. Elizabeth thinks, and I suppose she's right, that we can't kill the man in cold blood. You see, the point is that we don't *want* to kill him : we're being stampeded into it out of funk, when you come to think of it."

" But I do want to kill him, and I'm sure my friend the chemist does. What's the good of gassing him out if we don't ? He'll simply come back again."

" I know," said Buller wearily. " If we had any sense we'd kill him, of course. But other things enter into it. Elizabeth has all sorts of loyalties and decencies which one can understand. In the last resort she'd rather be killed herself than kill somebody else for fear of it."

" Then she's a fool," said the surgeon.

" No," said Buller. " Or if she is, so am I."

" Naturally."

" In any case, it's definitely decided. We're going to chase him out of the house alive, and let the future look after itself."

There was a tone in Buller's voice which left the surgeon no other course except to shrug his shoulders helplessly.

" I've been thinking," Buller continued, " that we might be able to do without the gas attack altogether. That creature has been living in the chimneys for two days. I don't suppose he has any provisions with him, and he can't have brought sufficient water. He hasn't needed to. He's had access down the kitchen chimney to all the provisions of the household, and any one of a dozen taps in different sinks and bathrooms can keep him watered. Water's the main problem after all. He may have brought some concentrated form of food, as far as that goes, but the water he can't have brought. It's a hundred to one that he comes through the fireplace into one bedroom or another, every night, and goes through the side door into the bathroom for a drink. What I suggest is that we should lay for him to-night, and then perhaps we shall be able to do without the gas to-morrow."

" And when we catch him what do we do ? "

" Knock him on the head with a thick stick, I suppose, and turn him out into the road."

" And what then ? "

" Don't ask me. I suppose the family goes off in a yacht and becomes nomadic until they hear of his death. It's a wretched situation, but I agree with Elizabeth."

" Well," said the surgeon, " if it's got to be done it's worth trying. But we haven't enough people to watch all the bathrooms."

" No. We shall have to trust to luck. We'll need two in each room, and we'll have to pick on the most likely. Charles will have to look after himself for once. We'll give him a fire and tell him not to sleep a wink. If you don't mind, we won't tell Elizabeth. She'll be better sleeping as usual, with Kingdom in the passage outside. She'd better have a fire too. And we'll leave one of the gardeners outside the maids' bedrooms. That'll leave you ; Smith ; the gamekeeper ; two grooms and myself. We'd better leave the rest to take turns out of doors."

" It seems an inadequate number for watching all the taps."

" Actually, I think we've got a good chance. We'll leave you and Smith in the kitchen. That's a likely spot because there's food there as well as drink. Then I'll make a little tour, now, before dusk, in the best approved style with my detective's magnifying glass. Although the chimneys have just been swept, and whatever precautions the man may take, he can't move about indefinitely without traces of soot. He probably cleans up mighty carefully after him, but its beyond human possibility for him to be absolutely clean. I ought to be able to pick up some signs or other in the bathroom or rooms which he generally favours. We'll post the other traps according to that. Any suggestions ? "

" No. Except that if he chooses the kitchen he's going to have a headache."

CHAPTER XIII

THE third night of darkness at Pemberley found the garrison as silent as the house which surrounded them. Buller's search had revealed three suspect areas besides the kitchen : one for each main chimney stack. One of these was a bedroom and bathroom which were not in use, within three doors of Charles's own room in the same passage. This area seemed to Buller the most likely after the kitchen, and he selected it for his own post, taking the gamekeeper to watch with him.

The two grooms were posted at the far end of the façade, the bedroom known as Queen Caroline's room, over the museum. This left a suspicious sink in the servants' quarters unguarded ; but, as Buller said, it was three to one that the fox would visit one of the other bolt-holes.

Wilder and Smith sat in the kitchen, in wooden chairs on either side of the wide fireplace. The chairs were solid and comfortless, but they were too strongly built to creak. So the two watchers in the darkness were able to alter their positions every twenty minutes or so, when the cramp became intolerable. The cockroaches scuttled over the brick floor undisturbed, giving to the

black stillness a pianissimo background of miniature life, and a tabby cat crouched over a possible
mousehole in taut and patient attention.

The kitchen clock—half an hour wrong, as
usual—ticked out the minutes with a tinny noise,
and Mrs. Bossom's own alarm clock on the
dresser answered antiphonically. The two separate
counters combined in Wilder's head, making
endless rhythms and varied reiterations. He
remembered the train wheels of his childhood,
which had always repeated " I-think-I-can. I-
think-I-can," on the up grade, and "I-thought-I-
could. I-thought-I-could. I-thought-I-could," as
they came down hill. Mrs. Bossom's clock now
mentioned to him " Per-haps He-will. Per-haps
He-will. Per-haps He-will " through the interminable hours of the night.

Buller, in the bathroom upstairs, was in a worse
plight. He had nothing to sit down on but a bathroom chair with a rush bottom, which sounded at
every movement. The gamekeeper, on the other
side of the door, had nothing to sit on but the rim
of the bath itself, and this he disdained. He stood
erect on his own feet for three hours, without
apparent movement.

The plan of this couple was to lay their trap on
either side of the bathroom door. Buller was afraid
to wait in the bedroom itself, in case some chance
movement should discover them to the intruder

before he was fairly away from the fireplace. He wanted Mauleverer to come right across the room and into the bathroom for his drink, before they chanced their leap upon him.

The two grooms were in the same position at the other end of the façade. They conversed in whispers about Vitty Kerumby and how she had been a waller before Elizabeth took her in hand.

· · · · · ·

Mauleverer happened to visit the kitchen first. He came down the chimney as silently as death and reached one foot over the cooking range. He was within two feet, on either side, of the seated figures ; but he did not see them. Neither did they see him. He sat on the range for a moment, making some adjustment. Then he stepped off on to Wilder's toe.

Wilder moved it with a jerk and a muffled exclamation. Smith whispered quickly " What is it ? "

Wilder hissed : " Did you touch me ? "

" No."

The light of a torch sprang through the darkness, picking out the kitchen range and chimney. There was nothing to be seen.

· · · · · ·

The grooms were still confabulating about horses. One of them was telling some story about

a former master. " Ah, he says, Chippy, you get
up on 'im while they're a-holding of his 'ead (and
mind, I'm telling you, he was a nappy one : a-
waltzing round of us the 'ole time like a primer
balleriner and all but a-bitin' of 'is own tail) and
then when yore up, Chippy, 'e says, I'll 'and you
this 'ere soda water siphon afore 'e gets away.
Yes, 'e did, the old so-and-so. Them very words.
Mincing-like, you might say. So I thinks to myself : All right, me old cock, we'll see who's who—
Hullo ! So I touches me cap, respectful-like, and
when I sees me chance I'm up on the old barstad
before he know'd what'd 'it 'im. And the old man,
'e's 'opping round like a turkey, clasping this 'ere
siphon to 'is bosom and 'ollerin' to me to catch a
hold. Which I did before we begins to buck : and
then hoy-hullo ! round that tan we goes like the
fox in the 'en 'ouse. Well, when we'd cleared the
air a bit we fetches up in front of the gov'ner—'e
was up in the 'arf-a-crown seats by then, you may
imagine—and 'e yells out as if he was dying :
Chippy, 'e's going to rear ! Get the siphon ready,
Chippy, 'e says, and when I shouts out Now !
give 'im a squirt. Don't do it before I says, 'e says,
or you'll ruin the 'ole experiment. So then this
'orse—'e was a raking great skewbald with an eye
like a rhinoceros—this 'orse begins to stand up for
'is country, and the gov'ner 'e squeals out Now !
and I ups with the soda water siphon and catches

'im a fair beauty. All over 'is silk 'at, it was, and down behind 'is spectacles. That was the only experience I ever 'ad of curing an 'orse with soda water."

The darkness outside the bathroom door became a shade less dense, and the smallest wisp of soot fell shortly afterwards in the chimney.

.   .   .   .   .   .

Buller had been motionless for forty minutes. His limbs, he found, sooner or later passed the period of sensation and petrified into agony. The discomfort became less unbearable when one had forgotten what comfort was. He interested himself in the drip of water from the bath tap, trying to discover if there was any complicated temporal relationship between the drops. He counted between the drops. Twenty-one. Nineteen. Seven. Nine. Nineteen. . . . There seemed to be no equation. One would have to count all night, if the recurrent was widely spaced, before one could hope to establish a sequence. And yet there ought to be. His mind wandered off among capillary attractions, and water pressures at the reservoir.

A vague shape came through the door. He waited and it pressed his shoulder. It was the gamekeeper. How on earth, Buller wondered, did he get out of the room in the first place without my noticing him?

The gamekeeper talked softly into his ear, without whispering, but as quietly as the wind of night.

" Something stood in the doorway, sir," he said, " a moment agone. I waited for 'im to come in, but he cleared again. I've just been into the other room, but there's nothing there."

Buller whispered : " Are you sure ? "

" I couldn't make him out," said the keeper, " but he was there right enough. His hands was there as plain as day."

" If you're sure you saw him——"

" I saw him plain, his hands before him in the darkness and his eyes big : big like an owl's. He'd be a black creature, seemingly ? "

" But why did he go again ? "

The keeper moved deprecatingly in the dark : " That chair, sir," he said, " he's a difficult one to be silent with."

Buller said : " Well, if we've scared him away from here, there are still the others. Perhaps he'll visit them. And again, he may not have seen us at all. He may have gone away for something else. After all, he's got no reason to be suspicious and he can't see in the dark any more than we can. Are you sure you saw him ? "

" He was a black creature," said the other slowly, " in the black of night."

" Well, we'll stay in case he comes back."

. . . . . .

In the kitchen Wilder was muttering to Smith :
" God knows what it was. It might have been the
cat, I suppose. Anyway we'll wait here. We don't
want to go clattering about the place. Even if it
was him, and we've scared him away, he may try
one of the other traps ; and we don't want to
queer their pitch."

.   .   .   .   .   .

In the far wing the grooms were still talking.
Their voices had risen now beyond the last
vestiges of concealment. The rise and fall of the
monologues was audible, not only in the other
room as it had been before, but even in the
passage. " —and 'e said : That 'orse is lame in
the left 'and front leg, I seen it as it was passing
through the square. Oh, is it, I says, and I 'as
'em all out in the yard and walks 'em up and
down in front of 'im. Now, I says to 'im, in a civil
tone of voice you understand, would you know the
'orse as was lame in 'is near fore ? I says . . ."

.   .   .   .   .   .

The keeper moved over to Buller's elbow and
breathed quietly, in his ear : " There's somebody
been moving about outside, in the passage."

Buller answered : " Kingdom's there : outside
Miss Elizabeth's door."

" Kingdom never moved like that."

" What is it then ? "

" Something dragging. Hark. . . . It's stopped now."

Buller started to his feet. " This is no kind of game ! " he exclaimed out loud. " Either you've got nerves or I'm wasting my time."

He threw open the door into the passage, and started back, jerking his hand nervously above his pocket.

A figure was sagging in the entrance, sharply outlined against the electric light. It was propped up against the door jamb. The head hung forward over the chest, while something dripped monotonously from the collar, dripped into a wide and sluggish pool which spread and spread along the passage.

CHAPTER XIV

Buller lowered Kingdom's body gently to the floor, and stepped over it into the passage, wiping his hands. He was feeling sick, but conscious that the keeper was watching him for a lead, wondering what they ought to do. There was nothing to do.

Buller made a noise as if he were clearing his mouth of a foul taste and said :

" Help me to clear this up."

They fetched pails and did their best, laying the body inside the bathroom in case Elizabeth should wake and come out of her room.

On the bathroom door four words had been smeared in blood—smeared, as Buller realised, whilst they had been sitting inside. The message was cryptic :

NO WATER DRINKS BLOOD

Buller said : " Faugh ! An old man like that ! " He wiped the door clean viciously, and added : " Dabbling about like a muck-puppy ! "

Charles had heard them moving about, and opened his door cautiously. He looked at Buller with an expression of enquiry. Buller nodded

sourly towards the bathroom door and Charles
went across.

The old man's throat had been cut like the
porter's. He looked shrivelled and useless, horrid
not because of his connection with humanity but
because of that connection tragically wasted :
because what had once been human was now a
grotesque thing. Charles stayed there so long that
Buller went in to see what he was doing. He had
folded the old man's hands and smoothed the
twisted face into a picture of dignity. Charles
was as white as the dead man.

He said : " How did this happen ? "

Buller said : " I don't know. We'd better
collect the others."

He sent the gamekeeper to call in the watchers
at the other traps. Wilder came and made his
report. The grooms reported nothing.

Buller said : " Mauleverer must have visited
the kitchen first. When he blundered into Dr.
Wilder he nipped up the chimney in a second.
That put him on his guard and he was just as
much on the *qui vive* as we were. I expect he
visited the grooms' post, and the keeper here
says he visited ours. He twigged before we did.
Kingdom was alone in the passage. This was his
idea of reprisal."

Charles said : " Kingdom was sixty-nine years
old."

The party stood round in an atmosphere of constraint. They were all thinking of the stealthy footfalls in the passage, under the unwinking electric light ; of the mad face grinning with expectation, and the knife. Nobody would mention these things, however.

Buller said : " Now is the moment when we call in the police, or not. Elizabeth said yesterday that we were not to kill Mauleverer, and I agreed with her. But this makes a difference."

Charles looked round the circle of faces. He was grim now and almost cheerful.

" I think we are agreed," he said. " Is there anybody here who would rather have the police ? "

Buller added, unnecessarily : " If we get in the police now, Mauleverer may have cleared out for fear that we should do so. You see, he will realise that if we do call them in we shall be able to search the house thoroughly, and the chimneys. As like as not, he's cleared off. Then we shouldn't find him. There would be endless trouble. Like Sir Charles's fat man in the night club, he wouldn't be believed in. Even if we were fortunate enough to get out of it without one or other of ourselves being hanged—remember this is an ex-convict's house—we should be no nearer Mauleverer. He has an alibi pat you may be sure. Then the police would know that there was some sort of a feud between Sir Charles and him, and we should never be able to get him afterwards. If he came back we shouldn't be able to act with freedom. The disappearance of Mauleverer, even if we were fortunate enough to pull it off, would automatically throw suspicion on Sir Charles. And Sir Charles would still be in exactly the same danger from Mauleverer——"

Charles cut him short.

"You have all seen poor Kingdom," he said. "I don't think we need argue about it."

But Buller added : "It's only fair that every-body should understand exactly what we are in for. If we don't call in the police we can't get a doctor's certificate and we shall have to bury Kingdom secretly in the grounds. If we are not able to explain this and keep it quiet afterwards we are all bound to get into very serious trouble, perhaps even the gallows——"

Wilder interrupted. He said : "I will give a doctor's certificate."

"That is absolutely unfair on you," said Buller. "It can't be done."

"Nevertheless, I'm going to do it. I can lay him out, too, so that he looks all right in a coffin. After all, if he was sixty-nine nobody can be very surprised about it."

The gamekeeper said : "Begging your pardon, Sir Charles, but whatever way it's settled I think we should all be agreed on doing without the policemen."

Smith said : " Yes, sir." They were surprised to note that he was crying.

·   ·   ·   ·   ·   ·

By the time Elizabeth woke up—she possessed the virtue of sleeping soundly—the passage was clear again and Kingdom was decently laid in one of the bedrooms. Wilder had dressed him in a white sheet, which curved about his neck, hiding the gash. The coffin was ordered, and the measurements enclosed, from Derby. Charles went into her room and broke the news before breakfast. She said nothing for a time and then asked :

" I suppose it was sudden ? He couldn't have known what was happening ? "

Charles hastened to assure her.

" He hadn't even time to cry out," he said. " Buller was within a few yards of him all the time and heard nothing."

Elizabeth exclaimed suddenly : " What an inhuman beast ! What a devil ! Poor old Kingdom. Chiz, I don't remember a time when there wasn't Kingdom at Pemberley ! " She began to cry, with bitter dry sobs.

Charles said : " Liz, darling, he was sixty-nine. He couldn't have lived very much longer. Don't cry, Liz."

Elizabeth stopped crying as if a tap had been turned off. " Of course we shall go for him, now," she said. " You haven't told the police or any-thing ? "

" No. We'll do it ourselves."

" Of course."

Charles told her about Wilder's arrangements.

" Thank goodness," said Elizabeth, " that we aren't popular in the village. That's one good thing about your drug business, darling. Pember-ley's been a place apart ever since then, and I don't think any of the servants have much truck with the local people. There'll be no interest or servants' gossip at any rate."

Charles assented.

Elizabeth returned to an earlier subject.

" Kingdom was with daddy," she said, " even when daddy was young. He was more a part of Pemberley than any of us."

" Don't worry about him, Liz."

" No, I don't. Even although it was our fault. This would never have happened to him if it hadn't been for us. But I know he wouldn't mind that. He'd be glad. Our business was his. Well, now his business is ours. Chiz, I know we shall kill that man now. I'm not afraid of him at all."

Charles said softly, looking out of the window : " We're going to get him." There was an odd accent on the penultimate word.

They sat in silence for a moment ; then Elizabeth rose to go down to breakfast. She spoke in an even voice, almost with a note of wonder.

" One of the first things I remember," she said, " was a white moustache."

.   .   .   .   .   .

Wilder rang up his friend in Manchester before breakfast. He said : " Hullo, is that Edgeworth ? "

" Hullo, this is Wilder speaking——

" Yes——

" Yes——

" Look here, I wonder if you can make an alteration ?

" Can you make it lighter than air *and lethal* ? "

.   .   .   .   .   .

Mr. Edgeworth arrived by an afternoon train. He was a leathery man with a drooping moustache who smoked endless cigarettes. His fingers were yellow, and the cigarette hung from his lower lip. He wore steel spectacles from behind which a pair of baleful eyes twinkled benevolently.

He said : " Your last minute alteration held me up a bit, but it makes it more amusing. Now where are these rats ? "

He insisted on referring to Mauleverer as " rats " during his whole stay, to such an extent that Elizabeth asked Wilder whether he really knew what they were after.

" Of course," said Wilder. " I told him the whole story. It was only fair. But this is his way of showing he can be discreet about it."

" But isn't this rather cold-blooded of him ? After all, it isn't his quarrel."

" He knows what he's up to, and he wouldn't do it without thinking about it first. He doesn't say anything about it, but he's thought it out. He's a queer fellow : most people think him a little mad. He has a different way of looking at things, and he trusts me. That's all there is to it." Wilder added after a moment : " Actually, he's a genius. Half his reason for coming here, I suppose, is the desire to experiment. It's an extreme form of vivisection. Ordinarily he has to work with guinea-pigs : when he's lucky he gets a monkey : but a man's a positive windfall. He's thinking in terms of science, you see, and Maul-everer's a unit in some equation."

Elizabeth said : " I don't like men who apply their science to making murderous weapons of war."

" But you'd like Edgeworth. He's the sincerest man, really, and an idealist. I gather that he doesn't believe in peace and does believe in nationalism. But for God's sake don't let's start an argument. I like Edgeworth personally, and he likes me. The main thing is to get Mauleverer."

Meanwhile Buller was talking to the assembled male members of the staff. He had selected the Wren summer house for his staff-lecture.

" I want you to understand the position," he said, " because it's only fair that you should know what you're in for. The man who did these Cambridge murders which you've read about can't be connected with them. I told Sir Charles who it was, and he decided to take the law into his own hands. He visited the man and told him he was going to kill him. He didn't realise at the time what that involved. Now the man has decided to kill Sir Charles, and that's what all the rumpus has been about in the past few days. We believe that the man has hidden himself in the chimneys. He has tried to kill Sir Charles with a tile from the stable roof, and he has been trying to scare the staff by putting a skull in Mrs. Bossom's bedroom and by drawing a skull on Miss Elizabeth's looking-glass. Last night we tried to trap him by posting guards in three of the four places where he usually seemed to go for water. He visited all these places without being caught and killed Kingdom where he was guarding the passage alone, as a reprisal. We have not informed the police, and Dr. Wilder has given a death certificate. The object of this is that we may revenge Kingdom ourselves, not entirely from animosity but so as to be sure of it. If what we have done leaks out to the police we are all liable to imprisonment, perhaps worse. I understand that you are all agreed to stand by Sir Charles ? "

Smith, speaking for the household, said : " We are all agreed, sir, and we want you to understand that there is nobody here who would not rather go to prison than let Sir Charles down or Mr. Kingdom go to his grave without being paid for."

The others murmured encouragingly.

Buller went on : " Very well. Sir Charles and Miss Elizabeth were quite sure that this was what you would say. In fact we have chanced it, for we have committed ourselves already. It was hoped that we could keep you out of it, more or less, but now that's impossible. What I want you to do now is to keep your wives out of it as much as possible. Cook and the maids are to go to the North Lodge this afternoon and we shall take tea and dinner there. We hope that you will be able to make them believe, or at least leave them *able* to believe, that Kingdom died from an infectious disease and that the house is being fumigated. It's a poor story, but it will have to do."

Buller took a breath and went on : " Dr. Wilder has brought a friend down who is an expert on poison gas. We are going to close and bolt all the windows and doors and then Mr. Wilder's friend will release this stuff in the hall and in all four of the main chimney stacks. The gas is lighter than air and will go upwards. You, meanwhile, will be posted in a cordon right round the house so that if this man tries to make a bolt for it you can stop him. I want you to shoot him dead. If he comes to a window to open it, let him have it. If he breaks from a door, bowl him over. Those of you who have to use shotguns wait till you can get a close shot and don't aim low. Shout if you get him, and I will finish him off if necessary. This is the most merciful thing. We do not wish to attack him with hatred, for he is mad. It is useless to do anything on account of Kingdom now ; revenge will do him no good. We are doing this for the sake of Sir Charles's safety. Does everybody agree and understand ? "

Everybody said : " I agree," the male voices making a steadfast and quiet rumble.

Buller added : " Just one thing more. We are afraid that the man may have escaped already. That was an additional reason for not calling in the police. In case he has we shall have to be prepared to carry on the defensive perhaps for a long time. He may come back again. In any case we shall give him the gas for two hours to make sure of him, if he is there. I hope he is, and I hope you will shoot straight if necessary. Sir Charles will issue the guns in an hour or so, when the gas cylinders arrive. They are coming by road. Does anybody wish to ask any questions ? "

There was a restless movement of feet, but nobody spoke.

" Very well," said Buller. " When the lorry comes I should like to have you all here. In the meantime, keeper, you might post a couple of look-outs just in case the man tries to bolt before we get going."

Buller left them and went in search of Elizabeth. It was the first time he had seen her alone that day, and he could not do without her.

" Come for a drive," he said. " Nothing can happen for a couple of hours yet. It will do you good."

Elizabeth asked : " What about Chiz ? He oughtn't to come out of his room like he did this morning till we're sure, ought he ? "

" Somebody had to break it to you," said Buller, " so I let him. But he's back there now, with a fire, and he won't come out till we start the gas."

" Is he alone ? "

" Yes, Wilder's talking to his friend. But it's all right. Nobody can get at him with the door and window bolted and the fire going. He's quite capable of looking after himself since last night.

Elizabeth said : " Well, I should love a drive."

As the car left the park gates Buller remarked wearily : " We've got out of that place for a bit, anyway."

" Thank God. Don't let's talk about it."

" It's a fine house, for all that. What have you been doing there all these years since Charles lost his wife ? "

" Waiting about, I suppose," replied Elizabeth. She took the cigarette from her lips with a sharp movement of her hand and looked out of the near window bitterly. Buller's eyes were on the road in front of them. He pressed the accelerator a little more.

" Well, I must say you're making up for the lack of excitement now."

" Yes," said Elizabeth.

" It seems silly to say you're being very brave about it. That's the sort of thing one says to children. You don't give one the impression that there's any reason why you shouldn't be. Women are different from what I was always given to understand they were."

" You should study them." There was no irony in Elizabeth's voice.

" I don't understand them."

" You aren't interested in them is what you mean."

" I suppose not," said Buller loyally, to the

only thing in which he was really interested in the wide world.

The speedometer crept to sixty.

. . . . . .

When they got back a lorry was standing in the drive, with Edgeworth beside it talking to a bright little man in horn-rimmed spectacles.

Edgeworth said : " This is my assistant Hankey. He is going to help us get rid of these rats." He added with a trace of significance : " Hankey has an open scientific mind like my own." Wilder had evidently been talking to him.

Buller said : " Well, if you'll start getting the windows closed and so forth I'll assemble the emergency rat-killers."

He went off to the summer house, where the men were sitting patiently, smoking their pipes. They put them in their pockets deferentially, and stood up.

The gamekeeper came forward, touching his hat.

" I beg pardon, sir," he said, and waited for encouragement.

" Yes ? "

" Sir Charles has given out the guns, sir, and what with the keeper's guns and the gardeners —we all does a little bit of rabbiting—there's something for everybody. Shotguns and that. But it's these two express rifles I was thinking of, them and the revolvers. Sir Charles was saying that there was three revolvers between us. That and the expresses makes five, and there's six doors on the ground floor in the main building. I was thinking, sir, that you, sir, and Dr. Wilder could watch the two doors on this side the house with your revolvers. Sir Charles was wanting to take the front door with his, and Smith and myself, sir, if you was willing, could cover the three doors on the stable side easy."

"You know the lie of this place better than I do," said Buller. "You'd better post the men yourself. We can put the shotguns further back, at the corners, as a reserve line."

He left the rest of the dispositions entirely to the keeper and went back towards the lorry. Elizabeth was still in the coupé. He leant in at the window and said :

"Wouldn't it be a good idea if you saw that the maids were behaving themselves at the North Lodge ?"

Elizabeth replied, with pardonable irritation : "My dear man, where on earth do you get your ideas about women from ? Your period's about 1850. I'm going to stay here and see the fun. Why should I be bundled off to the Lodge any more than you ?"

But Buller was adamant, and, for him, surprisingly guileful.

"It isn't a question of not being allowed to watch," he said. "I want you to go over there for just the reason I gave. We don't want to have the maids butting in on us and I'd like to be sure of their keeping to the Lodge by sending somebody there to keep them. After all, it's more in your line than anybody else's."

Elizabeth said petulantly : "But I shall be worried out of my life if I don't know what's going on."

"Well if you haven't the guts," said Buller, wondering if he could allow himself that word, "I'll send for one of the gardeners."

Elizabeth said : "Curse you for saying that." She turned the car and drove off towards the Lodge.

The cordon was drawn up and the two scientists came out of the front door.

Edgeworth came up to Buller rubbing his hands.

"The windows are all shut," he said, "and the cylinders are in the grates. I've put one in the billiard room as well as the hall, to make sure, for there looks as if there might be a different vent. Now, if your men are ready, Hankey and I will go in and set them off. If we give them two hours the house will have been permeated from cellar to attic. (I've put one in the cellar by the way.) You

must tell your men not to come within the length
of a cricket pitch, let's say, for the stuff is practically colourless. Actually there's no danger outside,
with the windows and doors closed, for it won't
spread as much as that. It'll go up. I hope nobody
will elect to fly over Pemberley just now." He
looked up cheerfully and bustled off to put on a
gas mask.

Buller stood on the lawn opposite his own door
and waited. He kept his hand in his pocket, strok-
ing the triggerguard of his revolver on the outside.
About twenty yards away, on the opposite side of
a yew tree, he occasionally caught glimpses of
Wilder moving about. Wilder had lighted a cigarette, and seemed nervous.

Buller was nervous too, but he stood quite still,
watching the door and windows. For a few moments he saw Edgeworth, or his assistant, moving
in the drawing-room. The mica goggles and
tubular snout made it impossible to recognise the
man, gave him an inhuman feeling of danger in
the pit of his stomach. There was death in that
quaint intent figure, a still suggestion of operating
surgeons and silent overtakings. Buller sniffed the
air with a faint nausea. He felt sure that he could
hear a minor hissing, scarcely tuned to human
ears. He cocked his head a little to one side. The
air smelt queer, he was sure of it.

He restrained an impulse to retreat another ten

yards for safety's sake. He stood still, three at least of his five senses at a high pitch.

Soon Edgeworth and the assistant joined him. They stood silently in a group, watching death trickle from the chimney pots, whilst Buller squeezed and squeezed, gently, at the outside of his triggerguard.

CHAPTER XV

After two hours Edgeworth snapped his watch shut with a click and turned to Buller.

" That's that," he said. " If the rats are at home they're dead. Still, I should have liked to see a bolt."

Buller moved restlessly.

" So should I. What do we do now ? "

" Hankey and I will go in and open all the windows. Also we'll light some fires on the ground floor to get an upward draught. It's six o'clock now. If you dine at eight in the Lodge the house will be ready for you after dinner."

" You'll be staying to dinner, I hope ? " Buller asked.

" No. Thank you very much. I should like to be back in Manchester to-night."

.   .   .   .   .   .

They were still discussing the situation after dinner.

Charles asked : " I suppose this stuff of your friend's was definitely lethal, Wilder ? There couldn't be any mistake about that ? "

" No. That's quite sure."

" It means, then, that either Mauleverer had cleared off last night or early this morning, for fear of the police, or that he's dead somewhere in the chimneys ? "

" It's not like Mauleverer," said Buller, " to be caught napping. One would have thought that he'd have heard all the bustle of shutting the windows and getting the stuff going. On the other hand, he must sleep sometimes. He's been doing his work at night, so perhaps he sleeps during the day time. He may have died in his sleep."

" I can't understand," said Elizabeth parenthetically, " how he could find anywhere to sleep in, in a chimney, still less how he managed to get about in them so well."

" The chimneys aren't all straight up and down. The four main shafts go straight up, and you can see the sky if you look up them. But the other rooms come into them at various angles. In fact there's a regular tissue of passages all through the house, with ledges and turns, just like the sewers or catacombs of big cities. He would find plenty of nooks to sleep in. It's more difficult to understand how he gets about in the sheer drops than how he can find a ledge."

" You speak as though he was still there."

" I hope he is there—dead. We shall have to make a thorough search for the body to-morrow, when it's light."

Wilder said : " Well, he had a good death if he died sleeping."

The talk took a more general turn.

" I don't think so," said Elizabeth. " Poor wretch, I'd rather do anything than die in my sleep."

Wilder was interested. " Why ? " he asked.

" Oh, I don't know. You wouldn't be ready. It would catch you just between wind and water."

" But you wouldn't know anything about it."

" Oh yes, you would."

Charles said : " Death is an extraordinary thing. I've thought about it a lot. I've even decided what the best sort of death is."

" And what would that be ? "

" I was an observer just at the very end of the War. Somebody could write a very interesting war book about observers. Imagine trusting yourself to a separate person, in a machine which might go wrong at any moment, in a situation which meant almost certain death if it did go wrong— and that quite apart from the dangers of actual combat. The observers were much braver than the pilots. It used to be interesting to see the old observers looking over the new pilots, wondering how safe they were. But this is apart from what I was trying to tell you. I never got to France, but I knew an observer who did. He was a shrivelled little man with bright eyes, like a bird's. His pilot was shot through the chest one day, over the lines. The man flew the machine back and landed his observer safely, a perfect landing. He was dead when the machine came to rest. That's a man I shall always envy. He had something to *do* when he was dying. He had a fight for it, and he pulled it off. He was busy and striving with death to the last moment, and he died in his triumph."

Wilder said : " And according to you, if the machine had crashed in the end, the observer's death would have been the worst kind—for he wouldn't have had a chance to fight it ? "

" Yes."

" I'm not sure that I agree with you. He had no responsibility. I can imagine that observer, if he was a brave man, leaning back and getting quite a kick out of it. Also, of course, there's an odd satisfaction about trusting people. I don't know."

" The kind of death I should like," said Elizabeth, " is rather like Chiz's. Only Chiz wants to die fighting and I want to die enjoying myself. I should like to be killed instantaneously, hunting. I suppose if I were Cleopatra or Faustine, I should choose some other form of death by enjoyment, but as it is I should like to break my neck at a double oxer. One can get quite close to what it would be like by thinking of the falls one's had. Joy till the last moment, and then a split second's anxiety, instinctive self-preservation : the faculties moving too quickly for emotion. One's last word would be ' Damn ! ' "

Wilder said : " Buller, what's your contribution to this question ? "

" I think it's a very silly question. I don't want to die at all. I want to go on living for ever, with more joy and more experience every day. I want to put my arms right round the world and never, never leave go."

" My dear Buller ! " said the surgeon. " I told you you ought to be a poet once before."

.   .   .   .   .   .

Pemberley was again in darkness, but the darkness was less hostile. Buller had wanted to keep up the system of watches for one more night, but his doubts had been overruled. " If the man's dead," Wilder had said, "he can't do us any harm, and if he did a bunk yesterday it's highly unlikely that he'll come back to-day. If he's bunked he'll come back, but not immediately. The danger of his coming back will increase as the days go by. To-day its at it's minimum. Anyway it's ten to one that he's dead in one of the chimneys, caught sleeping. We deserve a rest."

Buller, tired by his lack of sleep in the past few days, and worried by his own problems, had assented. But he could not sleep.

Too tired for immediate rest, and falling

between the stools of two questions, his mind
revolved in the darkness with aching concentration. His brain resembled that fabulous and leg-
less bird, circling wearily about the perch, but
defeated by its own structure of any hope of
peace. In the south of France, he seemed to remember, the enthusiastic Latins would employ a
decoy pigeon : a live bird tethered by the leg to a
sharply pointed pole, round which it would flutter
till it died, unable to perch because of the sharp-
ness of the point.

He wondered if Mauleverer were dead, but
could not believe it. He wondered when he had
left the house, and how soon he would come back.
He wondered how long the net of protection
which he had drawn round Charles would stand
the strain, and where it was weakest. He felt
thankful, at least, that he had himself lit Charles's
fire this evening, as a last concession to his fear
that Mauleverer might be there. If there should
be a secret chamber, he thought, and if Mauleverer had found it and hidden in it, would it have
been airtight enough to keep the gas out ? Edgeworth had assured him that there was not a pad-
locked cupboard or closed drawer in the house
which would not have been permeated. And if
Mauleverer had been hidden in some secret chamber, and had died there, perhaps they would never
find the chamber or his body. To-morrow's

search might well reveal no corpse among the chimneys, and that would prove nothing. Maul- everer might moulder in his secret room till the end of Charles's life, without being discovered. The shadow of uncertainty would never lift from Pemberley.

Concurrently with these thoughts Buller's mind was circling round Elizabeth. He wondered how much was behind the convention which forbade her to marry a policeman. He wondered at what point of affection the compensation of marrying the person one loved would redress the balance of this contrary convention. Above all he won- dered if she possibly could love him. She had said such curious things, which in the old days would have been construed as being affectionate. But nowadays that counted for nothing These bright young people called each other *darling* remorselessly. He was afraid. He did not under- stand. He was miserably in love.

Lying on his back in the darkness, amid a tangle of pillows, Buller put up his hand and felt the short hairs at the back of his neck. His fingers strayed over his face, tentatively, pressing the cheeks and feeling under the eyes. He was middle- aged, he supposed, and he had never been hand- some. He felt his hardening skin anxiously. He turned over in bed and pushed a pillow on the floor, exasperated.

Elizabeth's hair was mouse-coloured, and her lips were red. He got out of bed, saying to himself " I am a fool " ; and fetched the handkerchief with which he had wiped her mirror. He sniffed it, put it under the remaining pillow, and lay down again. Like a child who has been allowed to take his newest toy to bed with him, Buller felt comfortable again at once. Her eyebrows had a trick of lifting. It was indescribable. Buller snuggled his middle-ageing head deeper into the pillow. There were certain things, in short, that he would like her to like him to do to her. Buller was asleep, almost before he had reached the end of this complicated sentiment.

Elizabeth had been lying awake under similar problems. It was unmaidenly, she decided, to ask a gentleman's hand in marriage : but then she had never been a lady. She would ask Buller at once if she thought he wanted to and was afraid. But she was proud, too. She had dropped hints, cast straws to see which way the wind blew. There had been no wind, no response. She dared not believe that Buller was in love with her ; and, if not, she dared not face the situation of a proposal. Or dared she ? Nothing venture, nothing have. This kind of love must be worth risking a rebuff for.

She felt her arms in the darkness. They were empty. She was getting old, she supposed. She was getting fat. She must bant.

At this moment she became conscious that there was somebody in the room. Not only in the room, but by the side of her bed. She had thrown out her arm and touched something which moved.

She opened her mouth to scream, but a hand closed over it. Nothing came but a sort of exaggerated snore. She struck out with her arm, and it was caught. It was held between two knees. She tried to roll over, but as she moved there was a faint stab above the elbow in the held arm. She struck with the free arm, struggling for breath. The man was hurting her nose and she was suffocating. Her knuckles struck him in the face, but against something hard, which cut them. Then her free arm was caught too, and a body lay across her, pinning her down. She struggled to throw it off. There was an interminable pause, whilst her mind battled on the brink of consciousness, and then her arms were cautiously released. She would get up and shout for help.

Her body would not move.

She became conscious that she must be dead.

CHAPTER XVI

Buller dreamed that there was a gas attack in the trenches, and he was suffocating. The Germans were black men with white hands, whose bayonets were as sharp as razors. They were swarming over the parapet, and surrounded him with their cutting points in deadly attitudes. He had been wounded and was paralysed. But he must sound the gas alarm. The gong was a shell case hanging from the trench wall. He could reach it by crawling on his stomach, if he moved without being observed. He crawled between their black legs, stealthily, dragging his paralysed spine behind him. Evidently his back was broken, but he could move his arms. They saw him as he reached the gong, and sprang to stab him. But he reared up like a broken snake and beat it with the butt end of his pistol, in agonising measured strokes. It sounded thrillingly through the house ; for each trill the black men stabbed him in the back.

Buller woke up in a muck sweat to the last stab of the telephone bell downstairs. The bed-clothes swept to the right and his legs to the left in the same moment. He did not wait to thrust his bare feet into slippers even, or to snatch a dressing-gown.

Wilder's tousled head looked over the banisters as he reached the instrument.

" Hullo ? "

" Yes."

" Hullo ? Hullo ? "

" Yes, what is it ? "

" No. When ? "

" Which way did he go ? "

" To Burton. Right. Which car did he take ? "

" Will you get the others out at once, and running ? "

Buller slammed down the earpiece whilst the small voice was still rattling, and came up the stairs three at a time.

Wilder said : " Well ? "

" It's Smith, from the garage. He says the Bentley has just gone out, and wanted to know if it was all right. About five minutes ago."

He was past Wilder and through the morning-room before the latter could speak.

Charles threw the door open with a jerk as he tapped on it. He had his revolver in his hand.

Buller said : " Good. Ask Wilder." And was away down the passage before Charles could open his mouth.

He tapped on Elizabeth's door, but there was no answer. He tapped again, quietly. He must not frighten her. And yet, and yet, why didn't she answer ? He kicked the door noisily and cried

" Elizabeth ! Elizabeth ! " It was the second time he had ever addressed her by her Christian name. The room was horribly silent.

He threw his shoulder against the door, as he had done with Mrs. Bossom's, but the lock and bolt held it. He kicked it, but hurriedly this time and without success. The bolt held.

Buller immediately became quite calm. Wilder had come up, and the two of them lifted the lacquered cabinet which stood outside, bodily, and crashed it against the door with their combined weights. The cabinet went right through one of the panels of the door, losing a leg in the process, and the door still held. It must have been a strong door.

Buller put his hand through the broken panel and drew the bolt. The key was fortunately in the lock : he turned it.

The room was empty.

Wilder moved across to the curtains, and glanced at the fastenings of the window, whilst Buller cast his eye over the bed. Charles stood in the doorway. There was a split second of arrested movement.

Buller said : " In the car, obviously. He can't have a quarter of an hour's start of us. Perhaps only eight or ten minutes, if we hurry. Get coats, sweaters, trousers—anything warm."

He was out of his own room, dressed after a

fashion, before either of them. He stood in Wilder's doorway.

" Charles had better come," he said. " It's safer that he shouldn't be left alone, in any case, and besides we shall want all three cars if we're going to explore the crossroads. I think there's a good chance. I want the Chrysler coupé, and you can take the Daimler if you can drive it. I never knew what these people had all these cars for, but thank God they've got them. Charles will have to take the Studebaker. You're more useful than he is. The Bentley went towards Burton-on-Trent. If he's going any distance there aren't any important turnings before that. At Burton-on-Trent I want you to turn east and explore the Ashby-de-la-Zouch road, and Charles must go north to Uttoxeter. Stop anybody you see, except policemen, and enquire. I'm afraid there won't be many about at three in the morning. If the worst comes to the worst, stop a policeman : so long as you can make up a convincing story— something about a bet. Say it's something to do with this controversy over average speeds on long distances at night. You're a judge, or something, and have missed one of the entrants. You want to know which way he's gone. Speed Charles up and tell him all this. I'm off. Remember you're for Ashby and Charles for Uttoxeter. I'm going straight through to Lichfield."

Buller was clattering down the stairs as Charles came out of his room.

Smith was standing by the three cars, with their engines running. He had taken them out on to the drive and left them abreast, as if for the start of a race. He looked at Buller with such a pleading look that Buller said : " All right. Jump in."

The drive sloped gently away from the house and Buller started off in second whilst Smith was still on the footboard. He glanced at his wrist-watch as they shot round the curve in a roar of small pebbles. It was one minute to three.

" Tell me more about this," he asked.

" There's nothing but what I told you over the telephone, sir. Mrs. Smith woke me up at quarter to three, saying there was somebody moving about in the garage down below. I got out of bed to see if I could see anything from the window and saw that the big doors was open. I was just putting on my slippers to see who it was when I heard the engine started—it was a still night—and, going to the window, I hears the Bentley come out without lights. I thought there might be some-thing queer, so I stays at the window to see which way the car went if I could. From the top windows of that garage, sir, you can just see the lodge gates. Well, the car had no lights, and I was just thinking that 'twas no good watching any more when I see the lights turned up on the road outside, moving off between the trees towards Burton. He must have driven down the drive and opened the lodge gates in the dark, not trusting to his lights till he was well out on the road."

" I suppose we're not short of petrol ? "

" Full up, sir. I filled up all three of 'em when you spoke to me over the wire."

Buller said : " You're a stand-by, Smith. You're sure it was a quarter to three ? "

" Certain, sir. I looked at the alarm clock as I got out of bed."

" That gives him about fourteen minutes start ; less than that, really, for he had to feel his way down the drive. I think we might do it, with luck. What do you think ? "

" He has the legs of us, if he chooses to," said Smith, " but not by much. And he probably doesn't know that we're after him. I don't suppose he'll be pushing her along."

Smith looked back through the small window as a light came through, making the windscreen opaque. The broad fans of light from the two following cars dazzled him.

" Here's the other two coming," he said, " I'll shut the flap."

.   .   .   .

As the Bentley drew out of Lichfield, Maul-everer looked over his shoulder. His pale face showed thin in the faint light from the dashboard, but his eyes were bright. The light concentrated in them, so that they seemed to gleam with their own lustre. Scarcely more than half a mile behind him he could see a broad fan of light sweeping between the trees, catching them alternately, like an errand boy running his switch along a stretch of iron railings.

He smiled softly and stepped on the accelerator. The Bentley gathered speed with a succession of squattering detonations, and stormed up the hill.

.   .   .   .   .   .

Buller glanced at his watch as they came out of Lichfield. It showed thirty-seven minutes past three. There had been a loss of time at Burton-on-Trent, where he had waited to make sure that Charles and Wilder followed his instructions. He had been rewarded by seeing the two lights flit away, right and left handed, according to plan. In spite of this check he had averaged a little under thirty-eight miles an hour.

Smith said phlegmatically : " He's less than three quarters of a mile ahead." This startled Buller, for he had seen no lights. The chauffeur pointed them out and Buller trod on the gas.

Smith said : " He's going at a good lick. He must have been going slow before, for us to have caught up on him like this. He must have seen us."

Buller said nothing, but drove. Their bore of light seemed to tunnel through chaos, creating and abandoning its tiny universe in the same moment of time. The tunnel world of leaning trees and telegraph poles hurtled or poured towards them, snuffing itself out behind their backs in instantaneous night. The strip of road streamed under them, a resistless river of speed between the deep gorges of the dark.

The fork roads at Sutton Coldfield were blind. The Bentley reached them sixty seconds in advance of Buller, and almost smashed into a car coming from Birmingham. The Birmingham car went on, right handed, towards Tamworth, and the lights of the Bentley suddenly disappeared. Buller arrived a moment afterwards, in time to see the red light of the car from Birmingham vanishing up the road.

Smith said : " He's doubled back for Tamworth," and Buller brought the car round as quickly as he could, but it was a sharp corner and he lost time. He drove hell-for-leather, saying : " With luck we might catch him between two fires. If Wilder has discovered he didn't go through Ashby-de-la-Zouch, he'll most likely have turned south, to try and strike our line again. In that case he'll be coming through Tamworth, towards us, on this road."

This was exactly what had happened. Wilder had found a constable outside Ashby, who fell for his story about the average-speed test, and told him that no car had been along that road in the last forty minutes.

At five minutes to four Buller saw Wilder's light coming towards him, on the far side of the car he was chasing. The latter was only a couple of hundred yards ahead.

Buller signalled by switching his headlights on and off, rapidly, without decreasing speed. Wilder replied in the same way. As the two opposite courses converged, the quarry in the middle became brightly illuminated. It was a harmless Sunbeam, bringing back its slightly drunken owner at top speed from a dance near Birmingham. The latter was to give up champagne for quite a week, because he said that it made headlights look as if they were doing the morse code afterwards.

Wilder and Buller drew up on opposite sides of the road and held a hurried conference.

Buller said : " I chased him to Sutton Coldfield for sure. Nothing but the Bentley could have kept up the speed of our last mile. Then he must have switched off his lights and gone on to Birmingham, whilst I followed the only lights visible— this other car. We'd best make for Birmingham as quick as possible. It may not be too late."

" There's a choice of three roads after Birming-ham," said Wilder, " and we shan't catch him before."

Buller thought quickly.

" Look," he said, " will you 'phone from Birm-ingham to Pemberley with a message for Charles in case he has the sense to ring up ? He's north-west of this road somewhere. Leave a message for him to bear south and explore the Birmingham – Wolverhampton road. We shall just have to leave that one to chance and hope for the best. Then, if you'll go on towards Worcester, I'll bear south-east for Warwick. Report whenever possi-ble to Pemberley by 'phone. Is there anything else ? "

" No. That's O.K. Good luck."

Buller turned his car in a fever of impatience, but Wilder was almost out of sight before he could get away.

.   .   .   .   .   .

Mauleverer saw Buller's car slew left on the track of the red herring from Birmingham, and smiled faintly. He decelerated to thirty and drove on comfortably, smiling and smiling.

.   .   .   .   .   .

Wilder leapt out of his Daimler in Birmingham, and threw himself on a telephone box. He got through, much to his surprise, very quickly, and left the message with Mrs. Smith. She appeared to have been up and waiting.

" Hullo, is that you, Mrs. Smith ? Good. Will you take this message very carefully. It is for Sir Charles, in case he rings up. Will Sir Charles kindly bear south and comb the Birmingham – Wolverhampton or Birmingham – Shrewsbury roads ? Tell him the time of the message. Thank you."

He hung up the receiver and ran across the road to the car. He had seen Buller roar past in the Chrysler as he stood in the box.

Wilder's average from Birmingham to Ombersley was good, for he arrived there at 4.51, and caught a market gardener's lorry making for Birmingham. He stopped it, repeating the story of the bet as quickly as possible.

The driver of the lorry was a young man who personally owned a motor bicycle, and knew about cars. Yes, he had seen the Bentley not ten minutes ago. In fact it had stopped and the driver had asked him the way to Tewkesbury.

Wilder was doubly fortunate at Ombersley, for there was a telephone box as well. He got through to Pemberley.

" Yes, this is Dr. Wilder. Has Sir Charles rung up ? No ? Well, here's another message—for Mr. Buller, this time. Don't muddle them. Tell Mr.

Buller that the Bentley has certainly taken the Worcester road and that I am going on to Tewkesbury. Tell Mr. Buller to come back westwards. Have you got that? Right."

Wilder drove for Worcester as fast as he could go, but in an unhappy frame of mind. Mauleverer was a cunning devil, and had almost certainly stopped that lorry on purpose. The hint that he was going to Tewkesbury was valueless. But it was impossible to weigh up how far he would work the double-cross. He would probably guess that his pursuer was sensible enough to see that the question about Tewkesbury might be a blind. He might carry this further and conclude that his pursuer, guessing so far, would decide to take the Malvern road instead of the Tewkesbury one. In this case he would go to Tewkesbury just as he had said. But he might carry it further still, and expect the pursuer to follow the argument even as far as that. Then he would go to Malvern. Eventually it became merely a matter of chance again.

Wilder reached Worcester at two minutes past five, and the sky was already lightening.

In Worcester he had an idea and tried westwards towards Leominster, in case Mauleverer had meant neither Tewkesbury nor Malvern. In a couple of minutes, however, a new thought struck him. He remembered the strategy of flight as laid down in the Universities. When pursued by a proctor with his bulldogs (that is, by more than one person) the undergraduate is recommended to fly as nearly as possible in a straight line. Then his speed may help him. If he dodges to left or right he is wasting his forward lead, for the bulldogs are said to be trained to run on parallel courses on either side of the line of flight. By doubling sideways he may simply run into the arms of a pursuer who has been running forward all the time, on a side course. Much the same thing was happening with the present chase—Sir Charles was west of the line and Buller east—and Mauleverer probably realised it. He would be likely to keep straight on.

So Wilder turned back, and was making for Tewkesbury five minutes later. The complicated red and green traffic lights of Worcester had received short shrift, even when they stood at CAUTION.

.   .   .   .   .   .

Buller reached Warwick at five minutes to five and telephoned to Pemberley. He received Wilder's message and decided to take the Oxford – Worcester road. He was in a tearing bad temper, now that he was definitely off the trail and Wilder on it, and drove like a demon for Chipping

Norton. He averaged fifty miles an hour exactly, and turned west.

.   .   .   .   .   .

Wilder reached Tewkesbury at 5.40, in broad daylight, and found a belated milkman who could swear positively that no private car of any sort had passed through in the last hour. The milkman also directed him to a telephone, and he got through to Pemberley, after much delay, for the third time.

" This is Dr. Wilder again. Another message for Mr. Buller. Yes, Mr. Buller. Will you tell him that the Bentley has not gone through Tewkesbury but perhaps through Malvern and is probably making for Ross. Yes. R. O. S. S. I am going through Ledbury. Mr. Buller had better make for Ross through Gloucester. Yes. Will you repeat it? Right. Has Sir Charles rung up? If he does you must tell him we're somewhere round Ross. The other message is no good by now."

Five miles out of Ledbury Wilder had a puncture. He leapt out of the car, cursing like a maniac, and began to change wheels. As he had no notion where the tools were kept and was not accustomed to Daimlers, besides having had no breakfast and very little sleep, his time of eight minutes was brilliant.

He reached Ledbury at 6.8, and turned south for Ross.

.   .   .   .   .   .

Buller made bad time from Chipping Norton to Broadway, and 'phoned from there at six o'clock. He received Wilder's message from Tewkesbury and made straight across to Gloucester, through the most beautiful country in England. But the country was beautiful in vain, for by now Buller was nearly mad. He was miles and miles from the line and every minute might be taking the field further away from him.

He reached Gloucester at half past six, having averaged fifty-two miles an hour on roads which were no longer deserted. He was surprised to find that the muscles of his jaw had set so tightly that it required a mental effort to unclench his teeth.

Meanwhile Wilder had reached Ross at twenty-eight minutes past six and had 'phoned to Pemberley. Buller got on to Pemberley within two minutes of the message, and received it from Mrs. Smith. " Yes," she said, " another message from Dr. Wilder, sir. 'E says that the Bentley 'as gone to Ross for certain, for 'e's spoken to a garage there where it filled up about 'alf an 'our ago. 'E can't find which way it's gone since Ross and is making south for Monmouth. 'E said as 'ow, if you was coming in on the Gloucester road, and 'ad seen nothing there, you might cut across, sir, on the Abergavenny road, and try there."

When Buller got back to the car Smith was sitting in the driver's seat. As he had been driving for three and a half hours he made no comment.

" Ross," he said, " and then Abergavenny."

For the last two hours their conversation had been in monosyllables.

They reached Ross at ten to seven and cut straight across without stopping.

Buller said : " Our scent's cold, but it's surprising that we've kept it so long. We can't keep it much longer in daylight. Now that there are other cars on the road we shall be lucky to get news of the Bentley. I wonder what luck Wilder's had towards Monmouth ? If we don't do something in the next hour we shan't do anything at all."

Smith said : " Well, he wasn't on the Gloucester road, sir, and Monmouth and Abergavenny are the only other main roads. We've got a car on each, sir. I don't think the chances are bad. The only other things he can have done would be to take some side turning and cut across country— or he may have doubled back to Hereford."

" Unless he keeps to the main roads," Buller said, biting into his pipe-stem, " it's a needle in a haystack. I can't think why he's kept to them so far."

They reached Abergavenny at 7.20 and spent
ten minutes in fruitless and hurried enquiry.
Buller was getting desperate when the chauffeur
suggested ringing up Pemberley.

Mrs. Smith's news was to be as bad as it could
be.

" Dr. Wilder's rung up, sir," she announced,
" and Sir Charles. Sir Charles has given me a
number and is waiting to speak to you. I've given
'im Dr. Wilder's last message, sir, so if you care to
talk to Sir Charles 'imself no doubt 'e could give
it you in the course of your talk."

She gave the number—in Ludlow—and Buller
got through.

Charles's voice came distantly, mechanised and
apologetic.

" I say, Buller," it said, " I'm sorry I didn't
think to ring up before. This has been an awful
waste of time. No, of course I ought to have
thought of it. Yes, I'll tell you at once. He's come
to an absolute check in Monmouth. No, nobody
seen the car at all. Yes, he did leave a message.
He says he's coming back to Ross and then on to
Hereford. He says the Bentley may have broken
back that way. He was hoping that you'd find at
Abergavenny, but he thought best to stop the
earth at Hereford in case you didn't. No, I realise
that you haven't. No, he didn't say anything
else. Well, I'm at Ludlow. I've been through

Newcastle-under-Lyme and Shrewsbury. I didn't know what to do. Yes, sickening. Yes. Well I thought I might cut down to Hereford in the hopes. You see, he *may* have cut back towards Hereford, and there's nothing else we can do. That is if Gloucester, Monmouth and Abergavenny are blank as you say. Yes, of course if he's cut off on a bye-road we're done. There seems nothing else for it. Right-oh. Then we'll meet at Hereford. Let's say the post office."

Buller went back to the car.

" Dr. Wilder's drawn blank at Monmouth," he said, " and it's no good here. Nobody seems to have seen him. The only hope is that he's doubled back towards Hereford, and Wilder's following him there. The swine must have an hour's start besides the distance, if that's the case. Actually, it's much more likely that he's taken some side turning and given us the slip altogether. But we might as well try all the possibilities before we give it up. At least we're certain that he was at Ross somewhere about six o'clock."

Smith asked : " Where do we go next, sir ? "

" There isn't anything we can do here, so we might as well make for Hereford too. We ought to get there twenty minutes or half an hour after Dr. Wilder. And the Bentley *may* be round about there. We might be useful. Sir Charles is making for Hereford also."

" There's a second-class road according to the map," said Smith, " from here to Hereford, through Pontrilas."

" Take it."

At the tiny village of Llanvihangel Crucorney, Buller said : " This is wild country. He might well have been making for Wales."

Smith said : " We might stop at Pandy, sir, to buy a bit of chocolate and cup of coffee. If we're lucky enough to keep this chase going we might be glad of it."

In the small grocer's at Pandy, where Buller was making his purchase, it suddenly occurred to him that there would be no harm, at any rate, in enquiring after the Bentley on the off chance. They were only twelve miles from Hereford, and about the same distance from Ross. Maul-everer had disappeared at Ross, so he might be anywhere. He asked, casually, as the old lady handed him his change.

" Why, yes," said the old lady, " there was a gentleman in not an hour ago, buying chocolate just the same as you. In one of them long open motor cars. Black it was, I think."

Buller asked, in a voice which he was scarcely able to control, what the gentleman looked like ?

A medium-sized gentleman, she thought, just the ordinary sort of gentleman.

Was he clean shaven ? Yes, so far as she could

remember he was clean shaven. Not very well shaved, perhaps. Had he glasses? Yes—here she was definite—he had horn-rimmed ones. And, now she remembered it, he was very dirty. Buller raced out of the shop, checked himself on the step and demanded:

" Which way did he go? "

" He asked the way to Longtown, to be sure," said the old lady.

.   .   .   .   .   .

Buller found the village post office and rang up Pemberley. " Tell either of them," he said, " that the Bentley was seen at Pandy an hour ago. He asked the way to Longtown, which is on a small road leading to Hay." He slammed down the receiver almost before Mrs. Smith could open her mouth, and picked it up again at once. He asked for the post office at Hereford.

" Now could you be an angel," he said flirtatiously, " and give a message to two friends of mine if they happen to enquire? You might see them waiting outside, in a Daimler and a Studebaker. I was to meet them at the post office. Could you tell them that Mr. Buller's had a breakdown near Pandy, and can't come? Tell them to come here, or better still, to ring up Pemberley."

He waited to see that the girl had got it right, and to ensure that she would remember to give the message by making himself pleasant to her. Then he scrambled into the car and they spun round the side turning towards Longtown.

· · · · · · ·

When they had covered eight miles on a sad road, and passed Longtown without seeing anything, Smith remarked :

" Lonely bit of country this, sir."

Buller had been studying the map.

" There's not a village," he said, " between Longtown and Hay—or not that you could speak of. Certainly not a church, anyway. That's getting on for nine miles."

" All them mountains," remarked Smith, jerking a thumb towards Twyn Du. " It's pretty, I daresay, but what a country for dark deeds."

Buller said : " You're romantic, Smith. They're called the Black Mountains, certainly, but I don't think you'll get many dark deeds in Wales. Not beyond lechery, swindling, and toll gates at every turn."

Smith opened his mouth to make some defence of a possibly maligned people, but he got no further.

The gallant Chrysler groaned inwardly, made

a grinding noise with its wheels, and lurched clumsily to rest.

Smith said : " Puncture," and got out to look. Then he added : " All four," and began to walk back along the road. Buller joined him, and they stood together, looking down at what must have been quite half a crown's worth of excellent nails.

CHAPTER XVII

BULLER said : " That's dished it."

Smith added, unnecessarily : " It's a put up job, of course."

" Yes. It's the sort of thing an urchin would do in this god-forsaken country. But this time it's not an urchin."

" I suppose there's nothing else but to try and mend them ? They'll be shot to pieces, but it might be possible."

" I think you'd better," said Buller. " As far as I can see this is the end of the chase, and it's now merely a question of getting the car home. We must be seven miles at least from the nearest garage. In the meantime I'm going to walk back towards Longtown. The others should be following and we may be able to do something about it. He had an hour's start to begin with, but still . . ."

Buller thought for a moment, then added : " No, I'm afraid it's hopeless. I'll stay and help with the tyres. If we hear the cars coming one of us will have to run back and warn them."

" Or preferably," added Buller, in a final afterthought, " sweep the road."

Whilst they were working, Buller soliloquised.

" God," he said, " he chose a marvellous place to maroon us in ! Now why did he want to maroon us ? Obviously he's just led us here, by the noses, like little pigs. If he'd wanted to he could have slipped off at any small turning and lost us at once. And on top of that he had the fastest car and ten minutes start. He must have waited for us, almost, every time we lost the scent, and left little hints all the way. He can't have been averaging more than thirty, except in that sprint from Lichfield to Sutton Coldfield, or he'd have been here hours ago. That's it. Whenever we were hot on the trail he pushed her along, and when we were lost he waited for us. Now why ? "

" Would you think, sir," Smith suggested, banging at an obdurate tyre, " that he wanted to entice us away from Pemberley ? "

" That's it, of course. I suppose he thought I should come away alone, or with Dr. Wilder, leaving Sir Charles unguarded. Then he hoped to finish him off."

After some time Buller added : " Though why he should expect us to come, and not Sir Charles, is more than I can fathom."

" Perhaps he thought it was worth chancing, sir, just to see what happened. And as far as he can know, sir, it's what has happened. Sir Charles hasn't been with us since Burton-upon-Trent. Don't you think, sir, as how he's probably now making back for Pemberley as fast as that Bentley can run ? "

" My. gosh ! You're right as usual, Smith. When he saw us at Lichfield there was only one car following him. He'll think that Sir Charles is still at Pemberley, and now's his chance ! "

" Except," said Smith, " that he wouldn't know who was in the car following. For all he knows it may be Sir Charles that's chasing him and us that's staying at home."

This was a poser.

" Actually," said Buller, " he may have hung about in Ross to see us go by. Then, whilst Wilder was off to Monmouth and we were trying Aber-gavenny, he slipped up here through Bagwy Mydiart and Pontrilas. He'd know then that Sir Charles wasn't in the hunt."

They banged the wheel in unison and then Buller remarked :

" I think you're right after all, Smith. He wasn't trying to get Sir Charles left alone. This is what happened. He had Miss Elizabeth on his hands, and he wanted to get her away. The best place to hide her was somewhere here in Wales. Out of pride, and to humiliate us—that's typical—he's lead us right out into the wilds as far as he can afford to let us come. Then he's cut us off like a lot of babies. Miss Elizabeth will be somewhere out here, in some filthy little cottage of his, where

she'll never be found. There's the Mynydd
Eppynt or the Forest Fawr—a hundred thousand
places where we'll never get at her without ten
miles of beaters."

Smith said : " There's ports in Wales, too, sir.
What price Cardiff ? "

Buller suddenly sat down on the tyre and, in a
curiously strangled voice, made the time-hon-
oured protestation.

" Smith," he said, " what does he want with
her ? What is he going to do to her ? What's he
done to her ? God, if that so-and-so's hurt a fibre
of her body I'll wring his bloody neck till his
head comes off."

.   .   .   .   .   .

The job was easier than it had threatened
to be. By the time that the two following cars
roared over the hill-brow from Longtown it was
finished.

Charles and Wilder got out stiffly, and walked
over. They heard the news in silence.

Charles asked : " What do we do now ? "

Buller replied : " I don't know what we can do.
It's no good carrying on with this chase any
further. He might be eighty miles away by now.
There's nothing to do at all, except, I suppose,
to go back to Pemberley."

" But he must be somewhere about here. He

wouldn't have come here otherwise. What's the sense of going back again ? "

" I admit that he's probably within an eighty-mile radius, but even that's not certain. He may have led us here in order to double back himself, by train perhaps, in exactly the opposite direction. Elizabeth may be gracing a wild-fowler's hut on the Wash by this evening. We just don't know why he's brought us here or where he is. There's nothing to do, so we might as well go home."

" But we can't *give up* ? "

" Not finally. But we must for the moment. Sooner or later we shall hear from the police that the Bentley has been found abandoned in the Mynydd Nallaen or left in a car park at Swansea or something of that sort. They'll identify it by the registration number. You'll write back and say : Thank you very much, I left it there by mistake. You'll have to pay the fine. When we know where it was left we may be able to get something by making enquiries in the district. On the other hand, probably we won't."

Buller looked dejected and added slowly : " But the main hope is this. Mauleverer must have kid-napped Elizabeth for a purpose. If he'd done it merely out of spite against you it isn't likely that he'd have gone to the trouble of kidnapping her. He'd have murdered her and saved a lot of bother."

The voice faltered. " He's a devil," he con-
cluded, " and of course he *may* have kidnapped
her in the realisation that the uncertainty would
be almost worse than finding her dead. He may,"
and here Buller spoke with an unnatural pre-
cision which deceived nobody, " he *may* have
killed her and hidden her to prolong the agony.
But what we must hope for is that he's taken her
as a hostage. He hasn't been able to get at you,
Charles, in the past few days. So he may intend
to deliver some sort of ultimatum."

" You mean that he'll ring us up or send us a
note saying that unless I go to a certain spot
alone at a certain time Elizabeth will be done
in ? "

" Something of that sort," said Buller. " And
in that case we shall have a hint of his whereabouts at any rate. We may be able to think
something up by then."

" Which all points," Wilder summed up, " to
our getting back to Pemberley as quickly as
possible, so that we can be available to his telephone message and to the police notification
about the finding of the car."

.   .   .   .

At Pemberley they had a late luncheon and
Buller spent the afternoon in the garden. He
walked restlessly about the tennis courts, sat

down on garden seats, and got up again almost before he had crossed his legs. The wildfowl on the lake retreated to the further shore as he approached them, and had no sooner ventured out when he approached again. He smoked pipes in an endless succession, filling and lighting them nervously, with jerky movements of his hands, and relighting them absently as they went out.

At teatime he came in with a determined air and took Wilder by the second button of his coat.

" Look here," he said. " We can't let this go on. We must notify the police and get a wide net out at once." He looked at Wilder anxiously.

" I've thought about all that," he continued, before the surgeon could reply. " Even if there are enquiries and an awkward situation about Kingdom I can take the responsibility. If they don't believe in Mauleverer—as I'm afraid they can't—we ought to be able to work out a story which holds water. I don't mind saying that I killed Kingdom myself. In half an hour we could get everybody word perfect to back up my confession——"

Wilder broke in good-humouredly.

" You forget," he said, " that my burial certificate is already out. Have I got to be hanged as an accessory ? "

Secretly Buller had hoped that he might offer to be.

" Well——" he said.

Wilder dashed his hopes to the ground.

" I don't want to be hanged at all."

" Listen," he added, and took Buller's arm. " You're upset about this, old man, and I don't blame you. Everybody's noticed you and Elizabeth. But you mustn't let yourself get rushed by your feelings. If we get the police in now we're all in a criminal position. Everybody's in it. It isn't only you or I. It's Charles and the servants and even more or less unconnected people like Edgeworth and Hankey. There isn't a hope for your concocted confession. For one thing nobody would back you up. If anything's going to be told we'll tell the truth. And then, on top of that, all your arguments against police protection are still operative, and, finally, the police may not be able to do any more good than we can."

He paused for emphasis and then continued :

" If we must get the police in we can do it tomorrow. By then we may have received Mauleverer's ultimatum. We must give the present situation a chance of development. It may turn out, when we hear from Mauleverer—as we're bound to—that we can do without the police after all. We may be able to ambush him whilst he's ambushing Charles at whatever rendezvous he appoints."

Buller said : " But it may be too late by to-morrow."

" Now, be sensible. If it's going to be too late by to-morrow, it's too late to-day. If Mauleverer meant to kill Elizabeth, since we must face it, he'd have killed her already : and if he has killed her, it's no good running our heads into nooses simply for the satisfaction of finding her body a little sooner. You're off your head with worry, old man, and I don't blame you. But you mustn't be rushed into hasty action on that account. If Elizabeth's dead, wouldn't you rather make him pay for it yourself ? And if she's alive, you'll save her best by giving the enemy time to reveal his position."

" But think what he may be doing to her now."

" Bosh. Elizabeth's able to look after herself. You're jealous. Come and have tea, and don't be a fool. I tell you what. If we don't hear from Mauleverer in the next two days I'll back you up in any confession you like to concoct and we'll swing together."

With this concession Buller had perforce to be content.

The subject was not re-opened at tea or dinner, and the household went to bed in sad disquiet.

.   .   .   .   .   .

Buller lay in bed. He was far too tired to sleep, had forgotten almost how to. His brain was swinging in his head, whilst the imagined roads of last night's chase swung to left and right before his smarting eyes. He was driving a car, endlessly, at impossible speeds, along roads which forked and turned in every direction. The crossroads leapt at him, filled with approaching cars, and reeled backwards menacingly, to be succeeded immediately by equal dangers.

Buller decided that he would soon be mad. In all the cars Elizabeth was huddled, her face pale, her red lips bloodless. She sagged beside the maniac at the wheel, impotent, enigmatic, possibly dead.

Buller wrenched his mind from the nightmare, laid his body straight out on the bed. He tried to relax his muscles, to lie quietly, to think visually instead of problematically. If only he could apply his mind to some subject of the eye alone, to the recollection of a view or the design of a picture, he might be able to sleep. And sleep he must, if he were to help Elizabeth to-morrow.

With the repetition of the name her whole body and action solidified before him, a compost of a thousand words and gestures, so that he writhed in the bed and started up, cursing.

He must do something. He must think. He must review his strategy, or anything, rather than be haunted by that image, in lovely flesh and undecided danger.

First of all, he had been a fool not to insist that somebody should sleep with Charles wherever Mauleverer might be. This was the third night that Charles had slept alone. It had all been inaugurated by the necessity of watching the bolt-holes on that fatal night when Kingdom had been butchered. But on the two succeeding nights he had seen to it himself that Charles kept up a fire. To-night he had been too worried, and if he understood Charles the latter would have been too forgetful. It was a warm night, for the spring had come at last, and Charles would probably have decided against a fire even if he had remembered it.

Buller got out of bed creakingly, put a hand to his forehead in a gesture of utter weariness, and shuffled with his slippers. He struggled into an ancient coat and padded off along the passage.

Charles's door was not locked or bolted. The day's confusion had broken down all precautions. Buller swayed slightly in exhausted annoyance and opened the door.

The light was on. Charles was lying motionless on his back. At the foot of the bed, leaving him like a surprised and reluctant vampire, a black figure writhed already towards the fireplace. It was clad from head to foot in black : in a black high-necked sweater, long black stockings, and black drawers. The feet were in black beach-shoes, the head in a black mask with mica goggles and a nozzle. The hands were in white kid gloves.

Even as Buller sprang forward the figure melted into the great fireplace, the thin black legs jerked for a moment in an upward leap. It had moved across the pile carpet as soundlessly as death itself, and vanished like the shade.

CHAPTER XVIII

Buller was across the room in two strides, and stared down at Charles for a divided second. The man's eyes were open and he appeared to be breathing. Buller seized his wrist and felt for a pulse. He found it. He did not wait to undo the buttons of the pyjama jacket, but tore it open, sending the buttons flicking across the room to fall soundlessly on the carpet. There was no visible wound.

Buller acted callously, but his mind was racing to a new idea. He felt in Charles's pockets on the chair and snatched his revolver. Then, turning in the same movement from the bed, he was across the room and peering up the chimney.

The fire had never been lighted, as he feared. Within the stretch of his arms was a blackened ledge. He rammed the revolver in the pocket of his coat and jumped.

The sooty brickwork crumbled and cut painfully into his hands. His knees barked against the uneven ridges of the mortar, tearing his trousers as he jerked spasmodically for a hold. He had forgotten his weariness now and was ready for all comers.

He gained the ledge, finding it was a horizontal

platform which led back to a sheer drop. Evidently the chimney of Charles's room came into the main vent at a right-angled bend over this platform.

He moved forward, stooping cautiously in the pitch darkness, through the oily smell of soot, until his hands touched the corner bricks where the flue of the side passage entered the vertical shaft. Here he paused, carefully yet quickly feeling the surface all round.

He knew that there was a vertical drop before him, right down to the fireplace of the main dining-room. He was not sure of the breadth of this shaft and dared not trust himself forward into the void.

If it were narrow enough he could support himself, and work himself upwards with his back against one side and his feet against the other, like a mountain climber in a fissure. He tried to guess its breadth by picturing the dining-room fireplace, but he could not remember, and the breadth of the chimney might alter between that point and this. All this time Mauleverer was presumably making his escape.

Buller sat down and reached out across the shaft with his feet, hoping to touch the other side. He touched nothing.

He rose to his full height and did the bravest thing he had ever done. He did it without the faintest doubts and was not afterwards able to see that it required any courage. In fact, it probably did not, for it was a means to reach Elizabeth. He would have leapt off the Eiffel Tower for that object, without qualms, for the object dimmed any consideration of possible consequences.

Buller slowly launched his body forward into the empty well of night, throwing his hands in front of him as if he were diving. For a terrible second there was nothing, and then they rasped against the brickwork. His shoulders reached the opposite side. He slipped down a couple of feet and righted himself. The main shaft was narrow enough to work himself upwards.

Buller began to wriggle furiously, gaining six inches at a time. He worked as nearly as possible in silence, quelling his laboured breathing with an effort, though the soot and smoky reminder of last night's fires left him gasping for breath.

He had covered a few feet, carrying his revolver pocket in his straining lap to prevent it banging against the walls, when his hand touched hemp. A rope dangled down the main flue beside his elbow.

He tested it softly, trusting only a small part of his weight to it at a time. It held.

Buller began to work himself upwards more quickly, hand over hand, but still keeping his back to one wall and his feet to the other. He passed an opening in the chimney where a side flue came in from one of the bedrooms.

After a few more yards his head struck an overhanging ledge, where the chimney narrowed, apparently to admit the large sloping shaft from the morning-room.

He had to abandon his horizontal pressure of leg and back in order to negotiate this, and was trusting himself entirely to the rope when the rope gave.

The man above him must have severed it at the critical moment, as if he could see in the dark. But Buller had one arm over the ledge, and clung there, kicking with his feet against vacancy whilst the rope rattled past him. A coil flicked against him, almost dislodging his precarious hold. He kicked himself into safety, his jaw set in determination : even in grim relief. At least he knew that the man was there.

He sat on the ledge panting silently, trying to still the thunder of his heart so that he could listen. He remained absolutely motionless till he could hear the soft sifting of the falling soot. He wondered if Mauleverer would believe that he had fallen. There was the faintest hope that he might, if he gave no sound, although the body would presumably have raised a great clatter as it crashed into the dining-room fireplace. He tried to imagine the sound that a body would

throw up a forty-foot shaft by striking the bottom
of it. The rope had given a sweeping thump.
Would that be enough ?

Buller sat perfectly still for nearly five minutes,
straining his ears in the darkness, differentiating
with anxious attention between the small sounds
of night.

He could be sure of nothing. The darkness
itself seemed to have a sound : the welling void
sound, almost, of a seashell lifted to the ear. It
oppressed and engulfed him, weighing him down
into the abyss.

Buller secretly and patiently stretched out his
legs to reassume the upward tussle. He moved
now with infinite caution, slowly winning his
progress, inch by inch, as silently as a bat.

A new flue gave him some difficulty, and he
paused beside it, listening intently. He must
not pass his enemy and let him take him in the
rear.

He stayed beside it until he had picked out the
crepitation of every brick and could swear nobody
was breathing, no heart beating except his own.
Then he crawled upwards into the night.

He kept his head back, peering intently at the
faint square of starlight above him. The morning-
room ledge had blotted it out before, but now he
could distinguish the faded heaven, pricked into
being by two stars, unnaturally bright. If anybody

should move across that background he would fire. The revolver weighed heavily on his thighs.

After an eternity of motion, when his heart would burst, Buller reached another shaft which sloped in at a gentle angle from a bedroom in a higher storey. The last storey before the dormers of the attic.

He paused here, as before, and waited for his pulses to allow the silence. There was no silence. There was breathing within an arm's length of his ear.

·   ·   ·   ·   ·   ·

Buller remained motionless, holding his breath to make sure that it was not his own. The breathing seemed to stop. Almost certain that it was an echo, he breathed again : the echo seemed to start before him. He took a deep respiration, the other breath seeming to inspire at the same moment, and held it as long as possible. But he was short of breath from his exertions and had to let it out. In the middle of the expiration his ear seemed to catch the outlet of the other.

Buller made a great effort and prolonged his breath, listening intently. Within reach of his hand a different person quite separately inhaled.

He drew the revolver from his pocket and weighed it in his hand, altering his position so that his shoulder was against the bricks and his head inclined over it towards the opening of the flue. It would be a simple matter to thrust the revolver sideways into that dark lair and with one percussion end the breaths for ever. But a wild guess restrained him. He slewed round slowly, so that his back was against the adjacent wall of the chimney and the opening of the shaft lay on his right hand. Then, holding his revolver pointed in his left, he softly stretched his right arm into the gap.

His hand touched soot, gently grated on the rough surface of bricks, then descended full on a warm face.

Buller started perceptibly, but the face remained without movement. His hand slipped up and felt the hair. It was fine—and soft—and long.

He slipped the revolver back into his pocket and wriggled sideways like an eel, climbing into the side shaft feet foremost till his body lay side by side with the silent body, and his hands were fluttering over it in a fever of impatience.

Elizabeth was lying on her back, breathing regularly and deeply. He felt her all over with a sort of shamefaced tenderness and anxiety. There were no cords or bonds of any sort to account for her stillness. She was alive, loose and apparently insensible.

Buller, with an ungovernable impulse, and under the supposition that she would never know about it in any case, laid his head beside hers with an audible sigh of gratitude and kissed her nestling ear.

From that moment he became insane. Fortunately he had no matches or he would have struck one to make sure. He felt her face with trembling fingers, like a blind man reading in Braille, straining his mind to recollect her profile as it would appear to the sense of touch. He convinced himself that it was she.

He felt and kissed her cold hands, whispering in her ear an incoherent message of encouragement.

Then bumping his head sharply against the ceiling of the shaft, he turned over on hands and knees and crawled for the main chimney.

He grinned in the darkness with savage triumph and determination. He was ready and bursting to pay off all scores with Mauleverer in a single blow. He drew his revolver and crawled with it in his right hand, cocking it as he went. The hammer came back with a vicious snap which spilled the darkness. He reached the main shaft and stretched out his left hand, feeling against the wall for a purchase.

His hand fell on warm cotton, which moved. He swung his revolver round as a strange hand fell on his shoulder, tilting him forward into the well of the chimney.

The life preserver wrapped itself round the base of his skull with an almost silent thud, and he felt himself pitching forward into the tunnel of night.

.   .   .   .   .   .

Mauleverer caught him as he lurched on the brink, and thrust him back into the hole. From far below came the clatter of the revolver, as it struck the fender of the dining-room.

The startled house resumed its silence instantly, like a surprised guest who has laughed at the wrong joke, and Mauleverer began to move with the unseen agility of a spider.

He had been propped sideways in the chimney, supporting his weight between legs and back, waiting for Buller to emerge. Now he quickly scrambled round and sidled feet first into the same flue which contained the two bodies. But he slipped out again in a moment, and made a quick upward journey, to return almost at once. The journey was repeated and followed by another in the opposite direction, downwards, to the dining-room fireplace.

In these hurried activities, more than ever in the darkness, he was the gloating and eager spider : running to and fro along its web, strengthening

the meshes, binding in a gleeful haste the cap-
tured trophies in an increasing filament.

As he slid into the sloping flue again for the
last time, the darkness of Pemberley was animated
by a trilling chuckle.

CHAPTER XIX

Buller's head felt as if it would cave inwards under the tight hoop of pain which banded it. He opened his eyes in the darkness, wondering if he were dead, and smelt the stink of soot without reflecting on the corollary of hell fire. He moved his shoulders experimentally and grunted as the pang stabbed at his skull.

He could do no more than grunt, he discovered, for a gag drew the flesh of his cheeks cruelly backwards. He could do no more than move his shoulders, for his feet were bound together with the ankles crossed ; and his hands were tied behind him. His fingers throbbed and his toes ached, but the pain in his head was enough to make him sick.

At his second groan a soft voice fanned the darkness by his ear. It was a low voice, modulated to an exaggerated music.

" Inspector Buller," it said, " my dear Inspector Buller. Are you conscious, are you in great pain ? "

It paused for an answer, and then :

" But of course you can't speak. That cruel gag. I must really, really apologise for all this suffering.

Really, it is against my nature. I suffer for you, Inspector Buller, I assure you I do. But you thrust it upon me. How can I loose you when you carry a revolver to take my life ? How can I ungag you when you would so impetuously seek to rouse the household with a yell ? "

The question was rhetorical.

" That blow on the head," the voice trickled on, " it cost me a pang to give it. I'm sure your head must ache so dreadfully. And yet it was calculated with such anxiety. I said to myself : If I strike too hard I may crack the skull, I may preclude for an eternal future all possibility of conversation with my dear friend Inspector Buller. And yet, I said, perhaps—and I do so beg of you to excuse the indelicacy of the remark—perhaps the Inspector's skull is *thick*. Perhaps the Inspector—but of course I was only joking—is a *bonehead*. I must be sure to strike him hard enough to be certain of insensibility. You do see my dilemma, I feel so sure ? Yours is a forgiving and honest nature which will overlook an action, a distasteful action, thrust upon me by the hard necessity of circumstance ? "

" But I trifle," added the douce voice, " I plague you with questions which I know you cannot answer. Forgive my importunity."

There was a faint sigh in the darkness, and the voice ran on conversationally :

" I have been looking forward to this quiet chat, Inspector, for a variety of reasons. Hearing you talk over my affairs, in the various rooms of this fine house, so often lately, I have longed to correct your theories : to put in that word of explanation which will so clear them up, so relate them to one another in a connected whole. My attachment to you, Inspector, has been one of which I daresay you would never have dreamed. We murderers have our pride. Fame for us must be anonymous —such are the sad rules of society—and yet we seek our fame. You are the only living being who has been permitted to follow my whole career. I had hoped to treasure you as a sort of live repository for my successes. Then, when I felt lonely in my achievements, when the necessary neglect of my trophies by the wide world weighed upon me, I could think to myself that one man at least was following my career and appreciating my triumphs. It was vain of me, I know, but that was my desire."

Mauleverer sighed again.

" I had hoped for a living chronicler, a sort of inverted Dr. Watson who could never prove anything against me and who would be actionable for libel if he tried. And now circumstances have combined against me—at least so it seems, at least so I fear—and my living repository must become a mausoleum. This is a sad setback to all my hopes. I shall have to seek a new disciple and begin all over again. Perhaps Dr. Wilder would be eligible."

He considered this idea for some time in silence.

" In the meantime," he continued, " I owe it to you that the whole of my tactics up to the present should be explained. I can at least satisfy myself in this. I can be sure that you understand everything that has happened so far. I shall pour into your brain the full realisation of every situation up to the present moment, and then, with the casket full, the safe, I might say, stocked to the last shelf, I insert my little key and lock it. I lose the combination and leave the treasure house, full, perfected, and never to be ransacked. I often think that even the dead brain, like a gramophone record without the machine to play it, retains its impressions in an eternal secrecy."

Buller moved restlessly, conveying to the maniac's mind some feeling of contempt by this fettered shrug.

Mauleverer continued briskly : " Come now, Mr. Buller, you have always been rude to me. Now you must really consent to pay attention. I cannot be responsible for your death unless you are a perfect record. Besides, you ought to be interested."

The voice became angry.

"You have bungled your affairs sufficiently, I should hope, to be interested in the real course of events. Don't you think you have danced on my strings long enough to wish to know how they were pulled ? Now listen to my story.

"When that young fool the baronet downstairs first came to call on me I was annoyed. I decided to kill him at once in some manner which could be attributed to the act of God. Naturally I thought at once of tiles, and tiles mean roofs and roofs are best approached by chimneys. I looked up Pemberley in a guide to Derbyshire, and was delighted to find, I must admit by a stroke of luck, that the chimneys here were highly suitable. I set about providing myself with an outfit suitable for chimneys. Black, of course, so that one would not be noticeable at night. And then the other adjuncts. People who move about in chimneys are liable to be dirty, and dirty people leave traces. I brought with me, to counteract this tendency as much as possible, a plain oil-cloth cover such as is used to protect tennis racquets from the damp. In this receptacle I packed a clean white pair of gloves, white so that I could see at once when, where, and if they began to be dirty ; a change of light rubber-soled shoes ; a *soft* clothes-brush ; and certain chemical accessories. Whenever I left a chimney for a room I used to brush myself in the grate (I was doing that when I sat for some time in the kitchen grate between your friends Wilder and the chauffeur : the soft brush was fortunately quite silent), change my shoes and don my gloves. I was further assisted in my efforts at cleanliness by the lucky circumstances that our hostess here had caused the chimneys to be swept in her spring cleaning before you arrived. So much for the oddities of my costume, which I also made as athletic as possible so that I might have freedom of movement. I only brought two other things : a rope and a gas mask. Let us pause a moment on the latter. You tried, my dear Inspector, two days ago, to rid yourself of the brooding genius of Pemberley by using gas. Cudgel your brains for a moment and consider whether this was logical. In me I believe you recognised a person of some small intelligence, and you believed that I had taken up residence in your chimneys. Has it occurred to you that chimneys are sometimes, I might even say frequently, connected with smoke ? With the fumes of coal gas at least, and, if coke is used, possibly of carbon monoxide ? Would it not have seemed likely to you, if you had given the matter that penetrating consideration which has always so distinguished your activities, that a wise person who came to establish himself in a chimney might bring a gas mask ? Your gas attack was futile from the start. I had not fled the house or hidden in an air-locked secret chamber. It may interest you to know that I slept through it, on this very ledge. I have been short of sleep in the past few days, and the gas was an admirable opportunity. It ensured that I should not be disturbed, since you all had to keep outside the house."

Mauleverer rested for a moment.

"I don't claim," he went on, "to have outwitted you by forecasting your use of gas in advance. For one thing I hoped you would never realise I was in the chimneys. But I do think that you might have given me credit for the sense to bring a gas mask, simply against the chimney fumes. But I must go on with my story. I arrived here, fully equipped, on the night of Sir Charles's visit to Cambridge. This was quick work, for I had been forced to motor to Wales that day, before I came back. I arrived in the early hours of the morning, left my ordinary clothes in a neat bundle in a culvert outside the grounds, and found no difficulty in effecting an entrance through the postern door into the old smoking-room. I brought my ropes and arranged a neat system of rapid communication down all four of the main stacks. Next morning, as you know, I made my way to the stable roof in a heavy storm of rain (which, I hope, washed away any small traces of soot that I may have left) and dropped my tile. I missed him, but it was not a bad shot when you reflect on the difficulty of sighting when the mark is hidden by a gutter and moving as well. Then, later in the day, I had the pleasure of listening to your forecast of my probable methods of execution. That forecast, as Dr. Wilder so penetratingly remarked, put me on my mettle and made me decide to adopt none of the methods which you had mentioned. I decided on a little preparatory amusement and indulged myself with those little jokes of the toothbrush, the lipstick and the skull. Over the last I was unfortunate. You must realise by now, Inspector, that I am not a lucky man. Remember those fingerprints on the tone-arm and the coincidence of that young puppy at the window in Copper Street. Trials are sent to me so that I may triumph over them. In this case the unlucky chance was the light sleeping of Mrs. Bossom. She woke at the very moment that I touched her bed with the skull, and I only had time to nip up the chimney before she was yelling the house down. I had no time to open the door. You will remember that in each case, prior to that, I had been careful to leave some entry open so that you would not be forced to conclude that I had entered from the chimney. But now, by ill luck, I had positively forced the chimneys on your attention.

" The next night you attempted to trap me at my drink, and I was compelled, so much against

my will, to give you a warning lesson. I was by
no means daunted, as you will by now have
realised, although the discovery of my line of
communications, forced on you by the accident
of the cook, made you think to keep up a fire
in Sir Charles's room. I could have reached
him fairly easily before, when I was in play-
ful mood, but now it was impossible without
strategy.

"On the next day you tried your amusing gas
attack. Although this made no difference whatever, in itself, I was quick to realise that you
would institute a thorough search of the chimneys, to find the supposed body, as soon as it was
light enough next day. I could easily have slipped
away from this search, for you lacked the numbers
to guard all the bolt-holes, but it would have
meant taking down my ropes (they were at-
tached by hooks, I may mention) and much
inconvenience. If I had fled it would have
given me all the trouble of coming back again,
and then by no means with the certainty
that Sir Charles's room would be without a
fire.

"And so, my dear Inspector, I had recourse to a
little experiment in psychology. I reckoned that
you would expect me to be gassed or gone, and it
turned out that I had reckoned rightly. The sweet
Miss Darcy, here, had omitted to light her fire.

It was a warm night—rosy cheekèd spring, you know, is here—and I suppose she was feeling stuffy. I had no difficulty in entering her room and treating her with an innocuous drug. You will have noticed that she lies limp and apparently unconscious. But she is not unconscious. She is enjoying our conversation just as much as you are. My little drug is a first cousin to stovaine, and much more easy to administer since it can be injected into the blood-stream instead of into the spinal fluid. Its effect is to paralyse the higher centres of conscious motion. Miss Darcy is at present suffering from total paralysis, although she is perfectly conscious."

At this point Buller blushed deeply at an unfortunate recollection. Mauleverer was running on without a pause.

"When Miss Darcy was quite relaxed I managed to get her up the chimney to this ledge, though with great difficulty, by means of ropes. I then made my way to the garage, after picking up my outdoor clothes, and took the liberty of borrowing Sir Charles's Bentley. I had no qualms about leaving Miss Darcy, for the drug is potent for ten or twelve hours. I need not go into details of the chase. I believe that it will have dawned on you by now that had I chosen to I could have shaken you off in the first ten miles. And yet I

led you as far as the Black Mountains before
I found it necessary to lose you. I may say that I
had the greatest difficulty in keeping you on my
track. At Worcester particularly, when the
Daimler went off to Tewkesbury and you were
careering about further east than ever, I thought
you would never catch up again. I had to leave
a very definite clue at that garage. However,
all's well that ends well (excuse the proverb),
and I managed to get you all beyond Longtown.

"I wonder if you have any inkling of my motives?
First of all, and most important, I had to take you
away from Pemberley before you instituted the
search for my asphyxiated body. Secondly, I
needed one more night (to-night) in which to
finish off the baronet. Thirdly, though this is a
minor point, I had a little shopping to do and an
alibi to tend. Why, you will ask, did I take the
trouble to lead you all the way to Pandy? The
answer is simple. I wanted to waste your day.
I did not want you to go back and start prying
about the house. I was afraid that you might
start looking for Miss Darcy (I fear I over-
estimated your intelligence) if you had a whole
day of idleness before you. But that was not my
main reason. You will realise that I had to *re-enter*
Pemberley, and for that reason I preferred that
you should not be here. Now it was essential to

me that I should reach a certain spot in Wales—
I'll explain why later—and get back before you.
So, remembering that delightful stretch of road
between Longtown and Hay (which was close
to my destination), I took you with me and
marooned you when we were nearly there. I exe-
cuted my business and was back long before you.
The Bentley is in a garage at Hay. I came back
by train and taxi, and got in whilst the servants
were having dinner.

"Now think it over. Before I started this wild
goose chase I was up a chimney which you would
search in a few hours. After I had finished it certain benefits had accrued. To begin with, you
knew that I was alive and thought that I had
abducted Miss Darcy to Wales. So you would be
unlikely to search the chimney. But there were
other benefits. I had laid in another dose of Miss
Darcy's little drug (my shopping) and I had paid
a visit to Dreavour (where my alibi lives). Also I
had got back whilst you were still pulling nails
out of your tyres. And the last benefit of all (this
was where my incursion into the realms of psychology justified itself) : the defence was disorganised. You thought I was well away, or at least
Sir Charles did, and there was no fire in his room
to-night.

"But about that alibi—my reason for wanting to
visit Wales. It's a poor alibi, but then it's difficult

to prove that one's in a different place for days at a stretch. I'm ashamed of that alibi, and yet it was the best I could do in a hurry. I told you that I had to visit Wales on the day I first came here. I drove to Dreavour with my humble Morris Oxford, and a tent, which I erected. I took with me a supply of empty condensed milk tins (I had emptied the condensed milk down the sink in my gyp room) and other open tins of salmon, meat, fruit, etc., the contents of which I threw out of the car on my way.

"Dreavour is a lonely place, where one can camp for days without seeing a soul. But one's tent would be noticed. At a pinch people would be ready to presume that one had been staying there, what with all this hiking. Colour might be added to the story by the empty tins of provisions. It was a poor alibi, but at any rate it was a possible one. It was better than not being able to explain where one had been at all. And it would be considerably strengthened if one could be seen in the village the day before the murder—just at the time when one was supposed to be hiding in the chimneys here. You see, I was seen to arrive and I wanted to be seen once in the interim. Hence my trip to Wales, to buy eggs from the nearest farm house.

"But we'll dismiss that subject as quickly as possible. As an alibi it's disgracefully fallible. It will just do as a weak way of explaining where I was, if necessary.

"We have got back to Pemberley. I gave Miss Darcy another dose and waited for the household to go to bed. As I expected, you were tired, bluffed and disorganised. I went down to Sir Charles's room, was pleased to find no fire, and gave him a little of his sister's medicine. He will be able to think things over on that bed for the next few hours. I was just having a chat with him when my bad luck cropped up again and you blundered into the room. However, that's been remedied, and a stitch in time saves nine (I beg your pardon). Since making you comfortable here, I've been down to the room again and corrected my mistake in not locking and bolting the door. To tell you the truth I never suspected the baronet of being such a fool as to leave the door open in the first place, besides forgetting to light the fire."

Mauleverer took a deep breath and relapsed into silence. The faint rancid smell of coal enveloped them.

The voice broke out again suddenly, but now with such a harsh and brutal intonation that Buller almost started.

" But time passes, my fine Inspector, and there's much to do. You've had the stupid impudence to pit yourself against me, and you'll learn your lesson. Listen now to what's in store. That puppy down below is helpless, waiting for the knife. It will be the knife. I've had the pleasure of telling him so, and now he's had the pleasure of waiting. Let him wait. I've something still to tell you. What shall we do with you and your pretty lady, that's the question ? "

The words stirred close to Buller's ear. The breath touched his cheek, smelling slightly of cachous.

" That's the question," it repeated, and a gentle hand stroked lightly at his hair ; stroked, twisted round a lock, and softly, increasingly, brutally pulled.

" That's the question, my mannikin, that you lie there in your silence meditating upon."

The pressure on the lock was loosened and the voice went on enchantingly :

" Do you remember, my pretty policeman, a little talk which you once had with your lovely Elizabeth about the ghosts of Pemberley ? She said that the house was not haunted. That the dead Darcys pressed very little upon it ? We shall see now whether the mysteries of Pemberley may not be increased by a little, whether the memory of me, her only genius, may not be kept green by a few succeeding generations. I should like the story of a lover and his lass to add amongst the others."

The banter dropped and the voice became fiercely urgent.

" Listen, Buller, to what I have in store for you. Because you have been the witness to my endeavours since they started I am disinclined to kill you. Your mistress shall share your immunity. It is Charles only that I am teaching. But I cannot let you go. So I have thought out a clever plan for you, a little joke of my own devising. It's in the nature of an experiment, or an offering to the goddess of chance. The flue in which we lie so comfortably leads to the fireplace of an upstairs bedroom which has long boasted no fire. There are no noxious gases here to hurt you. But I am going to carry you down now, one at a time, and hang you in the kitchen chimney. Not so as to strangle you, you know. There is a convenient ledge where I can truss you. Miss Darcy shall be tied as well. I wish I could do you the favour of letting you share her injections, but my little tennis bag is not an inexhaustible cornucopia and the last dose was used for Charles. I shall leave you together above the kitchen. The cook will light the kitchen fire, I suppose, some time before the household rises and long before Dr. Wilder becomes anxious about Sir Charles. They say that the good witches and warlocks who were burnt in the old days usually suffocated in the smoke before the fire reached them. That's a matter of conjecture. You will be able to make sure. I don't suppose the fire itself will burn you, though it's a large fire in a large grate and it may roast you very uncomfortably. Your deaths, I should say, would take place within the hour, and from suffocation. If they search the chimneys when Charles's body has been found they ought to find you dead. You may survive long enough, one or both of you, and then you'll be fortunate. That is why I say it's an offering to the goddess of chance. But on the other hand, even if you do survive, they may never search the chimneys, and then you'll starve to death. I like to make the situation quite clear to you. They will have no reason to think that Buller is up a chimney. Nobody saw him go. In whatever case, I'm quite contented. You will die not by my hands but by the hands of your own cook, lighting her fire, or by the negligence of your servants in leaving the chimneys unsearched. You, Miss Darcy, will have the satisfaction of dying in your own home, surrounded by your own servants. They will be within a few yards of you on every side, searching for you or going about their own business. If you were not to be gagged, how easily you could call to them ! If you were not bound, how few steps would take you to safety ! And both of you will have the satisfaction of dying in one another's company. Lastly I shall have the very great poetical stimulus of reflecting upon the new Glamis legend of Pemberley, and of thinking of the old sooty bones wedged safely, but forgotten, in the bosom of this lovely house."

CHAPTER XX

Buller lay on his back with his eyes open, staring blindly upwards and listening to the preparations of Mauleverer.

The voyage to the kitchen chimney entailed a passage over the roof, for the kitchen was beneath the servants' wing at the other corner of the U. Mauleverer would have to drag them up the main chimney stack off which they now lay, would have to carry or trundle them along the sharp edge of the V-shaped roof above the dormers, and would finally have to lower them down a fresh stack. It was an effort which required preparation and forethought. He was busy at the moment bringing in the ropes from the other two chimneys to aid him in his task.

He scuttled about his business cheerfully, humming to himself in tuneless amusement and sidling in every few moments, to pay Buller a visit where he lay. He was delighted with Buller and could scarcely bring himself to leave him. Now he would come back to turn him over and feel the knots about his wrists ; now he would wriggle in with an idea which had just struck him, to whisper it in his ear. " Smoked bacon," he whispered, on one of these visits. " Think of it ! You may be preserved. Like a haddock or something. Not sooty bones but the fair flesh itself, shrivelled but recognisable, for the generation which discovers the secret of Pemberley ! " And another time : " Charles is still waiting, still wondering. I shan't go near him till I've taken you both to your tomb."

Buller waited patiently, chafing his hands behind his back to keep the circulation. At last the system of ropes was ready and Mauleverer slid in for the last time.

" It's getting late," he said. " I shall have to be off in a hurry as soon as all this is settled."

He stroked Buller's hair affectionately.

" I should like to put off my parting with you, Inspector, to the very last moment. Old acquaintance, you know. I can't think why, but I have a feeling of real affection for you which makes me want to see you to the last. When I was a boy I always used to leave the best parts of the fruit salad till the end.

" I think," he added reflectively, " that I shall take Miss Darcy to the kitchen first, and then pay my final visit to Sir Charles. Then I can come back for you and tell you all the news, whilst we're on our way. Charles's last moments, you know, and how he enjoyed them. My little mausoleum, my house of fame, my finished gramophone record, would be stocked up to the last moment in that case. Yes, that is what I shall do. And after that I shall really have to be going."

He busied himself with a rope beneath Elizabeth's armpits, and hauled her out backwards, remarking, as his voice echoed in the main shaft :

" Ladies first, if you'll excuse the proverb."

. . . . . .

Buller tussled in the darkness for three minutes. He arched his body, supporting himself between his heels and the back of his neck, and fumbled upwards behind his back with his bound hands. He grunted and sawed for a moment, and his hands were free. He sat up in the darkness, and bumped his head, but took no notice. He was working against time.

The cords binding his ankles were off in a moment, but the circulation was gone from his feet and he could not stand. He kicked his heels violently against the brickwork, and rubbed his insteps fiercely, pawing downwards, away from the heart. He was rewarded by agonising pain, succeeded by pins and needles, but he worked with redoubled energy.

After the three minutes he was free and could move. The stiffness would work itself off whilst he was busy.

Buller's brain had been calculating at top speed as he moved. Mauleverer was away with Elizabeth. He could not accomplish his task of moving a second body up and down those chimneys, and along the roof, in less than five minutes. But he knew the ground he was working over, and had arranged his system of ropes, so it was not safe to expect that he would take longer. In about five minutes from his exit he would return to slit Sir Charles's throat. Three of those minutes were already gone, and Buller was unarmed. The revolver which had clattered from his senseless grip into the dining-room fireplace had been appropriated by Mauleverer.

The only way in which he could get another would be by scrambling down the chimney through two storeys to Sir Charles's room, by letting himself out of that—it would be locked on the inside—and fetching the weapon from his own bedroom. The advantage of this course would be that he could raise the alarm on the way. He could not reach his room through the empty bedroom above which he lay at present, for the door of that room, like all the others in the house, was locked : and Charles had the key.

Buller had taken off his wrist watch when he went to bed. Time was a matter of guess. He could not be sure that he had not taken more than three minutes in freeing himself. He had no time to waste in making decisions. Given that his calculations were correct, he had two minutes to reach his own bedroom through Charles's, *and to get back again.* He must catch Mauleverer, if possible, at a point when he would be too far from Elizabeth to return and do her a mischief, and he must be between Mauleverer and Charles.

Buller decided that he had no time to get the gun. He would have to do without the alarm, and to surprise Mauleverer, unarmed, on his way back from the kitchen stack.

Buller was not entirely unarmed. He had a small penknife.

He opened both blades of this, holding it by the ivory in the middle, and thrust himself out into the main flue. Mauleverer's ropes were useful, and he worked himself upward silently, a black panther in the night.

The stars were out, and the tang of the wind before dawn freshened his matted hair as he rose above the chimney. The faint starlight just illuminated the sliding planes of the grey roof, picked out the other three stacks as they loomed upwards, leaning to heaven. The smell of the young leaves in the park ran with the soft wind, and, far below him, a silver glint slept on the lake. A few drowsy birds were stirring, and, from the distant stable, sounding tiny in the stillness of the night, came the sharp clatter of a hoof moved restlessly in a single stamp.

Buller writhed out of the chimney with a deadly motion, and curled himself behind it like a snake.

His hands fluttered to his throat, raising the collar of his dilapidated coat so as to show as little white as possible. Mauleverer would be much more invisible than he, for his pyjama trousers were of a light material and his face uncovered. Fortunately he had made a firm acquaintance with the soot.

Buller waited, glaring round the base of the chimney stack with an intent and animal concentration. His body was firm and lithe ; his broad chest nestled the brickwork. The little blades in his right hand pointed upwards.

There was not long to wait. The chimney at the other angle of the U seemed to move, definitely grew taller and subsided. Mauleverer was stepping along the roof towards him. The chimney gave him a background, so that it was difficult to make him out. Buller was seized with an agony of apprehension lest he would not be able to see him well enough to strike. He trembled with excitement, as he had done in the butts at his first drive, waiting for his first covey to come over. He must calculate his moment, not leap too soon.

Mauleverer came to the chimney chuckling. He puts his hands on the ledge and sprang upwards, leaning forwards to catch his body on the rim.

Buller was on the other side of the chimney and could not see the movement, but he guessed it. He rose to his full height and the two men were face to face.

Although Buller was prepared, Mauleverer moved more quickly. He slipped backwards even as Buller lunged, and dropped with a soft thud on the other side. He was clawing at his pocket as he landed, and the starlight ran at once with a dull gleam along the barrel of his revolver.

He dodged to the right of the chimney at the same moment that Buller dodged to his left. The two men were again face to face.

Buller made no attempt to stab him this time (he had dropped his knife), but plunged in a kind of falling rugger tackle, to muffle the revolver. Mauleverer was raising it as he closed, and a detonation seemed to burst between the two of them, holding them motionless in its shuddering crash.

Buller felt no pain and did not hear the singing in his ears. He hugged Mauleverer like a bear, falling forward on the slope of the roof and bringing Mauleverer to his knees. The man was as slippery as an eel, and worked the revolver round even as they fell, so that it pointed full at Buller's chest.

But however quickly one may swing a revolver round, it takes time to pull the trigger, especially the stiff trigger of an old Webley. For the first shot the hammer had been cocked, for the second it had to be brought back by the action of the trigger. Buller caught the magazine as the hammer reared to strike, and slewed it away with his right hand over his right shoulder. The percussion burst in his ear, like a physical slap, almost stunning him in a roar of light and thunder. He was dogged now, half insensible and wholly mad.

He caught the revolver arm before Mauleverer could level it again ; but he was no longer attempting to prevent him. His object ceased to be to disarm the madman. He did not mind how often he was shot. He was not trying to prevent Mauleverer shooting him, but to achieve the revolver so that he might shoot Mauleverer. The gun became his objective, not something to be feared.

The change from the defensive to the offensive touched Mauleverer as well. He felt the body in his arms stiffen and swell with purpose, felt its gain in power and his own corresponding loss. The revolver was being twisted from his grasp. It became no longer a weapon of attack, but a desirable object, to be retained if possible : something which was passing beyond his reach and must be striven for. Mauleverer felt the touch of panic. The pale face looming in the starlight thrust nearer and nearer to his own, the hot breath panted triumphantly on his neck. The mica goggles of his mask flashed before it, his eyes behind the goggles narrowed with terror and hate.

It was useless to pull the trigger now, for the barrel pointed outwards, far over the tennis courts in front of the house. The hand over his own hand was crushing the fingers cruelly on the butt.

Mauleverer made a desperate change of tactics. He abandoned the revolver to the crushing hand, and, twisting his body sideways with a sudden writhe, sent Buller sliding down the incline of the roof. He was on his feet in the same moment, and running for the other chimney along the sharp edge of the roof. He ran crouching and sure-footed, like a creature of the night.

Buller slid—there was something slippery which helped him—but without caring whether he slid or not. He caught the brow of the roof automatically with his left hand and levelled the revolver with the other.

The first explosion tore his heart with fury and despair. It was a miss. Mauleverer was already leaping for the chimney down which Elizabeth lay. Buller knew at once that he would kill her as he fled. His head cleared with the knowledge and his shaking hand steadied at once.

Mauleverer's black shape rose against the star-light, clearly outlined as he crouched over the chimney for his downward plunge. Buller aimed deliberately and fired. He did not hear the explosion. The black shape hung still, as if arrested. Buller raised the muzzle again and pulled the trigger.

The figure dissolved before his eyes. The upper part of the body collapsed to the right, the lower part to the left. The whole crumbled from its eminence and tumbled to the roof. It bounced slightly, in a strange attitude, rolled sideways with a gathering impetus, and shot out over the edge.

Dr. Wilder who, at the first shots, had rushed out into the garden and was now prancing about in an agony of impotent anxiety, was nearly crushed by it, as it crunched on the gravel within a few feet of him. He leapt aside with a startled exclamation, and the wild recognisable voice filtered down from the chimney pots :

" Got 'im, by God ! Got 'im ! Got 'im ! "

.   .   .   .   .   .

They found Buller at dawn, after a painful and dirty journey up the chimney, sitting across the brow of the roof with one leg on either side. His left leg was numb and roughly bandaged, the tight soaked trouser glistening with blood. He was in tearing spirits and greeted Wilder's dishevelled head with a recitation of the "Ode to the Skylark."

They lowered him down the chimney and

Wilder examined the wound. It was the result of the first shot.

Wilder said : " Well, that's not much. There's a muscle torn, that's all. A close shot though. It was cauterised as it was made."

Buller was not interested.

" I had a bright idea on that roof," he said, " whilst I was waiting for you. It's an extraordinary thing how one thinks of things in the morning. You know that little mare's nest of the Master's drugs which we stirred up in Cambridge? Hasn't it struck you that it might lead us to Charles's fat man if we followed it up ? "

CHAPTER XXI

THE day after Kingdom's funeral Elizabeth took Buller for a drive. This time she had to drive the Chrysler herself, for his leg was still useless. They were talking about the excitements of the past few days.

Buller said : " We buried Mauleverer in the grounds, or rather Wilder and Charles did, yesterday. Till then we kept him locked in Charles's bathroom and nobody knew about it. I told Smith that I'd missed him on the roof. Wilder managed to rake up some quicklime from somewhere, so it'll be all right. I told him to be careful it wasn't slaked. One of my murderer friends once buried a body in lime, to get rid of it, but he got hold of slaked lime by mistake. And that's an excellent preservative."

" But surely he'll be missed ? "

" He'll be missed all right, but then he's been at great pains to manufacture his alibi at Dreavour, and that's where he'll be looked for. It's very bad for your engine not to change down when it's knocking."

Elizabeth changed down obediently.

" I've wanted to know one thing very much,"

she said. " How on earth did you get yourself
undone in that chimney ? "

Buller laughed.

" It was rather a swindle, I'm afraid," he said.
" I don't claim to be a Houdini, though there is
a way of holding your hands when they're going
to be tied which forces the tier to use a certain
knot which makes the ones on top of it useless.
Any way I was stunned when he triced me up,
so I didn't have a chance of that."

Elizabeth prompted him.

" Well ? "

" The explanation is, I'm afraid, that I've
always been incurably romantic. I used to read
detective stories far too much, and the hero always
gets tied up in them at one time or another. It
occurred to me that all heroes ought to have a
little pocket in the jacket of all their suits, in the
lining at the back, in which they could conceal
penknives."

" And do you mean to say you had that ? "

" Yes," said Buller defensively. " It wasn't
ridiculous.   I've always liked to work alone and
one gets into queer positions doing that sometimes.
I liked to think that I was prepared for emer-
gencies. Why shouldn't a detective think out a
useful easy equipment just as much as somebody
going on a walking tour ? As a matter of fact I
once amused myself by inventing all sorts of

little improvements on my suits. I always wear my cigarette case in a waistcoat pocket over my heart, even now—silly, I admit, but look at that governor or somebody that they tried to assassinate in India—and I have had occasion, once, to strap an automatic under my armpit like they do in America. When one worked on one's own, one liked to have little dodges of one's own. It made one feel more equipped to meet the unexpected. In my sleeve, for instance, here, there used to be a key which fitted the usual brand of handcuffs— sewn in at the cuff."

Elizabeth said : " I didn't know that detectives behaved like that."

" They don't. I'm afraid I've never been able to use any of my little dodges before. They were a sort of talisman, really, to keep my spirits up. And, as you see, there was no harm in my romances. The long shot came off for once. The lucky thing was that I slipped on my coat instead of my dressing-gown. The dressing-gown was at the other side of the room and I was too tired to fetch it."

Elizabeth said : " Well, I think it all sounds very improbable."

" As regards the ordinary murder, yes. No ordinary murderer or thief would think of tying you up. But I used to have to deal as well, sometimes, with gangs of racing toughs—vicious young

limbs from Glasgow, who carry razors and stab
you with broken bottles and call themselves
" The Bloody Hand " or something of that sort.
They are the people who are likely to tie you up.
They're nourished on penny dreadfuls and behave
as such. I served my apprenticeship in Glasgow
before I went to Cambridge. That's where I had
the old coat made which I was wearing."

Buller added apologetically : " I haven't got
a back pocket in this one. It was made in Cambridge."

Elizabeth seemed mollified and started on a
new tack.

" There's one more thing," she said, " which I
want an explanation of."

Buller wilted in the pause.

" What," she demanded, " were you doing to
my ear ? "

" When ? " asked Buller weakly.

" You know perfectly well."

Buller said : " Oh, I was—I was *whispering*."

" What about ? "

" About ? How do you mean what about ? "

" About what ? "

" Oh. Yes. About Mauleverer."

" What did you whisper about Mauleverer ? "

" Well, I didn't whisper. I—I hadn't a chance."

" Why ? "

Buller said : " Well—I——"

" If you wanted to whisper anything else," said Elizabeth, " my ear's still there."

For a detective Buller was obtuse, but he rose to the occasion.

.   .   .   .   .   .

After a bit he said : " Couldn't we stop for a minute and have a talk ? "

.   .   .   .   .   .

After the talk the base voice in Buller said : " Wouldn't it be marvellous if we could be married ? " The weak voice of timid morality added hastily : " Or something ? "

Elizabeth said : " Well, I'd *rather* be married."

.   .   .   .   .   .

On the way home Elizabeth said, " Do you know, I don't even know your Christian name ? "

" I know, Liz, but you see——"

" What is it ? "

" Leonidas Jeremiah Buller."

" I shall call you Buller," Elizabeth said emphatically.

THE END

A CATALOGUE OF
SELECTED DOVER BOOKS
IN ALL FIELDS OF INTEREST

A CATALOGUE OF SELECTED DOVER

BOOKS IN ALL FIELDS OF INTEREST

RACKHAM'S COLOR ILLUSTRATIONS FOR WAGNER'S RING. Rackham's finest mature work—all 64 full-color watercolors in a faithful and lush interpretation of the *Ring*. Full-sized plates on coated stock of the paintings used by opera companies for authentic staging of Wagner. Captions aid in following complete Ring cycle. Introduction. 64 illustrations plus vignettes. 72pp. 8⅝ x 11¼.   23779-6 Pa. $6.00

CONTEMPORARY POLISH POSTERS IN FULL COLOR, edited by Joseph Czestochowski. 46 full-color examples of brilliant school of Polish graphic design, selected from world's first museum (near Warsaw) dedicated to poster art. Posters on circuses, films, plays, concerts all show cosmopolitan influences, free imagination. Introduction. 48pp. 9⅜ x 12¼.
23780-X Pa. $6.00

GRAPHIC WORKS OF EDVARD MUNCH, Edvard Munch. 90 haunting, evocative prints by first major Expressionist artist and one of the greatest graphic artists of his time: *The Scream, Anxiety, Death Chamber, The Kiss, Madonna,* etc. Introduction by Alfred Werner. 90pp. 9 x 12.
23765-6 Pa. $5.00

THE GOLDEN AGE OF THE POSTER, Hayward and Blanche Cirker. 70 extraordinary posters in full colors, from Maitres de l'Affiche, Mucha, Lautrec, Bradley, Cheret, Beardsley, many others. Total of 78pp. 9⅜ x 12¼.   22753-7 Pa. $5.95

THE NOTEBOOKS OF LEONARDO DA VINCI, edited by J. P. Richter. Extracts from manuscripts reveal great genius; on painting, sculpture, anatomy, sciences, geography, etc. Both Italian and English. 186 ms. pages reproduced, plus 500 additional drawings, including studies for *Last Supper*, Sforza monument, etc. 860pp. 7⅞ x 10¾. (Available in U.S. only)
22572-0, 22573-9 Pa., Two-vol. set $15.90

THE CODEX NUTTALL, as first edited by Zelia Nuttall. Only inexpensive edition, in full color, of a pre-Columbian Mexican (Mixtec) book. 88 color plates show kings, gods, heroes, temples, sacrifices. New explanatory, historical introduction by Arthur G. Miller. 96pp. 11⅜ x 8½. (Available in U.S. only)
23168-2 Pa. $7.50

UNE SEMAINE DE BONTÉ, A SURREALISTIC NOVEL IN COLLAGE, Max Ernst. Masterpiece created out of 19th-century periodical illustrations, explores worlds of terror and surprise. Some consider this Ernst's greatest work. 208pp. 8⅛ x 11.   23252-2 Pa. $5.00

DRAWINGS OF WILLIAM BLAKE, William Blake. 92 plates from Book of Job, *Divine Comedy, Paradise Lost,* visionary heads, mythological figures, Laocoon, etc. Selection, introduction, commentary by Sir Geoffrey Keynes. 178pp. 8⅛ x 11.   22303-5 Pa. $4.00

ENGRAVINGS OF HOGARTH, William Hogarth. 101 of Hogarth's greatest works: *Rake's Progress, Harlot's Progress, Illustrations for Hudibras, Before and After, Beer Street and Gin Lane,* many more. Full commentary. 256pp. 11 x 13¾.   22479-1 Pa. $7.95

DAUMIER: 120 GREAT LITHOGRAPHS, Honore Daumier. Wide-ranging collection of lithographs by the greatest caricaturist of the 19th century. Concentrates on eternally popular series on lawyers, on married life, on liberated women, etc. Selection, introduction, and notes on plates by Charles F. Ramus. Total of 158pp. 9⅜ x 12¼.   23512-2 Pa. $5.50

DRAWINGS OF MUCHA, Alphonse Maria Mucha. Work reveals draftsman of highest caliber: studies for famous posters and paintings, renderings for book illustrations and ads, etc. 70 works, 9 in color; including 6 items not drawings. Introduction. List of illustrations. 72pp. 9⅜ x 12¼. (Available in U.S. only)   23672-2 Pa. $4.00

GIOVANNI BATTISTA PIRANESI: DRAWINGS IN THE PIERPONT MORGAN LIBRARY, Giovanni Battista Piranesi. For first time ever all of Morgan Library's collection, world's largest. 167 illustrations of rare Piranesi drawings—archeological, architectural, decorative and visionary. Essay, detailed list of drawings, chronology, captions. Edited by Felice Stampfle. 144pp. 9⅜ x 12¼.   23714-1 Pa. $7.50

NEW YORK ETCHINGS (1905-1949), John Sloan. All of important American artist's N.Y. life etchings. 67 works include some of his best art; also lively historical record—Greenwich Village, tenement scenes. Edited by Sloan's widow. Introduction and captions. 79pp. 8⅜ x 11¼.
23651-X Pa. $4.00

CHINESE PAINTING AND CALLIGRAPHY: A PICTORIAL SURVEY, Wan-go Weng. 69 fine examples from John M. Crawford's matchless private collection: landscapes, birds, flowers, human figures, etc., plus calligraphy. Every basic form included: hanging scrolls, handscrolls, album leaves, fans, etc. 109 illustrations. Introduction. Captions. 192pp. 8⅞ x 11¾.
23707-9 Pa. $7.95

DRAWINGS OF REMBRANDT, edited by Seymour Slive. Updated Lippmann, Hofstede de Groot edition, with definitive scholarly apparatus. All portraits, biblical sketches, landscapes, nudes, Oriental figures, classical studies, together with selection of work by followers. 550 illustrations. Total of 630pp. 9⅛ x 12¼.   21485-0, 21486-9 Pa., Two-vol. set $14.00

THE DISASTERS OF WAR, Francisco Goya. 83 etchings record horrors of Napoleonic wars in Spain and war in general. Reprint of 1st edition, plus 3 additional plates. Introduction by Philip Hofer. 97pp. 9⅜ x 8¼.
21872-4 Pa. $3.75

THE EARLY WORK OF AUBREY BEARDSLEY, Aubrey Beardsley. 157 plates, 2 in color: *Manon Lescaut, Madame Bovary, Morte Darthur, Salome,* other. Introduction by H. Marillier. 182pp. 8⅛ x 11. 21816-3 Pa. $4.50

THE LATER WORK OF AUBREY BEARDSLEY, Aubrey Beardsley. Exotic masterpieces of full maturity: *Venus and Tannhauser, Lysistrata, Rape of the Lock, Volpone,* Savoy material, etc. 174 plates, 2 in color. 186pp. 8⅛ x 11. 21817-1 Pa. $4.50

THOMAS NAST'S CHRISTMAS DRAWINGS, Thomas Nast. Almost all Christmas drawings by creator of image of Santa Claus as we know it, and one of America's foremost illustrators and political cartoonists. 66 illustrations. 3 illustrations in color on covers. 96pp. 8⅜ x 11¼. 23660-9 Pa. $3.50

THE DORÉ ILLUSTRATIONS FOR DANTE'S DIVINE COMEDY, Gustave Doré. All 135 plates from Inferno, Purgatory, Paradise; fantastic tortures, infernal landscapes, celestial wonders. Each plate with appropriate (translated) verses. 141pp. 9 x 12. 23231-X Pa. $4.50

DORÉ'S ILLUSTRATIONS FOR RABELAIS, Gustave Doré. 252 striking illustrations of *Gargantua and Pantagruel* books by foremost 19th-century illustrator. Including 60 plates, 192 delightful smaller illustrations. 153pp. 9 x 12. 23656-0 Pa. $5.00

LONDON: A PILGRIMAGE, Gustave Doré, Blanchard Jerrold. Squalor, riches, misery, beauty of mid-Victorian metropolis; 55 wonderful plates, 125 other illustrations, full social, cultural text by Jerrold. 191pp. of text. 9⅜ x 12¼. 22306-X Pa. $6.00

THE RIME OF THE ANCIENT MARINER, Gustave Doré, S. T. Coleridge. Dore's finest work, 34 plates capture moods, subtleties of poem. Full text. Introduction by Millicent Rose. 77pp. 9¼ x 12. 22305-1 Pa. $3.00

THE DORE BIBLE ILLUSTRATIONS, Gustave Doré. All wonderful, detailed plates: Adam and Eve, Flood, Babylon, Life of Jesus, etc. Brief King James text with each plate. Introduction by Millicent Rose. 241 plates. 241pp. 9 x 12. 23004-X Pa. $5.00

THE COMPLETE ENGRAVINGS, ETCHINGS AND DRYPOINTS OF ALBRECHT DURER. "Knight, Death and Devil"; "Melencolia," and more—all Dürer's known works in all three media, including 6 works formerly attributed to him. 120 plates. 235pp. 8⅜ x 11¼. 22851-7 Pa. $6.50

MAXIMILIAN'S TRIUMPHAL ARCH, Albrecht Dürer and others. Incredible monument of woodcut art: 8 foot high elaborate arch—heraldic figures, humans, battle scenes, fantastic elements—that you can assemble yourself. Printed on one side, layout for assembly. 143pp. 11 x 16. 21451-6 Pa. $5.00

THE COMPLETE WOODCUTS OF ALBRECHT DURER, edited by Dr. W. Kurth. 346 in all: "Old Testament," "St. Jerome," "Passion," "Life of Virgin," Apocalypse," many others. Introduction by Campbell Dodgson. 285pp. 8½ x 12¼. 21097-9 Pa. $6.95

DRAWINGS OF ALBRECHT DURER, edited by Heinrich Wolfflin. 81 plates show development from youth to full style. Many favorites; many new. Introduction by Alfred Werner. 96pp. 8⅛ x 11. 22352-3 Pa. $4.00

THE HUMAN FIGURE, Albrecht Dürer. Experiments in various techniques—stereometric, progressive proportional, and others. Also life studies that rank among finest ever done. Complete reprinting of *Dresden Sketchbook*. 170 plates. 355pp. 8⅜ x 11¼. 21042-1 Pa. $6.95

OF THE JUST SHAPING OF LETTERS, Albrecht Dürer. Renaissance artist explains design of Roman majuscules by geometry, also Gothic lower and capitals. Grolier Club edition. 43pp. 7⅞ x 10¾ 21306-4 Pa. $2.50

TEN BOOKS ON ARCHITECTURE, Vitruvius. The most important book ever written on architecture. Early Roman aesthetics, technology, classical orders, site selection, all other aspects. Stands behind everything since. Morgan translation. 331pp. 5⅜ x 8½. 20645-9 Pa. $3.75

THE FOUR BOOKS OF ARCHITECTURE, Andrea Palladio. 16th-century classic responsible for Palladian movement and style. Covers classical architectural remains, Renaissance revivals, classical orders, etc. 1738 Ware English edition. Introduction by A. Placzek. 216 plates. 110pp. of text. 9½ x 12¾. 21308-0 Pa. $7.50

HORIZONS, Norman Bel Geddes. Great industrialist stage designer, "father of streamlining," on application of aesthetics to transportation, amusement, architecture, etc. 1932 prophetic account; function, theory, specific projects. 222 illustrations. 312pp. 7⅞ x 10¾. 23514-9 Pa. $6.95

FRANK LLOYD WRIGHT'S FALLINGWATER, Donald Hoffmann. Full, illustrated story of conception and building of Wright's masterwork at Bear Run, Pa. 100 photographs of site, construction, and details of completed structure. 112pp. 9¼ x 10. 23671-4 Pa. $5.00

THE ELEMENTS OF DRAWING, John Ruskin. Timeless classic by great Viltorian; starts with basic ideas, works through more difficult. Many practical exercises. 48 illustrations. Introduction by Lawrence Campbell. 228pp. 5⅜ x 8½. 22730-8 Pa. $2.75

GIST OF ART, John Sloan. Greatest modern American teacher, Art Students League, offers innumerable hints, instructions, guided comments to help you in painting. Not a formal course. 46 illustrations. Introduction by Helen Sloan. 200pp. 5⅜ x 8½. 23435-5 Pa. $3.50

THE ANATOMY OF THE HORSE, George Stubbs. Often considered the great masterpiece of animal anatomy. Full reproduction of 1766 edition, plus prospectus; original text and modernized text. 36 plates. Introduction by Eleanor Garvey. 121pp. 11 x 14¾.   23402-9 Pa. $6.00

BRIDGMAN'S LIFE DRAWING, George B. Bridgman. More than 500 illustrative drawings and text teach you to abstract the body into its major masses, use light and shade, proportion; as well as specific areas of anatomy, of which Bridgman is master. 192pp. 6½ x 9¼. (Available in U.S. only)
22710-3 Pa. $2.50

ART NOUVEAU DESIGNS IN COLOR, Alphonse Mucha, Maurice Verneuil, Georges Auriol. Full-color reproduction of *Combinaisons ornementales* (c. 1900) by Art Nouveau masters. Floral, animal, geometric, interlacings, swashes—borders, frames, spots—all incredibly beautiful. 60 plates, hundreds of designs. 9⅜ x 8-1/16.   22885-1 Pa. $4.00

FULL-COLOR FLORAL DESIGNS IN THE ART NOUVEAU STYLE, E. A. Seguy. 166 motifs, on 40 plates, from *Les fleurs et leurs applications decoratives* (1902): borders, circular designs, repeats, allovers, "spots." All in authentic Art Nouveau colors. 48pp. 9⅜ x 12¼.
23439-8 Pa. $5.00

A DIDEROT PICTORIAL ENCYCLOPEDIA OF TRADES AND INDUSTRY, edited by Charles C. Gillispie. 485 most interesting plates from the great French Encyclopedia of the 18th century show hundreds of working figures, artifacts, process, land and cityscapes; glassmaking, papermaking, metal extraction, construction, weaving, making furniture, clothing, wigs, dozens of other activities. Plates fully explained. 920pp. 9 x 12.
22284-5, 22285-3 Clothbd., Two-vol. set $40.00

HANDBOOK OF EARLY ADVERTISING ART, Clarence P. Hornung. Largest collection of copyright-free early and antique advertising art ever compiled. Over 6,000 illustrations, from Franklin's time to the 1890's for special effects, novelty. Valuable source, almost inexhaustible.
Pictorial Volume. Agriculture, the zodiac, animals, autos, birds, Christmas, fire engines, flowers, trees, musical instruments, ships, games and sports, much more. Arranged by subject matter and use. 237 plates. 288pp. 9 x 12.
20122-8 Clothbd. $13.50

Typographical Volume. Roman and Gothic faces ranging from 10 point to 300 point, "Barnum," German and Old English faces, script, logotypes, scrolls and flourishes, 1115 ornamental initials, 67 complete alphabets, more. 310 plates. 320pp. 9 x 12.   20123-6 Clothbd. $13.50

CALLIGRAPHY (CALLIGRAPHIA LATINA), J. G. Schwandner. High point of 18th-century ornamental calligraphy. Very ornate initials, scrolls, borders, cherubs, birds, lettered examples. 172pp. 9 x 13.
20475-8 Pa. $6.00

ART FORMS IN NATURE, Ernst Haeckel. Multitude of strangely beautiful natural forms: Radiolaria, Foraminifera, jellyfishes, fungi, turtles, bats, etc. All 100 plates of the 19th-century evolutionist's *Kunstformen der Natur* (1904). 100pp. 9⅜ x 12¼.   22987-4 Pa. $4.50

CHILDREN: A PICTORIAL ARCHIVE FROM NINETEENTH-CENTURY SOURCES, edited by Carol Belanger Grafton. 242 rare, copyright-free wood engravings for artists and designers. Widest such selection available. All illustrations in line. 119pp. 8⅜ x 11¼.
23694-3 Pa. $3.50

WOMEN: A PICTORIAL ARCHIVE FROM NINETEENTH-CENTURY SOURCES, edited by Jim Harter. 391 copyright-free wood engravings for artists and designers selected from rare periodicals. Most extensive such collection available. All illustrations in line. 128pp. 9 x 12.
23703-6 Pa. $4.00

ARABIC ART IN COLOR, Prisse d'Avennes. From the greatest ornamentalists of all time—50 plates in color, rarely seen outside the Near East, rich in suggestion and stimulus. Includes 4 plates on covers. 46pp. 9⅜ x 12¼.   23658-7 Pa. $6.00

AUTHENTIC ALGERIAN CARPET DESIGNS AND MOTIFS, edited by June Beveridge. Algerian carpets are world famous. Dozens of geometrical motifs are charted on grids, color-coded, for weavers, needleworkers, craftsmen, designers. 53 illustrations plus 4 in color. 48pp. 8¼ x 11. (Available in U.S. only)   23650-1 Pa. $1.75

DICTIONARY OF AMERICAN PORTRAITS, edited by Hayward and Blanche Cirker. 4000 important Americans, earliest times to 1905, mostly in clear line. Politicians, writers, soldiers, scientists, inventors, industrialists, Indians, Blacks, women, outlaws, etc. Identificatory information. 756pp. 9¼ x 12¾.   21823-6 Clothbd. $40.00

HOW THE OTHER HALF LIVES, Jacob A. Riis. Journalistic record of filth, degradation, upward drive in New York immigrant slums, shops, around 1900. New edition includes 100 original Riis photos, monuments of early photography. 233pp. 10 x 7⅞.   22012-5 Pa. $6.00

NEW YORK IN THE THIRTIES, Berenice Abbott. Noted photographer's fascinating study of city shows new buildings that have become famous and old sights that have disappeared forever. Insightful commentary. 97 photographs. 97pp. 11⅜ x 10.   22967-X Pa. $4.50

MEN AT WORK, Lewis W. Hine. Famous photographic studies of construction workers, railroad men, factory workers and coal miners. New supplement of 18 photos on Empire State building construction. New introduction by Jonathan L. Doherty. Total of 69 photos. 63pp. 8 x 10¾.
23475-4 Pa. $3.00

THE DEPRESSION YEARS AS PHOTOGRAPHED BY ARTHUR ROTH-STEIN, Arthur Rothstein. First collection devoted entirely to the work of outstanding 1930s photographer: famous dust storm photo, ragged children, unemployed, etc. 120 photographs. Captions. 119pp. 9¼ x 10¾.
23590-4 Pa. $5.00

CAMERA WORK: A PICTORIAL GUIDE, Alfred Stieglitz. All 559 illustrations and plates from the most important periodical in the history of art photography, *Camera Work* (1903-17). Presented four to a page, reduced in size but still clear, in strict chronological order, with complete captions. Three indexes. Glossary. Bibliography. 176pp. 8⅜ x 11¼.
23591-2 Pa. $6.95

ALVIN LANGDON COBURN, PHOTOGRAPHER, Alvin L. Coburn. Revealing autobiography by one of greatest photographers of 20th century gives insider's version of Photo-Secession, plus comments on his own work. 77 photographs by Coburn. Edited by Helmut and Alison Gernsheim. 160pp. 8⅛ x 11.
23685-4 Pa. $6.00

NEW YORK IN THE FORTIES, Andreas Feininger. 162 brilliant photographs by the well-known photographer, formerly with *Life* magazine, show commuters, shoppers, Times Square at night, Harlem nightclub, Lower East Side, etc. Introduction and full captions by John von Hartz. 181pp. 9¼ x 10¾.
23585-8 Pa. $6.00

GREAT NEWS PHOTOS AND THE STORIES BEHIND THEM, John Faber. Dramatic volume of 140 great news photos, 1855 through 1976, and revealing stories behind them, with both historical and technical information. Hindenburg disaster, shooting of Oswald, nomination of Jimmy Carter, etc. 160pp. 8¼ x 11.
23667-6 Pa. $5.00

THE ART OF THE CINEMATOGRAPHER, Leonard Maltin. Survey of American cinematography history and anecdotal interviews with 5 masters—Arthur Miller, Hal Mohr, Hal Rosson, Lucien Ballard, and Conrad Hall. Very large selection of behind-the-scenes production photos. 105 photographs. Filmographies. Index. Originally *Behind the Camera.* 144pp. 8¼ x 11.
23686-2 Pa. $5.00

DESIGNS FOR THE THREE-CORNERED HAT (LE TRICORNE), Pablo Picasso. 32 fabulously rare drawings—including 31 color illustrations of costumes and accessories—for 1919 production of famous ballet. Edited by Parmenia Migel, who has written new introduction. 48pp. 9⅜ x 12¼. (Available in U.S. only)
23709-5 Pa. $5.00

NOTES OF A FILM DIRECTOR, Sergei Eisenstein. Greatest Russian filmmaker explains montage, making of *Alexander Nevsky,* aesthetics; comments on self, associates, great rivals (Chaplin), similar material. 78 illustrations. 240pp. 5⅜ x 8½.
22392-2 Pa. $4.50

HOLLYWOOD GLAMOUR PORTRAITS, edited by John Kobal. 145 photos capture the stars from 1926-49, the high point in portrait photography. Gable, Harlow, Bogart, Bacall, Hedy Lamarr, Marlene Dietrich, Robert Montgomery, Marlon Brando, Veronica Lake; 94 stars in all. Full background on photographers, technical aspects, much more. Total of 160pp. 8⅜ x 11¼.   23352-9 Pa. $5.00

THE NEW YORK STAGE: FAMOUS PRODUCTIONS IN PHOTO-GRAPHS, edited by Stanley Appelbaum. 148 photographs from Museum of City of New York show 142 plays, 1883-1939. *Peter Pan, The Front Page, Dead End, Our Town,* O'Neill, hundreds of actors and actresses, etc. Full indexes. 154pp. 9½ x 10.   23241-7 Pa. $4.50

MASTERS OF THE DRAMA, John Gassner. Most comprehensive history of the drama, every tradition from Greeks to modern Europe and America, including Orient. Covers 800 dramatists, 2000 plays; biography, plot summaries, criticism, theatre history, etc. 77 illustrations. 890pp. 5⅜ x 8½.
20100-7 Clothbd. $10.00

THE GREAT OPERA STARS IN HISTORIC PHOTOGRAPHS, edited by James Camner. 343 portraits from the 1850s to the 1940s: Tamburini, Mario, Caliapin, Jeritza, Melchior, Melba, Patti, Pinza, Schipa, Caruso, Farrar, Steber, Gobbi, and many more—270 performers in all. Index. 199pp. 8⅜ x 11¼.   23575-0 Pa. $6.50

J. S. BACH, Albert Schweitzer. Great full-length study of Bach, life, background to music, music, by foremost modern scholar. Ernest Newman translation. 650 musical examples. Total of 928pp. 5⅜ x 8½. (Available in U.S. only)   21631-4, 21632-2 Pa., Two-vol. set $9.00

COMPLETE PIANO SONATAS, Ludwig van Beethoven. All sonatas in the fine Schenker edition, with fingering, analytical material. One of best modern editions. Total of 615pp. 9 x 12. (Available in U.S. only)
23134-8, 23135-6 Pa., Two-vol. set $13.00

KEYBOARD MUSIC, J. S. Bach. Bach-Gesellschaft edition. For harpsichord, piano, other keyboard instruments. English Suites, French Suites, Six Partitas, Goldberg Variations, Two-Part Inventions, Three-Part Sinfonias. 312pp. 8⅛ x 11. (Available in U.S. only)   22360-4 Pa. $5.50

FOUR SYMPHONIES IN FULL SCORE, Franz Schubert. Schubert's four most popular symphonies: No. 4 in C Minor ("Tragic"); No. 5 in B-flat Major; No. 8 in B Minor ("Unfinished"); No. 9 in C Major ("Great"). Breitkopf & Hartel edition. Study score. 261pp. 9⅜ x 12¼.
23681-1 Pa. $6.50

THE AUTHENTIC GILBERT & SULLIVAN SONGBOOK, W. S. Gilbert, A. S. Sullivan. Largest selection available; 92 songs, uncut, original keys, in piano rendering approved by Sullivan. Favorites and lesser-known fine numbers. Edited with plot synopses by James Spero. 3 illustrations. 399pp. 9 x 12.   23482-7 Pa. $7.95

PRINCIPLES OF ORCHESTRATION, Nikolay Rimsky-Korsakov. Great classical orchestrator provides fundamentals of tonal resonance, progression of parts, voice and orchestra, tutti effects, much else in major document. 330pp. of musical excerpts. 489pp. 6½ x 9¼.　　　　21266-1 Pa. $6.00

TRISTAN UND ISOLDE, Richard Wagner. Full orchestral score with complete instrumentation. Do not confuse with piano reduction. Commentary by Felix Mottl, great Wagnerian conductor and scholar. Study score. 655pp. 8⅛ x 11.　　　　22915-7 Pa. $12.50

REQUIEM IN FULL SCORE, Giuseppe Verdi. Immensely popular with choral groups and music lovers. Republication of edition published by C. F. Peters, Leipzig, n. d. German frontmaker in English translation. Glossary. Text in Latin. Study score. 204pp. 9⅜ x 12¼.

23682-X Pa. $6.00

COMPLETE CHAMBER MUSIC FOR STRINGS, Felix Mendelssohn. All of Mendelssohn's chamber music: Octet, 2 Quintets, 6 Quartets, and Four Pieces for String Quartet. (Nothing with piano is included). Complete works edition (1874-7). Study score. 283 pp. 9⅜ x 12¼.

23679-X Pa. $6.95

POPULAR SONGS OF NINETEENTH-CENTURY AMERICA, edited by Richard Jackson. 64 most important songs: "Old Oaken Bucket," "Arkansas Traveler," "Yellow Rose of Texas," etc. Authentic original sheet music, full introduction and commentaries. 290pp. 9 x 12.　　23270-0 Pa. $6.00

COLLECTED PIANO WORKS, Scott Joplin. Edited by Vera Brodsky Lawrence. Practically all of Joplin's piano works—rags, two-steps, marches, waltzes, etc., 51 works in all. Extensive introduction by Rudi Blesh. Total of 345pp. 9 x 12.　　　　23106-2 Pa. $13.50

BASIC PRINCIPLES OF CLASSICAL BALLET, Agrippina Vaganova. Great Russian theoretician, teacher explains methods for teaching classical ballet; incorporates best from French, Italian, Russian schools. 118 illustrations. 175pp. 5⅜ x 8½.　　　　22036-2 Pa. $2.00

CHINESE CHARACTERS, L. Wieger. Rich analysis of 2300 characters according to traditional systems into primitives. Historical-semantic analysis to phonetics (Classical Mandarin) and radicals. 820pp. 6⅛ x 9¼.

21321-8 Pa. $8.95

EGYPTIAN LANGUAGE: EASY LESSONS IN EGYPTIAN HIERO-GLYPHICS, E. A. Wallis Budge. Foremost Egyptologist offers Egyptian grammar, explanation of hieroglyphics, many reading texts, dictionary of symbols. 246pp. 5 x 7½. (Available in U.S. only)

21394-3 Clothbd. $7.50

AN ETYMOLOGICAL DICTIONARY OF MODERN ENGLISH, Ernest Weekley. Richest, fullest work, by foremost British lexicographer. Detailed word histories. Inexhaustible. Do not confuse this with *Concise Etymological Dictionary*, which is abridged. Total of 856pp. 6½ x 9¼.

21873-2, 21874-0 Pa., Two-vol. set $10.00

A MAYA GRAMMAR, Alfred M. Tozzer. Practical, useful English-language grammar by the Harvard anthropologist who was one of the three greatest American scholars in the area of Maya culture. Phonetics, grammatical processes, syntax, more. 301pp. 5⅜ x 8½.   23465-7 Pa. $4.00

THE JOURNAL OF HENRY D. THOREAU, edited by Bradford Torrey, F. H. Allen. Complete reprinting of 14 volumes, 1837-61, over two million words; the sourcebooks for *Walden,* etc. Definitive. All original sketches, plus 75 photographs. Introduction by Walter Harding. Total of 1804pp. 8½ x 12¼.   20312-3, 20313-1 Clothbd., Two-vol. set $50.00

CLASSIC GHOST STORIES, Charles Dickens and others. 18 wonderful stories you've wanted to reread: "The Monkey's Paw," "The House and the Brain," "The Upper Berth," "The Signalman," "Dracula's Guest," "The Tapestried Chamber," etc. Dickens, Scott, Mary Shelley, Stoker, etc. 330pp. 5⅜ x 8½.   20735-8 Pa. $3.50

SEVEN SCIENCE FICTION NOVELS, H. G. Wells. Full novels. *First Men in the Moon, Island of Dr. Moreau, War of the Worlds, Food of the Gods, Invisible Man, Time Machine, In the Days of the Comet.* A basic science-fiction library. 1015pp. 5⅜ x 8½. (Available in U.S. only)
20264-X Clothbd. $8.95

ARMADALE, Wilkie Collins. Third great mystery novel by the author of *The Woman in White* and *The Moonstone.* Ingeniously plotted narrative shows an exceptional command of character, incident and mood. Original magazine version with 40 illustrations. 597pp. 5⅜ x 8½.
23429-0 Pa. $5.00

MASTERS OF MYSTERY, H. Douglas Thomson. The first book in English (1931) devoted to history and aesthetics of detective story. Poe, Doyle, LeFanu, Dickens, many others, up to 1930. New introduction and notes by E. F. Bleiler. 288pp. 5⅜ x 8½. (Available in U.S. only)
23606-4 Pa. $4.00

FLATLAND, E. A. Abbott. Science-fiction classic explores life of 2-D being in 3-D world. Read also as introduction to thought about hyperspace. Introduction by Banesh Hoffmann. 16 illustrations. 103pp. 5⅜ x 8½.
20001-9 Pa. $1.50

THREE SUPERNATURAL NOVELS OF THE VICTORIAN PERIOD, edited, with an introduction, by E. F. Bleiler. Reprinted complete and unabridged, three great classics of the supernatural: *The Haunted Hotel* by Wilkie Collins, *The Haunted House at Latchford* by Mrs. J. H. Riddell, and *The Lost Stradivarious* by J. Meade Falkner. 325pp. 5⅜ x 8½.
22571-2 Pa. $4.00

AYESHA: THE RETURN OF "SHE," H. Rider Haggard. Virtuoso sequel featuring the great mythic creation, Ayesha, in an adventure that is fully as good as the first book, *She.* Original magazine version, with 47 original illustrations by Maurice Greiffenhagen. 189pp. 6½ x 9¼.
23649-8 Pa. $3.00

UNCLE SILAS, J. Sheridan LeFanu. Victorian Gothic mystery novel, considered by many best of period, even better than Collins or Dickens. Wonderful psychological terror. Introduction by Frederick Shroyer. 436pp. 5⅜ x 8½. 21715-9 Pa. $4.00

JURGEN, James Branch Cabell. The great erotic fantasy of the 1920's that delighted thousands, shocked thousands more. Full final text, Lane edition with 13 plates by Frank Pape. 346pp. 5⅜ x 8½. 23507-6 Pa. $4.00

THE CLAVERINGS, Anthony Trollope. Major novel, chronicling aspects of British Victorian society, personalities. Reprint of Cornhill serialization, 16 plates by M. Edwards; first reprint of full text. Introduction by Norman Donaldson. 412pp. 5⅜ x 8½. 23464-9 Pa. $5.00

KEPT IN THE DARK, Anthony Trollope. Unusual short novel about Victorian morality and abnormal psychology by the great English author. Probably the first American publication. Frontispiece by Sir John Millais. 92pp. 6½ x 9¼. 23609-9 Pa. $2.50

RALPH THE HEIR, Anthony Trollope. Forgotten tale of illegitimacy, inheritance. Master novel of Trollope's later years. Victorian country estates, clubs, Parliament, fox hunting, world of fully realized characters. Reprint of 1871 edition. 12 illustrations by F. A. Faser. 434pp. of text. 5⅜ x 8½. 23642-0 Pa. $4.50

YEKL and THE IMPORTED BRIDEGROOM AND OTHER STORIES OF THE NEW YORK GHETTO, Abraham Cahan. Film *Hester Street* based on *Yekl* (1896). Novel, other stories among first about Jewish immigrants of N.Y.'s East Side. Highly praised by W. D. Howells—Cahan "a new star of realism." New introduction by Bernard G. Richards. 240pp. 5⅜ x 8½. 22427-9 Pa. $3.50

THE HIGH PLACE, James Branch Cabell. Great fantasy writer's enchanting comedy of disenchantment set in 18th-century France. Considered by some critics to be even better than his famous *Jurgen*. 10 illustrations and numerous vignettes by noted fantasy artist Frank C. Pape. 320pp. 5⅜ x 8½. 23670-6 Pa. $4.00

ALICE'S ADVENTURES UNDER GROUND, Lewis Carroll. Facsimile of ms. Carroll gave Alice Liddell in 1864. Different in many ways from final Alice. Handlettered, illustrated by Carroll. Introduction by Martin Gardner. 128pp. 5⅜ x 8½. 21482-6 Pa. $2.00

FAVORITE ANDREW LANG FAIRY TALE BOOKS IN MANY COLORS, Andrew Lang. The four Lang favorites in a boxed set—the complete *Red, Green, Yellow* and *Blue* Fairy Books. 164 stories; 439 illustrations by Lancelot Speed, Henry Ford and G. P. Jacomb Hood. Total of about 1500pp. 5⅜ x 8½. 23407-X Boxed set, Pa. $14.00

HOUSEHOLD STORIES BY THE BROTHERS GRIMM. All the great Grimm stories: "Rumpelstiltskin," "Snow White," "Hansel and Gretel," etc., with 114 illustrations by Walter Crane. 269pp. 5⅜ x 8½.
21080-4 Pa. $3.00

SLEEPING BEAUTY, illustrated by Arthur Rackham. Perhaps the fullest, most delightful version ever, told by C. S. Evans. Rackham's best work. 49 illustrations. 110pp. 7⅞ x 10¾.
22756-1 Pa. $2.00

AMERICAN FAIRY TALES, L. Frank Baum. Young cowboy lassoes Father Time; dummy in Mr. Floman's department store window comes to life; and 10 other fairy tales. 41 illustrations by N. P. Hall, Harry Kennedy, Ike Morgan, and Ralph Gardner. 209pp. 5⅜ x 8½.
23643-9 Pa. $3.00

THE WONDERFUL WIZARD OF OZ, L. Frank Baum. Facsimile in full color of America's finest children's classic. Introduction by Martin Gardner. 143 illustrations by W. W. Denslow. 267pp. 5⅜ x 8½.
20691-2 Pa. $3.50

THE TALE OF PETER RABBIT, Beatrix Potter. The inimitable Peter's terrifying adventure in Mr. McGregor's garden, with all 27 wonderful, full-color Potter illustrations. 55pp. 4¼ x 5½. (Available in U.S. only)
22827-4 Pa. $1.10

THE STORY OF KING ARTHUR AND HIS KNIGHTS, Howard Pyle. Finest children's version of life of King Arthur. 48 illustrations by Pyle. 131pp. 6⅛ x 9¼.
21445-1 Pa. $4.00

CARUSO'S CARICATURES, Enrico Caruso. Great tenor's remarkable caricatures of self, fellow musicians, composers, others. Toscanini, Puccini, Farrar, etc. Impish, cutting, insightful. 473 illustrations. Preface by M. Sisca. 217pp. 8⅜ x 11¼.
23528-9 Pa. $6.00

PERSONAL NARRATIVE OF A PILGRIMAGE TO ALMADINAH AND MECCAH, Richard Burton. Great travel classic by remarkably colorful personality. Burton, disguised as a Moroccan, visited sacred shrines of Islam, narrowly escaping death. Wonderful observations of Islamic life, customs, personalities. 47 illustrations. Total of 959pp. 5⅜ x 8½.
21217-3, 21218-1 Pa., Two-vol. set $10.00

INCIDENTS OF TRAVEL IN YUCATAN, John L. Stephens. Classic (1843) exploration of jungles of Yucatan, looking for evidences of Maya civilization. Travel adventures, Mexican and Indian culture, etc. Total of 669pp. 5⅜ x 8½.
20926-1, 20927-X Pa., Two-vol. set $6.50

AMERICAN LITERARY AUTOGRAPHS FROM WASHINGTON IRVING TO HENRY JAMES, Herbert Cahoon, et al. Letters, poems, manuscripts of Hawthorne, Thoreau, Twain, Alcott, Whitman, 67 other prominent American authors. Reproductions, full transcripts and commentary. Plus checklist of all American Literary Autographs in The Pierpont Morgan Library. Printed on exceptionally high-quality paper. 136 illustrations. 212pp. 9⅛ x 12¼.
23548-3 Pa. $7.95

AN AUTOBIOGRAPHY, Margaret Sanger. Exciting personal account of hard-fought battle for woman's right to birth control, against prejudice, church, law. Foremost feminist document. 504pp. 5⅜ x 8½.
20470-7 Pa. $5.50

MY BONDAGE AND MY FREEDOM, Frederick Douglass. Born as a slave, Douglass became outspoken force in antislavery movement. The best of Douglass's autobiographies. Graphic description of slave life. Introduction by P. Foner. 464pp. 5⅜ x 8½.
22457-0 Pa. $5.00

LIVING MY LIFE, Emma Goldman. Candid, no holds barred account by foremost American anarchist: her own life, anarchist movement, famous contemporaries, ideas and their impact. Struggles and confrontations in America, plus deportation to U.S.S.R. Shocking inside account of persecution of anarchists under Lenin. 13 plates. Total of 944pp. 5⅜ x 8½.
22543-7, 22544-5 Pa., Two-vol. set $9.00

LETTERS AND NOTES ON THE MANNERS, CUSTOMS AND CONDITIONS OF THE NORTH AMERICAN INDIANS, George Catlin. Classic account of life among Plains Indians: ceremonies, hunt, warfare, etc. Dover edition reproduces for first time all original paintings. 312 plates. 572pp. of text. 6⅛ x 9¼.
22118-0, 22119-9 Pa.. Two-vol. set $10.00

THE MAYA AND THEIR NEIGHBORS, edited by Clarence L. Hay, others. Synoptic view of Maya civilization in broadest sense, together with Northern, Southern neighbors. Integrates much background, valuable detail not elsewhere. Prepared by greatest scholars: Kroeber, Morley, Thompson, Spinden, Vaillant, many others. Sometimes called Tozzer Memorial Volume. 60 illustrations, linguistic map. 634pp. 5⅜ x 8½.
23510-6 Pa. $7.50

HANDBOOK OF THE INDIANS OF CALIFORNIA, A. L. Kroeber. Foremost American anthropologist offers complete ethnographic study of each group. Monumental classic. 459 illustrations, maps. 995pp. 5⅜ x 8½.
23368-5 Pa. $10.00

SHAKTI AND SHAKTA, Arthur Avalon. First book to give clear, cohesive analysis of Shakta doctrine, Shakta ritual and Kundalini Shakti (yoga). Important work by one of world's foremost students of Shaktic and Tantric thought. 732pp. 5⅜ x 8½. (Available in U.S. only)
23645-5 Pa. $7.95

AN INTRODUCTION TO THE STUDY OF THE MAYA HIEROGLYPHS, Syvanus Griswold Morley. Classic study by one of the truly great figures in hieroglyph research. Still the best introduction for the student for reading Maya hieroglyphs. New introduction by J. Eric S. Thompson. 117 illustrations. 284pp. 5⅜ x 8½.
23108-9 Pa. $4.00

A STUDY OF MAYA ART, Herbert J. Spinden. Landmark classic interprets Maya symbolism, estimates styles, covers ceramics, architecture, murals, stone carvings as artforms. Still a basic book in area. New introduction by J. Eric Thompson. Over 750 illustrations. 341pp. 8⅜ x 11¼.
21235-1 Pa. $6.95

GEOMETRY, RELATIVITY AND THE FOURTH DIMENSION, Rudolf Rucker. Exposition of fourth dimension, means of visualization, concepts of relativity as Flatland characters continue adventures. Popular, easily followed yet accurate, profound. 141 illustrations. 133pp. 5⅜ x 8½.
23400-2 Pa. $2.75

THE ORIGIN OF LIFE, A. I. Oparin. Modern classic in biochemistry, the first rigorous examination of possible evolution of life from nitrocarbon compounds. Non-technical, easily followed. Total of 295pp. 5⅜ x 8½.
60213-3 Pa. $4.00

THE CURVES OF LIFE, Theodore A. Cook. Examination of shells, leaves, horns, human body, art, etc., in *"the* classic reference on how the golden ratio applies to spirals and helices in nature . . .. "—Martin Gardner. 426 illustrations. Total of 512pp. 5⅜ x 8½.   23701-X Pa. $5.95

PLANETS, STARS AND GALAXIES, A. E. Fanning. Comprehensive introductory survey: the sun, solar system, stars, galaxies, universe, cosmology; quasars, radio stars, etc. 24pp. of photographs. 189pp. 5⅜ x 8½. (Available in U.S. only)   21680-2 Pa. $3.00

THE THIRTEEN BOOKS OF EUCLID'S ELEMENTS, translated with introduction and commentary by Sir Thomas L. Heath. Definitive edition. Textual and linguistic notes, mathematical analysis, 2500 years of critical commentary. Do not confuse with abridged school editions. Total of 1414pp. 5⅜ x 8½.   60088-2, 60089-0, 60090-4 Pa., Three-vol. set $18.00

DIALOGUES CONCERNING TWO NEW SCIENCES, Galileo Galilei. Encompassing 30 years of experiment and thought, these dialogues deal with geometric demonstrations of fracture of solid bodies, cohesion, leverage, speed of light and sound, pendulums, falling bodies, accelerated motion, etc. 300pp. 5⅜ x 8½.   60099-8 Pa. $4.00

Prices subject to change without notice.

Available at your book dealer or write for free catalogue to Dept. GI, Dover Publications, Inc., 180 Varick St., N.Y., N.Y. 10014. Dover publishes more than 175 books each year on science, elementary and advanced mathematics, biology, music, art, literary history, social sciences and other areas.